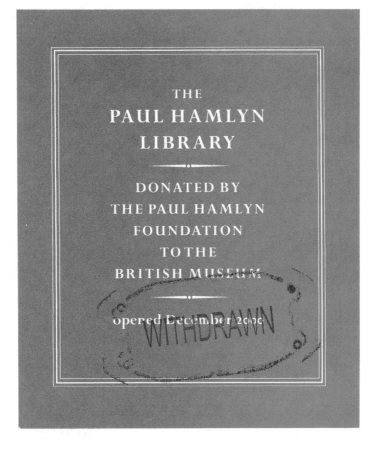

DEATH'S DARKEST FACE

DEATH'S DARKEST FACE

Julian Symons

*Death's darkest face is murder, murder that comes
Subtle and cruel and secret.*
Vortigern, William Ireland

**MACMILLAN
LONDON**

First published 1990 by
MACMILLAN LONDON LIMITED
4 Little Essex Street London WC2R 3LF
and Basingstoke

Associated companies in Auckland, Delhi, Dublin, Gaborone, Hamburg,
Harare, Hong Kong, Johannesburg, Kuala Lumpur, Lagos, Manzini,
Melbourne, Mexico City, Nairobi, New York, Singapore and Tokyo

ISBN 0-333-51783-0

A CIP catalogue record for this book is available from the British Library

Typeset by Wyvern Typesetting Limited, Bristol

Printed and bound in Great Britain by Billings Book Plan, Worcester

For Kathleen
again and always

CONTENTS

CONTENTS

A Sketch of Geoffrey Elder
by Julian Symons

The narrative that follows is not mine but Geoffrey Elder's. I have, however, shaped and tinkered with it in a way that calls for some explanation. It may be helpful also to describe briefly the impression he made on me and others, which was not identical with his own self-portrait in these pages.

In the Fifties and early Sixties my wife and I, with our son and daughter, lived in a house facing Blackheath, and during our years there I wrote several plays for television. A couple of them were successful (by which I mean that they had high viewing figures), but eventually I decided that the skills used in writing crime novels are not those needed for creating TV plays, and gave them up. At first, though, it was exhilarating to get out of the study and spend hours in draughty drill halls hearing one's words spoken by actors, arguing with them about changing phrases, and with directors about cutting passages or whole scenes. The shock of being told by a director that a scene doesn't play or by an actor that he doesn't understand his part, is salutary.

It was in one such drill hall, in the course of rehearsing a play called *The Guilty*, that I met Geoffrey Elder. The play was doomed to failure from the start, the rehearsals marred by a running battle between the director and the leading actor, another actor in a minor but important rôle then being taken ill and replaced by somebody hopelessly inadequate, and so on. Tension creates further tension. I found the director treating my suggestions more and more brusquely, and began to yearn for the safety of my study. At one of the lunchtime breaks for beer and sandwiches an actor on the next bar stool said, 'I shouldn't worry, none of it's real.' I asked what he meant. 'None of it's real acting, you only get that on the stage. And for you the real thing is the printed word, isn't that right? All this – well, we have to make a living.' With a smile somehow both bold and shy he said, 'Don't tell Bongo.' Bongo was the director.

This was my first meeting with Geoffrey, who was playing a plain-clothes detective in the TV play that, sure enough, turned out to be a disaster. As we went on talking through the rehearsals I found, as others did, something attractive in that blend of boldness and shyness, a modesty about his own achievements combined with something like arrogance about the importance of the actor on the stage, compared with the director, producer, or even the dramatist. In the narrative that follows he persistently, and misleadingly, remarks on the tiny parts he played. Misleadingly, for in his season with the Royal Shakespeare he played important parts in a way that earned much praise, Enobarbus in *Antony and Cleopatra* and Sir Epicure Mammon in *The Alchemist* being two of them. In conversation he would be likely to say, 'Oh, I'm an actor, you might have seen me in a bit of nonsense on the box.' There was nothing mock modest about this. It was rather that he was assured of his own abilities, but knew that if you were not a theatregoer you would have seen him only through cinema and TV, which he regarded as giving no scope for serious acting.

With *The Guilty* over and mercifully forgotten, he invited my wife and me to the shabby Pimlico flat he shared with Leila, and they came to drinks and dinner parties in Blackheath. His portrait of Leila in the narrative is, again, not quite like the impression formed by most of our friends. She was plump, fleshy, an ardent feminist and pacifist likely to burst into any conversation when key words or phrases like 'equal rights' or 'unilateral nuclear disarmament' were uttered. She would argue vigorously, even violently, for several minutes, lapsing into silence when the subject was changed to one in which she had no interest. Sometimes, especially at home in their flat, her eyes closed and she drifted into a light doze, from which Geoffrey would waken her by gentle pressure on arm or knee. I mustn't exaggerate. Leila was good-natured, unmalicious, an excellent cook of nourishing hearty soups and filling meat pies. But still, she was slovenly about the house to judge by the flat's untidiness, and as I thought not physically attractive. Others must have echoed my wife Kathleen's question, 'What *can* he see in her?', although I think the narrative answers that question.

Geoffrey himself was certainly attractive to women, again something that isn't apparent in his telling of the story. He was forty when I first met him, a man of medium height with regular but slightly rugged features, and a good head of completely grey hair. He rarely laughed but smiled a good deal, that smile both bold and shy I have already mentioned. In conversation he was almost always flatteringly attentive, yet behind the attentiveness there was detachment, as if only part of his mind was occupied by what you were saying, the rest given to some private concern. On the infrequent occasions when somebody remembered one of his stage performances he would show almost childlike pleasure, but praise for a TV performance rated only a brief smile. It was, I think, the withdrawn nature of his personality, the sense of something remote about him, that particularly attracted women. 'Such a charming man ... but somehow sad ... very reserved but so lovely you long to know him better ...' are comments I remember. All of them may be thought justified by what follows.

It was in the Sixties that he told me he was involved in something that might interest me. 'I'm being a sort of detective. Did you know Hugo Headley?'

'The poet who disappeared? I met him once at a party, didn't like him much. Didn't like his poems much either.'

'Somebody's writing a biography. It seems my father may have been mixed up in his disappearance.' I have a natural lack of curiosity about the lives and backgrounds of other people, and knew only that Geoffrey's father was dead, and that he had been an estate agent. 'I'm trying to find out about it, digging into Headley's past and my father's too. It can be fascinating.' I said it could be uncomfortable, and he smiled. 'I know the uncomfortable things already.' There he was wrong, as I gathered later on when I asked what progress he'd made. He said not much, then shook his head. 'No, that isn't true. I found out things, but you were right, I don't want to know them. You saw that piece in the paper about my being attacked, I expect. Of course you did, you and Kathleen sent flowers.' A pause as if he meant to say more, then the smile. 'You might say the enquiry's closed down.'

I liked Geoffrey, but it would be an exaggeration to say we

were close friends. In the Seventies I learned from a common acquaintance that Leila had died, and wrote what might be called the standard condolatory letter, which he left unanswered. Apart from that I'd lost touch with him, and it was a shock to read his obituary in *The Times*, which called him 'a steady, reliable actor who never aspired to major rôles or inspired emotional heights, but invariably turned in a worthy performance'. That would have rated one of his smiles. A few days later I received a large package, together with a letter from a solicitor saying that Mr Geoffrey Elder had asked that the enclosed papers, along with his explanatory letter, should be sent to me on his decease. In Geoffrey's neat clerkly hand the letter, dated a month before his death in August 1979, said:

Dear Julian

I wonder if you remember that, years ago, I told you I was being a sort of detective, an enterprise which ended when I was bashed over the head and spent some time in hospital? On the assumption that you do I'm sending what I wrote after the enterprise was over, with the vague feeling that I ought somehow to be able to make a book of it. Or perhaps I deceive myself, as all of us do so much of the time, and simply wanted to get some of my life down on paper. Or perhaps it was all self-justifying self-examination . . . perhaps.

Anyway, with Leila gone, and my own learned doctor's prognosis suggesting a distinctly short-term future for me, I've been sorting stuff out, and re-read this badly ordered account of my abortive detective work, and of what some writer or other calls my 'life as a man'. I should have shown it to you before. *Technique* is the thing in any art, it is what you must learn as an actor or you're never any good no matter how much passion you feel, and I'm sure the same applies to writing.

Somewhere, in what I see with astonishment on re-reading is in a way my life story, there is perhaps a book. Do you think so? I shan't be here for you to say *no*. Of course, the story may not interest you, but if it does (ah, you see my confidence) then feel free to do all the reshaping, cutting, etcetera that you like. (Remember Bongo, that ruthless cutter through whom we met?) One thing you'll have to do is change the names, and then – why, then no doubt you could claim it as all your own! But you're a man of honour, and will at least give me some credit.

My love to Kathleen. I remember good evenings in Pimlico and Blackheath.

Geoffrey

For some weeks I did no more than glance at the pile of manuscript, some of it typed, but most written in the same clerkly hand that at times became minuscular and, for all its neatness, hard to read. I was in the last passages of a crime story, almost always the most difficult part to manage, and that first cursory dipping seemed to offer no more than an unrevealing autobiography. Then, my book finished and with the publisher, I read with greater attention, came to the crucial event at Clempstone, and from that time on was absorbed by the story and by Geoffrey's quest.

Was there a book in it? Decidedly there was, but I could not see how to manage it, and put the manuscript aside again in favour of other things. This year, however, with all the principal figures dead, I set to work in earnest, and what follows is the result. Here is a brief account of the way in which it differs from the original.

Geoffrey's manuscript, of some six hundred typed and calligraphic pages, has been reduced by a quarter. I have cut out some repetitious passages, several pages about what he called the dying craft of acting that would interest only other professional actors, and some though not all of his comparisons between the present (the Sixties, in which he was writing) and the past. The purely autobiographical element has been cut down – for, even though Geoffrey reminded himself more than once that he was not writing an autobiography, he could not resist putting in a good deal that had nothing to do with the disappearance of Hugo Headley.

I have changed the names as he suggested. But the essential difference, which makes me feel I can justify putting my name on the cover, is that I have reshaped his straightforward chronology to emphasise the element of mystery, which I persuade myself is what he would have wished. The shifts in time from Thirties to Sixties are mine, as are the sub-headings. The newspaper cuttings were with the manuscript, but not placed at the beginning as they are now. And because he reached some wrong conclusions, I have added a postscript. In its essentials, however, this is Geoffrey Elder's manuscript.

Julian Symons

What the Papers Said

Daily Banner, Tuesday 10 August 1936

MYSTERY OF THE VANISHING POET

Friends tonight said they were concerned about the whereabouts of Mr Hugo Headley, the poet. Mr Headley's Austin car was seen on Sunday evening parked near the beach outside the Kent resort of Clempstone. Miss Ellen Corliss, a visitor, noticed it and assumed the owner had gone for a swim. When she saw the car still there on the following morning she notified the police. They are enquiring into the matter, but a bathing accident is regarded as unlikely. Mr Headley is known to be an eccentric character, and it is thought possible that he was suddenly afflicted with the divine afflatus, and wandered away in pursuit of a poem.

Daily Banner, Thursday 12 August 1936

THE MISSING POET: A TRAGIC ACCIDENT?

Nothing more has been seen or heard of Mr Hugo Headley, the writer who left his car beside the beach near Clempstone last Sunday, and police are now seriously concerned that he may have gone swimming and been the victim of underwater currents. Most of the beach is safe enough, according to locals, but there are strong currents in the sea near to Parker's Point, where Mr Headley's car was left. Inspector Lynton of the local constabulary says that while he is still inclined to the view that some other explanation of Mr Headley's disappearance is possible, the chance of a tragic bathing accident cannot be ruled out.

Daily Banner, Tuesday 24 August 1936

SUICIDE, ACCIDENT – OR PLANNED DISAPPEARANCE?

By Our Special Reporter

The little Kentish seaside resort of Clempstone is buzzing with rumours about the disappearance two weeks ago of the bohemian poet Hugo Headley. It was at first thought that he had gone for a late night swim near the local landmark known as Parker's Point, been caught in one of the treacherous currents known to local fishermen, and drowned. But no body has been recovered, and Inspector Lynton told me some of the unexplained aspects of the affair that lead him to doubt whether this straightforward explanation is the correct one. Here are some of the questions that have to be answered.

The mystery of the Austin car. Mr Headley's Austin 7 was parked near the beach, with his clothing inside it. The car had been left unlocked, which was why Miss Ellen Corliss, who saw it there on Sunday evening and again on the following morning, reported its presence to the police. But why was it there at all? The writer had a cottage at the other end of the village. Why did he take the car if he was just going for an evening swim? And why choose to swim at Parker's Point, rather than near his cottage?

Where was the towel? The missing man's clothes, jacket, trousers and undergarments, were neatly folded on the back seat of the car. There was, however, no towel. Did he take a towel on to the beach, and if so what happened to it?

The Inspector would not be drawn into speculating on what might have happened, but Clempstone itself is buzzing with rumours, among both residents and summer visitors. Mr Headley was a colourful character, and one opinion expressed to me was that to go bathing at night in a dangerous spot would have been typical of him. He was unmarried, and was staying alone in his small cottage, although he had frequent visitors. I learned also from local tradesmen that he was slow in settling bills, and owed money to several of them. However, his friend the actress

Mary Storm scouted the idea that he might have staged a deliberate disappearance.

'Hugo simply didn't worry about money,' she said to me in the course of an interview. 'He always thought something would turn up, and it usually did. When I last saw him, a few days before he disappeared, he was in high spirits and talking of going to Egypt and taking a trip down the Nile. He'd become fascinated by the civilisation of ancient Egypt.'

He had suggested that Miss Storm might accompany him, and she had asked whether that meant he was in funds. He laughed and said foreign travel was far cheaper than living in England. Miss Storm's view is that he has drowned. 'Hugo was a good swimmer, but not as good as he thought. I believe he swam out too far and perhaps got caught by the current, or got cramp.' She attached no importance to the missing towel. 'He just forgot to take one, I've known him to be similarly forgetful a dozen times. What would he have done? Just dried himself with his shirt.'

Opinion among the villagers, however, is inclined to the view that the disappearance may have been voluntary, and that the poet will reappear within a week or two.

Manchester Guardian, June 1939

(From a review of *Collected Poems* by Hugo Headley, with an introduction by Mary Storm.)

He came, he saw, he conquered – and he vanished. That might be the epitaph on Hugo Headley, who disappeared three years ago at the age of thirty, and whose two slim volumes of verse, along with a number of uncollected poems, can now be seen as a remarkable body of work. 'Of roaring sea and thundering sky I sing' begins one of the poems in *From a Hawk to a Handsaw*, his last collection, and as Mary Storm says in her introduction, it was the roaring sea he finally embraced. His body has never been recovered, and as one reads the poems today his end seems tragically appropriate. The Dionysian exultation of his

17

verse always had in it the throb and power of the sea, and it provided the imagery and the background for much of his finest work.

Headley's poetry was outside the conventions of his period. He owed nothing to T. S. Eliot, nothing to the concern of the fashionable Oxford poets with politics and psychology. His poetry is elemental, vital, bold, rhythms and rhymes descending on us in an ecstatic Swinburnian flood . . .

The Sixties

Kevin Duffy

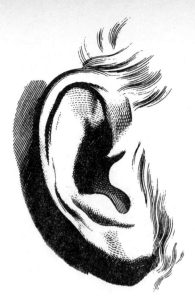

Kevin Duffy

'Just thirty years ago this month.' The young man sniffed. He had red hair, horn-rimmed spectacles, a sharp nose. His name was Kevin Duffy. He was a lecturer in English at a Midlands university, and was writing a book about the life and work of Hugo Headley.

He took the cup of tea offered him, looked at the plate of biscuits and shook his head. 'I suffer from hay fever,' he said as if that explained his refusal. 'It's good of you to spare the time to see me.'

'That's all right. At the moment I'm what's technically known as resting.' He gave a cut-off laugh, as if unsure whether I had said something funny. I asked how his research was going.

'I've been seeing people. Your aunt was good enough to grant me another interview. A remarkable woman. I had hoped also to see Mrs Winterbottom again, but she felt there was nothing more she could tell me.'

Ah Melissa, Melissa, I thought, how wise you are to deny the probing biographer. But how could you marry a stockbroker named Winterbottom? Melissa Winterbottom, what a self-evident absurdity of a name, although perhaps better stockbroker Winterbottom than an actor out of work a good deal of the time. And what did red-haired Duffy want from me, why had he said he would be most grateful if I could spare time to see him again? 'You haven't solved the mystery?'

'I beg your pardon?'

'The mystery. Of the disappearance.'

'No.' But the negative had a touch of affirmation in it. 'Inspector Lynton, ex-Inspector Lynton now retired, was good enough to talk to me. He thinks Hugo is still alive, living in some other country, perhaps in Africa, under another name. He always thought that, or so he says.'

'If he felt that at the time he concealed it pretty well. But you've had no letters from people who've seen Hugo Headley reading his poems in Egypt, or giving lectures in Rhodesia, that kind of thing?' He looked at me to see if I was serious, then shook his head. 'Because it's perfectly possible he could still be alive, he'd only be in his early sixties.'

'Sixty-one this year. But I've had no communications of that kind. The Inspector said in the course of our conversation that Hugo had been in great financial and other difficulties.'

'I'd have thought it was his constant state.'

'That is true.' He sipped his tea, I ate a cream biscuit. 'Would you be in agreement that what is known should be revealed?'

'Should a biographer tell, you mean? I suppose so, though I wouldn't have thought there was anything fresh to find out about Hugo. Everybody knows he got money out of publishers and editors for things he didn't write. And had lots of affairs. He used to dedicate poems to women at the end of the affair. There's a rhyme I heard long after he'd vanished:

> "After three months of fornication
> He signed her off with a dedication"

I expect you know that.'

He sniffed and didn't reply. I found him an irritating young man, so raw and awkward in manner that he might have been eighteen.

'The problem arises with some of the material your aunt kindly gave me.'

'If it concerns Aunt Aggie I'm sure you needn't worry. She always liked to conduct her love affairs with the maximum publicity. She was rather proud of snaffling Hugo and keeping him in tow for so long, when she was much older. I think she'd take an extended account of their affair as a tribute.'

'Certainly she's been very frank. She even told me Hugo once said to her, "You are my oldest lover, but this has been the most passionate affair of my life."' I didn't say so, but it seemed to me quite possible that Aunt Aggie, who had used Mary Storm as her stage name, had much embroidered any compliment of the kind Hugo paid her. 'And of course his poem, "The Eternal Muse", is dedicated to her. That is not the problem.' He paused, sniffed. 'We got on very well, she loves talking about the past. And this time, when I asked if there was any other information she could give me, she said there were some boxes in her roof loft and I could look at them if I wanted.' Aunt Aggie lived now in a tiny cottage outside Guildford, bought after she had a heart attack and was told she must give up the stage. 'So I did look, I spent a couple of hours up in the loft. Most of the things there were connected with her life in the theatre, but I found two boxes full of letters, most of them written to Hugo. I couldn't imagine why your aunt had them, but she said he used to leave his things anywhere, which of course I knew. He had no sense of possession, and often left stuff with her. I asked if she wanted to look at them, but she said they'd be of no interest to her now, and told me to take them away. Which I did.' He sniffed, took out a handkerchief, wiped his nose.

'It turned out there were all sorts of odds and ends in the boxes, some enlarging my knowledge of things I already knew a little about. He'd arranged to write a film script around the life of Rupert Brooke, there were a lot of notes for that, and several pages of dialogue. Apparently he never submitted a script outline and there were angry letters from the producer, Dennis Elmore. I wonder if you met him?' I shook my head. 'And some interesting letters from his father, going back to Hugo's youth. His father owned a chain of tobacconist and confectioners' shops, and wanted Hugo to come into the business. For a time he made Hugo an allowance, but cut it off when he realised his son had no intention of engaging in what he called "a steady gainful occupation". Unfortunately Hugo's replies haven't survived. Mr Headley died during the war, and I understand from his widow that father and son remained on bad terms. However, Mrs Headley has kindly said I may use the letters.'

I couldn't imagine why he was telling me all this. Now he took off his spectacles, wiped his eyes, and said, 'There are also some letters from Mrs Winterbottom.' He resumed the spectacles, blinked rapidly. 'Some are of an intimate nature. I have had them photographed. These are not the originals.'

He opened a slim briefcase, took from it two large envelopes, looked through one of them and selected a sheet which he handed to me. It was a single page torn off a pad, with no heading and no date. I read: 'Darling H, Coming down to C next week, longing to see you, love and kisses, M.' Was the sprawling hand

23

Melissa's? I had seen her writing, but could not remember what it looked like.

'C of course was Clempstone, and some of the other letters make it clear that Hugo and Melissa Paton, as she was then, were lovers.'

Yes, I thought, I should have known. Perhaps the knowledge had rested within me for a long time, as one is aware of an illness without wanting to discover its nature. My immediate reaction was of anger against the red-haired prodnose who came telling me what I did not want to know. Did I make the feeling apparent? If so, he was unaware of it.

'I sent Mrs Winterbottom copies of the letters. I asked her if she had any correspondence from Hugo, whether she would give me permission to quote passages, and if in any case I might talk to her about her perception of Hugo Headley's character. Unhappily, as I say, she has refused to see me.' And indeed he did look unhappy. 'The copyright in the letters rests with her, but she can't prevent the references to the affair that I shall certainly make. On the other hand it would obviously be helpful if I could quote directly. I believe you were a friend of hers, and perhaps an approach from you—'

'The answer is no. I've hardly seen her for years, but in any case I wouldn't dream of trying to make her change her mind. I have every sympathy with her point of view.'

He said he was sorry I felt like that, though he did not seem surprised. And he had not finished. He peered at me, sniffed, and said, 'There were also letters from your father. They suggest he was a rival for Miss Paton's affections.'

For a moment I did not take it in. Then I said, 'Nonsense. What bloody rubbish.' I got up, and he shrank back slightly in his chair. 'If you suggest anything like that I can tell you you'll be in trouble, and so will your publisher.'

'See for yourself.' He took some sheets out of the other envelope, handed them to me.

There was no doubt that Father had written the letters. I might not know Melissa's hand but I recognised even in these copies his old-fashioned, almost copperplate calligraphy, the downstrokes thick, upstrokes thin. There were three letters, all written from our London home in Kensington, the dates covering ten days in late July 1936. We had gone down to Clempstone early in August.

The letters were all short. The first said:

Dear Mr Headley

I can assure you that your suppositions are quite erroneous, and that my relationship with M was not what you suppose. You may accept this on the word of a gentleman, and as I take you to be one yourself, I trust no further reference to the matter is necessary.

Yours sincerely
Harold Elder

The second was different in tone:

Dear Sir

Your motives and assumptions are as unpleasant as your manners. I have said you are mistaken, and see no need to justify myself or go into details. If you continue to make these scandalous allegations I shall have recourse to legal action.

Yours faithfully
Harold Elder

The last, dated 31st July, was different again in tone, and unsigned:

Very well. It is my understanding that you wish to leave this country for a time, and it is possible that I may be able to assist you. In the meantime I shall be glad to have your assurance that the matter will remain private between us. I understand you will be at your Clempstone cottage next week, and since that is when we pay our annual visit, the matter can be discussed and settled then.

I said what was obvious. 'There's no indication at all that this M was Melissa Paton.'

'Who else could it have been?' He did not wait for me to answer, and indeed I could not have done so. 'I sent copies of these notes to her, along with copies of her own letters. She didn't comment on them. I thought that was significant.' He continued talking while I read the notes again. 'It's obvious Hugo was asking your father for money, and it looks like some sort of blackmail. Nobody would pretend Hugo was a very scrupulous character, especially where money was concerned. I can assure you I'm not out to do a whitewashing job. Can you think of any other explanation than the one I've given?'

'Not offhand. But you know what they talked about at Clempstone.'

'What your father *said* they talked about after Hugo had disappeared, and wasn't there to contradict him.' He gave a restrained smirk. 'Mrs Winterbottom, that is Melissa Paton, was staying with you. Doesn't that strike you as significant?'

I glared at him. 'She came down with her mother. Do you suppose my father would have been going to bed with Melissa while her mother was in the house?'

He smirked again. 'Such things have been known.'

'The idea's ridiculous. Ridiculous and insulting. You never met my father. Or Headley either for that matter. You don't know what you're talking about.'

The smirk was replaced by a wounded look. 'It's because I didn't know the people involved that I've asked your advice.'

'Very well, here it is. Forget it. Hanging out Headley's dirty washing won't be any use to anybody, you included.'

'I'm afraid I can't forget, just like that. You agreed that what has been discovered should be made known. And there's something else. Here's another of Mrs Winterbottom's notes.' He handed me another sheet in that scrawled wavery hand. It was headed 'Sunday', and read: 'Sorry for what I said, we mustn't quarrel, see you tonight, ten or as near as I can make it, can't wait, M.'

I didn't need sniffing Duffy to remind me that Hugo Headley had disappeared on a Sunday night.

'Of course this doesn't *prove* anything. But suppose it was written on that Sunday, and your father learned about it, found them together, fought with Hugo and somehow Hugo was killed. Accidentally, I mean. It seems to me something of that kind may well have happened. If you could remember anything at all that might be significant about your father's behaviour that night—'

At that point I told him to get out. I was standing by the mantelpiece, and must I suppose have looked menacing enough to alarm him, even though he was two or three inches over my height. He gathered his envelopes and put them back in the briefcase, said he was sorry to find I took such a Victorian attitude, thanked me for tea and departed, stumbling slightly as he went up the steps leading out of my Pimlico basement. I went back to the living room, sufficiently disturbed to light a cigarette. In theory I had given up smoking, and theory worked pretty well in practice except when my emotional equilibrium was upset. This had happened half-a-dozen times in the year since I gave up, when I lost a part I expected to get, when I had a row with Leila, and so on. Return to the weed never lasted more than a few days, something that seemed to me to indicate the strength of my character, although Leila said it showed weakness of will to need it at all. That led on to arguments about whether it's better to resist stress or bend under it.

I may as well sketch my present circumstances, since they will move in and out of this narrative. I'm a professional actor, have been for a good many years after trying journalism without much success. My physique and appearance, and if I'm brutally honest perhaps my abilities, don't bring major parts, I'm mostly a friend of the hero, junior counsel in a legal drama, minor suspect in a house-party thriller, that kind of thing. I have a good ear, can manage a variety of accents pretty well, country yokel, Cockney wide boy, clubman about town, plummy-voiced lawyer, Southern or East Coast American. I do quite a lot of voice-overs. To my accents I owe my living, you might say.

Leila and I live in a Pimlico basement flat, living room, bedroom, kitchenette, all mod cons, even what house agents have recently taken to calling a patio garden, paved space about twenty feet square in which Leila grows a variety of pot plants. Leila is the emancipated daughter of a canon, and we've been living in what she sometimes gleefully calls sin for nearly five years. I wouldn't mind getting married, but Leila enjoys living in sin too much to give it up, or so I sometimes think. She was married before, to a film producer who beat her up when he was drunk, which may have something to do with her reluctance to get hitched again. Leila is several years younger than me, still under forty, and has a job as advertising manager of a women's magazine. She sometimes says I depend on her and probably has finance in mind, but I could scrape along cashwise (an awful word people have recently started using) on my own. Really the dependence is emotional. If it's true, as I once read, that men always want to marry either their mothers or their kid sisters, I'm the kind who needs his mother and Leila, although so much my junior, is motherly. Why do I need a mother? Something to do with my relationship to Deirdre, no doubt. Leila, a big-breasted earth-mother type, fills the bill.

So much for the present, which is agreeable but not exciting. But red-haired Duffy's visit had taken me back to that passage in the past which had been exciting but not pleasant, to the summer of '36 when I believed myself in love with Melissa and the days at Clempstone which had been so crucial in my life, the days when, as I see it now, I grew up. Comparing this present with that past I realise that the past seems much more real, more genuine, when the contrary is true. The present is real enough, this slightly dingy flat, my not uncomfortable way of earning a living, the companionship of Leila in bed and out of it. I have lived like this for years, yet there is no feeling of permanence about it. One month runs into another, so that I couldn't tell you whether it was in June or August of last year that I played in a revival of Noël Coward's *Hay Fever*.

The past is different. It is preserved intact, secure and unchangeable as a ship in a bottle. At that time I was an adolescent more innocent than most, one who didn't know what passions and greeds move adults. What I experienced then was not real in the sense that my life now is real. My perceptions were often false, people not always as I believed them, yet the memories of that time have an intensity quite lacking in my life today. Do such memories have their own reality? That's the kind of speculation I'd have thought worth a couple of paragraphs in the journal I kept intermittently in August 1936.

The Thirties

(i) Myself, the House

My name is Geoffrey Wild Elder. In August 1936 I was still living in Manfield Terrace, where I had been born in November 1919. This is a short street in the pleasant part of Kensington bounded by the High Street, Church Street and Notting Hill. The house, along with two others, was destroyed in a flying bomb raid during the war and has been replaced by a block of flats, but I can summon it up readily in the mind's eye. A columned portico flanked by spiked railings, steps leading down to the basement entrance where the servants cooked and ate, on the ground floor drawing and dining rooms and a smaller squarish affair called the morning room, although it was not used in the daytime, but only occasionally by Father in the evening when somebody came from the firm on some matter connected with business. The drawing room had a wonderful glass chandelier, the pendant drops of which sparkled when the light was switched on. A curved staircase, wide with shallow risers, led to the first floor and to Father and Mother's bedroom which I rarely entered, their bathroom, and Father's study which had a big leather-topped desk and bookcases holding thick volumes about the management of estates and laws relating to property, alongside books by Dumas, Henty, Wells and Galsworthy which I was allowed to take up to my room and read. Ascend another flight of stairs, shorter and straight, and you were confronted by a series of doors to left and right numbered as in a hotel, although the comparison did not occur to me at the time. There were bellpushes in these rooms that rang in the basement, and the doors were numbered so that the maid answering the bell should not be confused about which room had rung. These were smaller, though still sizeable rooms with lower ceilings, two of them guest bedrooms and the third mine. There was a bathroom on this floor, and a separate lavatory. And then on the top floor, up another short and steeper flight of stairs, were the servants' rooms.

Our house, eleven Manfield Terrace, was one in a row built I suppose in the eighteen sixties or seventies, identical in exterior appearance, and mostly occupied by professional families. A barrister lived next door, a surgeon who was knighted in my early childhood opposite, my father was an estate agent. Most of the families were larger than ours. The barrister had three sons, the surgeon two sons and a daughter, I was an only child. And although I went to the same school as two of the barrister's and surgeon's children, I saw them little outside the classroom. Perhaps this was because an estate agent was not then thought to be on the same social level as a barrister or a knighted surgeon, but it may have been that offence was taken when, after I had gone to birthday tea parties at these and other houses, my mother did not respond with invitations on my birthday. Arranging a children's tea party, I heard her say to Father, really would be the dreaded end.

I was far from miserable. I went through the prep school, as through my good day school later, without distinction but also without disgrace, the truth being that I never found lessons very interesting. My emotional life was involved totally with the house, and the romantic fantasies I wove around it. I could write down today the number of stairs on each flight, and I once borrowed a tape measure and noted the exact dimensions of every room in the house including the basement and top floor. (I was surprised by the smallness of the servants' rooms, and by a heavy sourish smell in them that I did not then recognise as the smell of dried sweat.) With the measurements taken I tried to build a model of the house with some ingenious interlocking bricks called Wonderbuild. I invented fantasies about the house. After reading *The Ingoldsby Legends*, which were on the study shelves, I imagined that a ghost inhabited room number three on my floor, and told my favourite maid Annie that he had come into my room dressed in naval uniform, holding a curved sword. She said I should tell her if he appeared again, because she knew a magic spell that would get rid of ghosts. In Dumas's *Chicot the Jester*, also borrowed from the study, I read an account of the wounded Bussy d'Amboise, impaled on iron spiked railings, and then shot to death at the order of his treacherous patron the Duc d'Anjou. I imagined Bussy jumping from my room and hanging spiked on the railings in front of our basement steps.

Was I a particularly fanciful small boy? I doubt it, although the fact that my fancies were so closely connected with the house may have been unusual. Tears came to my eyes when, a few days after the flying bomb raid, I saw the place where I had spent my childhood turned to rubble.

I can't remember just when I realised that I was unusually good at two things outside the curriculum: acting, and playing tennis. From the moment I was chosen to act in a class play, that old favourite *Box and Cox*, it was obvious both to me and the teacher that I was a natural actor. I mean by the phrase somebody who is not embarrassed and awkward on a stage, but finds it the easiest thing in the world to speak words that are not his own, and temporarily merge his personality in another's. To be a natural actor is not to be a great actor. Perhaps it means that one has no particular character of one's own, something that has occurred to me more than once. In any case, from the age of thirteen onwards I took a leading part in the plays and dramatic extracts presented to the school and parents at the end of each year. I played Romeo, Othello and Brutus – the drama teacher never strayed from Shakespeare. Father came to all the plays, and said things like 'I never knew I had an actor for a son.' Mother came twice, did not mention the play or my perform-ance, but told me I looked positively handsome in fancy dress. I took this as a compliment, and believe she meant it as such.

And tennis. I was perhaps lucky in that mine was one of the few English schools interested in the game. I won the school championship when I was twelve, and went on from there. Two years later I won an under-sixteen tournament, and in the year about which I am writing, 1936, played in an early qualifying competition for Wimbledon, but lost to an eighteen-year-old who stood six foot three and had a cannonball service. There were half-a-dozen cups and medals on a shelf in my bedroom. Father took a great deal of interest in my tennis, Mother not. Hitting a ball over a net, she said, was just as ridiculous an activity as knocking one into a little hole with a stick.

I was fourteen when it was decided that I should take my place at table at dinner parties, beneath the dazzling chandelier, enclosed within a heavy world of red velvet curtains, walls papered with dark unidentifiable large fruits against a reddish ground, mahogany dining table and sideboard, and silver serving dishes never seen at any other time. The guests at these dinner parties were almost all Father's friends, although the word is not quite the right one, for most of them were connected with him through business. His firm was called Branksome and Elder, although there was no longer any Branksome, only a junior partner named Neil Paton. It was concerned not just with buying and selling houses, but with the management of large estates. Accordingly the guests were varied, including directors of auctioneering firms (Branksome and Elder were sometimes asked to dispose of a house's contents), local dignitaries, even on occasion a peer or two who had put some affairs in the hands of Branksome and Elder. There were times when the dining room was used less formally, when Mother's parents Grandfather Johnjohn and his wife Pat came to stay, and sometimes Father's old friend the antique dealer Dodo Everard would pay a visit when he was up from his home outside York, but it is the dinner parties I remember.

I found them deadly dull. Mother told me later that she agreed with me, saying that most of the men had never read a book or been to a theatre since they were children, and that the women would have been more at home astride a horse than with their legs under a dinner table. She was a splendid hostess, however, drawing out the men to talk about subjects in which she can't have had the slightest interest, and talking to their wives as if they belonged to a sisterhood that must be perpetually on their guard against predatory males. I sometimes saw Father looking admiringly at her down the table, without understanding the reason.

Very likely the guests found my company as tedious as I found theirs. Those placed next to me had been primed about my tennis, and talked to me on the subject dutifully for a couple of minutes before turning to their companion on the other side. I dare say they had been told I was a tennis prodigy, although that was far from the truth, and people are always uneasy with prodigies. The only guest who did not talk to me about tennis as a duty was Neil Paton. He actually played the game, and we sometimes had a set or two of singles, although I could beat him comfortably. This was at the Patons' house at Ham Common where they had a court in the garden, and where Neil said the air was fresher than in central London. Mostly, though, we played mixed doubles with his daughter Melissa, and one or other of her friends.

I thought a lot about tennis, and about being Wimbledon champion, beating Fred Perry and Jack Crawford. Father arranged for me to have private coaching from a professional, and he did his best to convert my backhand from a slice into a drive and to develop my service, which was limited by my height. I was only around five foot five and have stayed rather short, putting on only three inches. My service was good enough in junior tennis and very accurate, but it lacked devil. I suppose that might be said of me as a character.

Tennis in summer, acting in winter, that would have seemed to me a perfect life. I wanted to leave school and go to drama school, taking time off to play tennis. This was never seriously considered by my parents, which I suppose is hardly surprising. Father said I should go to Oxford, Mother that the word was not *should* but *must*. I said to her that Father hadn't been to a university, something he had let slip one day, and she replied that he had been deprived but there was no reason why I should be as well. Then she gave me a sidelong glance.

'I wasn't born in the purple, far from it. You're not a fool, you must have understood that.' And of course I knew her parents, Grandfather Johnjohn and Grandma Pat, were working class, although I had never thought much about it. 'But that's what life's about, moving up in the world. And having fun.' Her eyes sparkled, as they did at any prospect of pleasure. I asked if Father would agree, and she tapped my arm in the flirtatious way she used with men who came to dinner, and told me not to be impertinent.

I was in love, or thought myself in love which is very much the same thing, with Melissa Paton. Let me describe her, as impersonally as possible: nineteen, dark hair sometimes worn long and sometimes bunched on top of her head, a perfect faintly olive skin, small elegant hands and feet, slim legs, a voice unusually deep for a woman. An inadequate description? No doubt. How can one convey the emotion of being 'in love'? Not in terms of physical attraction, any more than by analysing the loved one's mentality. If I'd been concerned with the latter I might have realised we were temperamental opposites. Looking back, I can see foreshadowed even then the man who has chosen the easy option, settling down in Leila's comforting presence as into a warm bath, whereas Melissa then was a risk-taker, eager for the kind of experience I was inclined to shrink from. But if I had understood that I shouldn't have been any less in love. I went to the Patons' chiefly in the hope of seeing Melissa. She gave me a photograph which I carried around with me and showed to a friend at school, telling him she was my girl. 'What a cracker,' he said. 'But does she put out, does she do it?' I was shocked. My feeling for Melissa was not platonic – I had been overwhelmed when I kissed her at a party and she responded – yet it was not primarily physical. For that matter, I suppose my feeling for Leila isn't primarily physical either.

At that time I was sure I was unattractive to girls. I made occasional notes in a journal, and one read: 'The three worst things in the world are being short, having spots, being knock-kneed.' The fact that Melissa was a couple of inches taller than me was a worry, and I spent a lot of time in front of the mirror squeezing out blackheads and worrying about my acne, although then it was just called spots. The knock-knees? Perhaps I imagined them. They seem straight enough now.

So that was Geoffrey Wild Elder in August 1936. There were three things I cared about: tennis, acting, Melissa.

(ii) Father, Mother Becoming Deirdre

My father, Harold Silas Elder, looked like Buster Keaton, something I realised at once when I saw early Keaton silent films. He had the same cast of handsome clear-cut features that looked as if carved from wood, the same immobility of expression, and gave the same impression of a deep feeling yearning for release. He was a man of fixed habits. He left for the office punctually at nine in the morning five days a week, wearing a double-breasted dark grey or dark blue suit. He always walked to the office, which was rather more than half a mile away just off Notting Hill Gate, wearing a bowler hat and carrying an umbrella. In bad weather it was up, on dry days carefully furled. He walked like an automaton, left right, left right, umbrella regularly tapping the pavement.

At the dinners he moved more easi;,, as if his joints had been oiled, and the carved features sometimes cracked open in a smile, but he rarely initiated a conversation or expressed a view contrary to what Councillor This or Member of Parliament That might be saying. Yet the Councillors, the MPs and the others did not seem to find him dull, and although Mother sometimes made fun of him and said he did everything by the clock, she stopped when she roused him to irritation or impatience, as if she knew the unwisdom of provoking him further. For his part Father treated her, as he did other women young and old, with elaborate politeness, never contradicting any idea they advanced, no matter how self-evidently ridiculous. In her case it was more than politeness. I have mentioned his obvious admiration for the skill with which she managed dinner party guests, and at times his intense yet withdrawn gaze would rest on her as she sat on a sofa in a negligent attitude, reading a newspaper or a book.

To me also he was kind, although we had little to say to each other except about my tennis. He was delighted when I had any success, and sometimes drove me to the coaching sessions in his Armstrong Siddeley. He drove fast, cutting in on other drivers, as if sitting at the wheel released something in his personality, and at the school unbent so far as to exchange occasional jokes with the instructor. More typical, though, was his reaction when I said I wanted to play for England, help them win the Davis Cup.

'I hope you will. To play games well is a great social asset. A blue for tennis at Oxford will mean something later on, it will open all sorts of doors.'

'You didn't go to Oxford.'

'To my lasting regret. I had to make my own way.'

'I'm not sure I want to go either.'

We came to a red traffic light. He turned to look at me, no emotion showing on his face. 'That's a stupid thing to say. I can't impress on you too strongly—' He checked himself, changed the phrase. 'It will be immensely useful.' As an afterthought he added, 'You'll enjoy it.'

'I don't think I want to go.'

The lights changed. He said, 'We won't discuss it further,' and drove away too fast, so that he had to brake.

So much for Father, at least for the moment. And now Mother. In childhood and adolescence I called her Mother and not Mummy, as I said Father and never Dad.

'Deirdre, my girl, although I say it as shouldn't, you're a beautiful woman,' Grandfather Johnjohn said once when I was about ten. The remark surprised me. I suppose children never at that age think of their parents as beautiful or handsome. I liked Grandfather Johnjohn, whose name was John Wild (hence my own second name), and it was not easy for me to grasp that Mother was his daughter. Johnjohn was the works manager of a firm that made spare parts for cars, and neither he nor Grandma Pat made the pretence of being anything but – as I often heard him say – working class and proud of it. They lived in a little semi-detached house at Merton, on the fringe of London, and came to stay in Manfield Terrace no more than three or four times a year. Father treated them with his invariable stiff courtesy, but even as a child I understood that they were not easy in this big Kensington house. Grandma Pat worried that the sparks from Johnjohn's pipe would fall on carpets or sofa cushions, he hated having to wear a collar and tie all day, neither of them was happy in the presence of servants. When I was six I went to stay with them at Merton for a week, and returned clamouring for shepherd's pie like Grandma Pat made, and using phrases I had heard on Grandfather Johnjohn's lips, like

'Pull your finger out.' After that visits were not encouraged, though when I was a teenager I often went to see them, occasionally staying a weekend.

Back to Mother. She was beautiful, as Johnjohn said, with auburn hair which she generally wore coiled round her ears, a flawless white skin, large green eyes, and a full but fine figure. Although in childhood I was not aware of her beauty I did know that she smelled delicious always, but especially when she came up to say goodnight after Annie the nursemaid had put me to bed. Sometimes she was accompanied by a man who was taking her to the theatre or a dance, a man in dinner jacket or white tie and tails. The men varied, but were alike in the sleekness of their hair, and in their unlikeness to the people who came to dinner. These visits were brief. The man, Freddie or Toby or Jackie, would say, 'Come on now, old fellow, mustn't monopolise her,' or 'Deirdre, old thing, we should be going,' and Mother would bend over, kiss me, and be gone. On such evenings her eyes would sparkle more than usual, and her hair seemed to have particular lustre. Her evident excitement would communicate itself to me, so that I sometimes asked her to stay and read a story. This she never did, and in fact such a suggestion caused a slight recoil, even when she had no companion. Annie would read to me, she would say, and so Annie did, although she was no great reader and often stumbled over words. I can't remember Father or Mother ever reading to me.

In company she glowed with interest and good humour, but at home when there were no visitors she was irritable, snapped at the servants of whom there were three or four plus the cook, sometimes even snapped at Father. This was in the Twenties, when I was small. And then all this changed, when she started to run a flower shop just by Shepherd Market. I learned later that Father put up the money to start the business, perhaps to give her an occupation that might eliminate the Freddies and Tobys from the scene. The shop was a success from the start, in part because it interested Mother in a way running a house had never done. I went there sometimes, and saw how she charmed the people who came in to order flowers.

I write 'to order flowers', but often both Mother and the visitors seemed to regard their presence in the shop as an excuse for social gossip, some of it conducted in whispers and with muffled laughter. The actual taking of orders would be done by a girl assistant, Mother's rôle being almost that of a hostess, the part she played to perfection at home. There the servants changed with what was to me bewildering frequency, some perhaps because they could not put up with Mother's uncertain temper, others because she would make favourites of them and confide in them, then dismiss them for undue familiarity. What did I think of her? Did I wonder at her accent and her manner of talking, so different from that of her parents? All that, in my recollection, came later, for the truth is that in those years of growing up I had little to do with her. One of the maids gave me breakfast, saw me off to school and gave me tea when I returned, and I might well not see Mother until it was time for bed, and at times not see her at all during a whole day. Of course this changed as I grew older, attended the dinner parties, and was in general present round the house.

It was then that I began to realise how important clothes, entertainment, what is loosely called pleasure, were to her. Many women like buying and putting on new clothes, but for her it was not just a matter of admiring herself in the looking glass. She would feel the stuff she was wearing with a sensuous wondering pleasure. She enjoyed a visit to the theatre almost regardless of the play. Her preference was for musicals and revues – hence perhaps her lack of interest in the school's Shakespeare extracts – but she enjoyed the very whiff and make-believe of the theatre, the red plush seats and even the programme, which she read with a child's close attention. One of the reasons why she never cared for my school acting performances was, I think, because it destroyed what was for her the magical make-believe of the theatre to have her son acting a part. Occasionally the three of us went to see what she called a show at Christmas or in the holidays, but Father did not enjoy it. The very make-believe element she loved was alien to him, and he sat through the evening with graven Keaton face unmoving. I have wondered since whether things might have worked out differently if he had made more effort to understand her. But I dare say that's a foolish comment, since it would have meant doing something against his own nature.

When I was fourteen she said I should call her Deirdre. 'Now you're grown up, "Mother" does sound rather ghastly. As if I were ninety.' I asked how old she was. She tapped my arm. 'That's not the kind of question a gentleman asks a lady. But remember, from now on, it's Deirdre.' I asked whether I should call Father Harold, and she laughed. 'That's not the same thing at all. Anyway, I don't think he'd like it.'

It was now, too, that in the critical way of adolescents I compared Deirdre with her parents, and realised her determination to shed their working-class manners and language. Perhaps such shedding never seems perfectly natural, and there was something contrived about her use of current slang like *rather ghastly* or *too sickmaking*. She didn't cut herself off from Johnjohn and Pat, she just didn't want them around when other people were there. Very likely they didn't want to be around either, and they might well have been shocked by the Freddies, Tobys and Jackies.

I realised that she was much younger than Father when I saw a wedding picture in the house at Merton. Father was in uniform, strongly resembling Keaton in *The General*, Mother in her wedding dress looked like a young girl. She was smiling, he was not. I asked Pat why Father was dressed up like a soldier.

'Why, he was a soldier in the war. He could have stayed out of the Army because of his age, but he didn't, he volunteered. He was wounded, can't quite remember how—'

'Shrapnel in the shoulder, leading an attack, couple of weeks before the war ended,' Grandfather Johnjohn said. 'Bloody shame.'

'Language,' Pat said reprovingly. 'And our Deirdre, she was a nurse in the hospital where he went for convalescence. And they fell in love.' I asked when they had married, she said it was in the May after the war ended. Grandfather Johnjohn had a fit of coughing, and she stopped talking. Not very long afterwards I had to write my date of birth, 15th November 1919, on a school form, and realised why Pat had stopped. Deirdre had been three months pregnant when Father married her.

Reading over what I've written about Deirdre, I seem to have made her sound like a working-class girl posing as something she wasn't, just as I've made Father sound like a stuffed shirt. In both cases that was a long way from the truth.

(iii) Justin

The first glimpse I had that this view of Father wasn't the right one came from my half-brother Justin, when I met him at one of the Patons' tennis parties a couple of months before Hugo Headley disappeared. Two or three of these parties were given every summer, with perhaps twenty friends and neighbours there, most of them youngish. There was tea on the lawn and the tennis was mostly mixed doubles played for fun, though I'm sorry to say I sometimes took it seriously, poaching my partners' shots and crouching at the net as if I was playing against Tilden and Helen Wills in the final at Wimbledon. I found it hard not to take any game of tennis seriously then.

I came off the court pleased at winning a set while partnering a girl who hardly knew one end of a racquet from the other, and Neil beckoned me over. He was talking to a man with slicked-back patent-leather hair, and features that looked vaguely familiar. Neil said we must have met before, and was a little embarrassed when I said no. 'Justin Elder, Geoffrey Elder,' he said, and turned away.

'We meet at last,' the man said. 'You don't mean to say he's never mentioned me? Isn't that just like the old bastard?' I must still have looked bewildered. 'We share a father, worse luck. I'm your half-brother, but I can see you've never heard of me. I suppose I shouldn't be too surprised, it's typical. Sit down, I'll tell you about it.' And there, sitting in deck chairs on the Patons' lawn, he told me some family history that had been a closed book to me. Even that convenient cliché isn't right, because I'd never known the book existed.

As Justin talked in an enviably easy way about the family background, I realised why he had seemed familiar. There was a resemblance to Father, although Justin didn't have the same impassivity, he laughed a lot, almost everything seemed to amuse him. This is what he told me.

As a young man Father had been for some years with the firm of Branksome and Simcox, house and estate agents, first as a clerk, then as one of three or four young men dealing with house sales. Then he married Lily Branksome, the elder of two daughters, and became a junior partner. Two or three years after the marriage Branksome died suddenly of a heart attack, and Father used the money that came to Lily to buy out Simcox.

'That's the way to make your way onwards and upwards in life, Geoffrey, marry the boss's daughter and get control of the firm.'

'I thought—' I stopped, and began again. 'You mean Father didn't have much money when he was young.' Although I knew he hadn't gone to university, I'd always assumed he went to a 'good' school like me.

'You can say that again. Do you know what *his* father did? Kept an ironmonger's shop near Newcastle. The old b went to the parish school along with the rest of the family. Mind you I dare say he was bright enough, he and his brother Cornelius, your Aunt Aggie too I dare say, though I believe she was a trouble, the ironmonger being a bit sniffy about boy friends. Cornelius was something of a lad too, from what Mummy said, but she didn't know him, he'd chased off somewhere to make his fortune.'

'And did he?'

'No idea. Do you indulge? Shouldn't ask, you're too young, wish I didn't.' He produced an amber cigarette holder and a packet of Player's, made quite a performance out of lighting up, leaned back in his deck chair.

I felt a surprising need to defend Father. 'How do you know all this?'

He blew a smoke ring. 'When I wasn't there, you mean? Tales my mother told me, that's mostly how. The old b married her, to the tune of distinct disapproval on the part of the Branksomes, in '07. A different world, my lad, not the one we live in now where a duchess's daughter can marry a dustman without an eyebrow being lifted. Here was a girl from a good solid family marrying a penniless young upstart whose father was in trade. I mean, I ask you. When I said to Mummy why did you marry him, she said he had charm. Can you imagine?' Another smoke ring. 'The first and only pledge of their love – that's me – appeared on the scene a couple of years later.'

'And then what happened? I mean, why aren't they still married?'

'Because the old b drove her off her head, then had her locked up in a nuthouse.' I stared at him. 'They had awful rows, I was only a nipper but I remember. If she went round the bend it was because of him, believe you me. She stayed in the nuthouse till she died. I was eight years old then, and I'd been at a boarding school for three years.' He tapped me on the chest. 'If you have kids one day, and want them to grow up nice and normal, don't send them to boarding school when they're five.' He broke off. 'Hilda, how do you manage to play hostess to fifty people and still look radiant?'

'There aren't fifty, only thirty. I didn't think you knew each other. Aren't you going to have any tea?' Hilda Paton looked, as usual, dishevelled and far from radiant.

'We didn't, but now we do. And I believe Geoffrey knows my friend Hugo. Yes, I thought so. We may meet again perhaps, chez Hugo.' Hilda Paton took him away, and I went to look for Melissa, who was absorbed in conversation with a young man I recognised as being in the firm. Was this another case of making eyes at the boss's daughter? But of course Neil Paton wasn't the boss.

On the bus ride home I thought about what Justin had told me, with astonishment and indignation. It was almost impossible for me to imagine Father behaving in the way Justin had described. Obviously a good deal of what he said could be put down to dislike, but I didn't doubt the truth of the story about the previous marriage, and was upset that I should have learned of it through a chance meeting. I said something like that to Deirdre, who heard my complaint coolly.

'Why should you have been told? It's a long time ago.' I said something about having a right to know, to which she responded impatiently. 'It's nothing to do with me. His first wife was dead before I came on the scene. If you want to know about it you must ask him. My advice is, don't.'

I was reluctant to do so. Our relationship was not like that existing nowadays between fathers and sons. There was no freedom in it, our conversations being almost wholly confined to sport and school. Did he tell me the facts of life, as they were called? I can't remember, but if he did it must have been in such obscure terms that I didn't know what he was talking about. But still I did speak to him one evening, a few days after seeing Justin. After dinner he often retired to his study, and it was there among the books on estate management and the volumes of Dumas and Henty that I bearded him.

He was sitting in a leather armchair, wearing a plum-coloured smoking jacket (he often changed after dinner), and reading *The Times*. A glass of port stood by his side. He looked up as I entered and said, not impatiently but as if I were a subordinate in the office, 'You wanted to see me, Geoffrey?'

Yes, I said and then, standing awkwardly before him and speaking awkwardly too I have no doubt, I told him what I had heard from Justin. He listened, his expression unchanging. When I had done he said, 'How old are you now? Sixteen, yes. Old enough for a glass of port.'

He crossed to the table that held decanters of port and whisky, poured a glass, gave it me and told me to sit down. Then he moved behind his desk and sat there, almost as if he felt safer behind it, looking at the wine in his glass. He was still looking at it, not at me, when he spoke.

'I might have said something about this before. Perhaps I should have done. It must have come as a shock to learn you had such a near relative.'

'Yes.' I did not know what to say next. 'I liked Justin.' I sipped the port. I had never tasted it before, and was surprised to find it sweet.

'The marriage was not a success from the start, we didn't suit each other. Lily's temperament was – erratic. I was afraid she might do away with herself. She was properly cared for in the home. She died in 1917. Is there anything else you want to know?' He might have been a businessman apologising for a missing clause in an agreement.

'Why doesn't Justin come here, why haven't I seen him before?'

Now he did look at me out of deep-set eyes whose intensity contradicted his manner. The eyes had a candour that seemed both to ask for and express sympathy. 'Justin is not a desirable acquaintance. He has been in prison.'

'What for?'

'I don't know the details, nor do I want to. I couldn't possibly ask your mother to receive him.' That seemed to me ridiculous, and I gave a quickly smothered laugh which turned into a snort. 'You find it funny that I shouldn't wish your mother to meet a jailbird? You have an odd sense of humour.'

'He's good enough to go to Neil Paton's.' I stood up, on the verge of tears. There was much more I wanted to know, about his life and about Justin, but I didn't dare to ask further questions. Instead I said, with a consciousness of being childish, that I didn't like the port. At that he left the desk, came to me and put an arm round my shoulders.

'My boy, I see you're upset. It's my fault, and I'm very sorry. You must understand, there are things in everybody's life they don't want to remember. If Justin came here he would remind me of them.'

It was then that I realised for the first time his love for me, and knew too that I loved him. Perhaps he would have gone on, but this approach to intimacy was too much for me. I gave a wail, escaped from the encircling velvet arm, and rushed up to my room, where I lay weeping. After a few minutes I dried my eyes, and looked in a mirror. As I feared the tears, or perhaps the stress of what had been said, had made my acne worse.

46

This was in July, not long before we went to Clempstone. We did not refer to the conversation again.

(iv) Hugo

As Justin said I had already met Hugo Headley some three months earlier, when he came to school to read his poems.

The reading was arranged by our English master Paul Topley, who was keen on modern poetry. He was a tall thin man with a large Adam's apple that moved convulsively up and down when he became excited, as he did when reading any passage that moved him. He would stop in the middle of reading a poem by Auden or Stephen Spender to say, 'Isn't that a *wonderful* image – doesn't it send a *shiver* up your spine?' No doubt Topley was regarded as a crank by most of his colleagues, and some of the boys mimicked his mannerisms, the emphasis he gave to certain words and his habit of swaying about when reading a passage. The general view in the sixth form was that old Toppers was a bit potty about poetry, but there were a few of us who read some of the poets he recommended, and became almost as excited as he was about them. I was myself much keener on Elizabethan drama, especially when it was really bloodthirsty and rhetorical, and was ready to declaim great stretches of Marlowe which I knew by heart. It was acting rather than poetry that I enjoyed, and old Toppers wasn't much interested in the stage.

One of the things I realised at once about Hugo Headley was that he was quite an actor. He came along in an old pullover, and Oxford bags that were already out of fashion, a short dark intense-looking man with a mass of black hair that came down almost to his shoulders, something that seemed astonishing at the time. When Toppers introduced him, telling us that Mr Headley was one of the most *exciting* poets to have appeared for *years*, the boys were restless. I heard Jevons behind me whisper, 'I'm a poet, and don't I know it.' But it was different when he got up to read. His voice was rich and deep, and the first lines of the first poem made us all sit up and take notice:

'When you and I together lie,
Lip to lip and thigh to thigh,
And I press, and you sigh,
What thunderclaps of eternity shake us, what archangels try
To urge us to Nirvana as passion fades and we die,
Asking forever in this expense of spirit why
We call it lust in action'

It's safe to say that none of us knew he was talking about sexual climax or that the last two lines referred to a Shakespeare sonnet, but 'lip to lip and thigh to thigh' was exciting stuff. As the poem continued through several similar verses attention might have flagged but for the power with which the poet declaimed the most stirring passages, hair partly concealing his face, body thrust forward and then back, an occasional fine spray of spittle issuing from his mouth. Topley swayed from side to side in his chair like a charmed snake, and the audience stayed captive and silent as Hugo read 'The Ballad of the Deadly Trunk' (about a body found in a trunk left in a railway station) and less intelligible poems like 'Praise to the Life Force'. He knew everything he read by heart, and acted scenes where possible, crouching and baring his teeth when speaking in the person of the trunk murderer. Poetry readings were prim and decorous in those days, and we had never heard anything like it. Afterwards Toppers introduced three or four of us to him, and he fastened on my name.

'Geoffrey Elder, yes. I've seen you before. Naked too, I may say.' He clapped me on the shoulder. 'A joke, though it's true. You've got a house at Clempstone, right, go there for the summer, right? Sometimes go in for an early morning dip in the altogether when no one's about, don't you? I've got a cottage there, tumbledown shack more like, stay in it when I want to get away from people. I immerse in the destructive element myself,

saw you further along the beach.' He grinned, the grin trans-
forming his face so that he looked like a long-haired monkey. 'I
know your aunt Mary Storm. She is your aunt, right?' I agreed,
and added that Mary Storm was her stage name. 'Great actress,
wonderful woman.' I was aware of a warm rich smell coming
from him, and realised that he was not exactly dirty but grubby,
his shirt not quite clean, his nails blackened. When Toppers
came up he said we'd discovered we knew each other.

'I know his aunt, Mary Storm.'

'Ah yes, a *beautiful* actress.'

'I know her off the stage.' He gave his grin, then put his head
near to Toppers'. 'Must have a quick one, reading takes it out of
you.'

Toppers looked taken aback, swayed slightly, said something
about a glass of sherry in his room. Before he went the poet
winked at me. 'We'll meet again, I feel it in my water. Next time
make sure you're properly dressed.'

I had never met anybody like him before, and was fascinated
and repelled in about equal proportions. Fascinated by the
outspokenness, the willingness I sensed to do or say almost
anything, even by the sloppiness of his dress which, perhaps
unconsciously, I contrasted with Father's pillarboxical neatness. I sensed also a half-deliberate attempt to attract the person
he was talking to, that drew me like iron filings to a magnet. And
what repelled me? His dirtiness, though that is not quite the
right word, for it was more a matter of what seemed ingrained
grime, so that his skin looked intrinsically muddy. This muddi-
ness then, and the whiff of sweat about him, which some
women find attractive.

Beyond the fascination and repulsion, though, I was aware of
something reckless in him, reckless and (though I wouldn't
have used such a word then) dangerous. I put a note down in my
journal: 'Poet named Hugo Headley came to school. Must buy
poems. Talked afterwards, said he'd seen me bathing naked.
Extraordinary man. Didn't like him.' That about sums up my
reaction, though fear might have been a better word than
dislike.

(v) Grandison House

Grandison House at Clempstone is indissolubly linked to my childhood. I remember crossing the road from the house each morning and running down the steps to the beach, spending hours building sand castles and decorating them with shells and seaweed, running as it seemed miles over the sand to the sea when the tide was out, playing cricket on the beach, finding tiny crabs in rock pools, running screaming out of the sea after being stung by a jellyfish. There were other summer visitors, children I played with on the sands, sometimes fighting them when they trampled my sand castles, and a small girl who caused a scandal among our elders by her sexual inquisitiveness when several of us were playing doctors and nurses in a tent. I remember Walls ice cream vendors riding up and down the promenade pedalling four-wheel cycles, calling out, 'Wafers, cornets, snofrutes, they're lovely,' and the sign on their ice box that read 'Stop Me and Buy One'. Conventional enough memories, no doubt. And memory can play strange tricks. It was a shock to discover after Father's death that I was seven years old when he bought Grandison House. It seemed to me that I recalled being pushed across the road in a buggy by a nurse or a maid, something that can never have happened. And my belief that the weather on our summer visits was always fine, that too must have been an illusion.

It was a large cheerless rambling house. What particularly caught my child's imagination were the circular towers at the ends, each of which contained a small room reached by a spiral staircase leading out of the larger room below. Between the towers were attics on the top floor, some empty, others occupied by the two or three servants who came down with us. On the first floor were bedrooms, dressing rooms and two old-fashioned bathrooms, the hot water coming from geysers which sometimes made a tremendous bang when lighted. There was a covered verandah in front of the house, and above it a wooden balcony. I remember Deirdre sitting in a deck chair on this balcony, sometimes wearing a frilled striped dressing gown, reading novels, polishing her nails, looking at the sea. On the ground floor were dining room, drawing room with an old upright piano, study, sewing room – although no sewing was ever done in it. At the back lay a maze of passages, kitchen, pantry, larder, wine cellar, utility room, and behind them a large scrubby garden looked after by a man in the village named Passlove, and in the last two years of our visits there, after Passlove had a heart attack, by his son. Passlove senior, who still occasionally came up, pottered about the garden and ate his lunch in the shed at the bottom of it, was a fawning cap-touching little man. Passlove junior was a large loutish figure who seemed always to be stripped to the waist and leaning on a fork or spade rather than working.

Behind the house, within a couple of minutes' walk, was the Clempstone Golf and Tennis Club, the biggest in that part of the county, with a dozen grass and four hard courts. The links were well-known, but the tennis club was famous, at least locally. County tournaments were sometimes played there, and it was at Clempstone that I had first discovered I was a much better player than most boys of my age.

We never returned to Grandison House, or for that matter to Clempstone, after Hugo Headley's disappearance. The happenings on our last visit made that inevitable, and in the following year Father sold it. When I went back after Duffy's visit I saw the place for the first time in twenty years or more. The house had been converted into four flats, each with its separate entrance, but apart from the new entrances, two of which were at the back, the façade was unchanged. There was the balcony with a couple of deck chairs on it, one of which might have been waiting for Deirdre to come out of her bedroom, there were the towers. They were no longer impressive but absurd, and the whole house was much smaller than I remembered. It seemed to me now an example of English seaside architecture at its worst, a ghastly mixture of mock-Gothic and mock-Tudor with a touch of Dutch influence in the attic gables. That's what the house really looked like, you might say, though I'm not sure there's anything more 'real' in the later view of it than in my youthful impression. The Golf and Tennis Club was still there, approached now by a rash of bungalows, with some new hard courts and a squash club added. I stood and watched some teenagers for half an hour, and wondered whether I would have beaten them in my youthful prime.

During the holidays I spent a lot of time in the little room at the top of the left-hand tower. I'd lugged a small table up there, along with some bookshelves and a couple of chairs, plus bits of worn carpet. Photographs of tennis players past and present were stuck up round the walls, the Dohertys, Gerald Patterson, Tilden and the three Musketeers, Cochet, Lacoste and Borotra, with women represented by Lenglen and Helen Wills. There I read Webster, Ford and Tourneur, and above all Marlowe, thundering out bits of *Tamburlaine* in the belief that they would not be audible down below. I also read thrillers by 'Sapper' and Sydney Horler, and spent much time looking out to sea from the circular window, dreaming of Wimbledon, of treading the stage at the Old Vic, and of Melissa. I imagined her climbing the spiral stair, and her astonished pleasure at dis-covering what I thought of as my secret room. My thoughts never went beyond imaginary kisses, extensions of the real one at the party. No thought of going to bed with her crossed my mind, and in fact that was not a phrase used by boys before the war. It may be that I just wanted her to admire me. I longed for her to see me play and beat some really good tennis player, or watch one of the school plays and be overwhelmed by my acting.

Why did Father buy Grandison House? No doubt partly because it released something in the concealed part of his personality. He played a little golf, was a good swimmer and went in the sea almost every day, he wore shorts in sunny weather and casual clothes the whole time. Another considera-tion was that, as I discovered when going through papers after he died, it was very cheap. The previous owner was a retired Indian Army colonel, a breed often found inhabiting unfashionable and inexpensive English seaside resorts in the days before the war. Branksome and Elder handled the disposition of his estate in collaboration with his solicitors, and when the place went unsold at auction Father bought it, as they say, for a song. Looking at the papers I saw that when it was sold he got quadruple the sum he'd paid for it a decade earlier.

We used the house for a month or six weeks in the summer, and for occasional weekends in spring and autumn, but it was shut up for the rest of the year, and in the care of the Passloves. We went there once for Christmas, but the weather was bad, the house damp, the cook left, and the experiment was never repeated. In 1936 I looked forward to our visit with particular excitement. My journal gives one reason in a sentence: 'Melissa staying with us at G H this year!' She was coming down with her mother who had not been well, Neil following a day or two later. Deirdre also was coming down only at weekends. There was a new girl at her shop A Joy For Ever, who needed to be shown the ropes and, as she often said, Clempstone was deadly dull.

If you were looking for urban amusement that was perfectly true. The village had one street of shops, butcher, baker, post office and general store. There was a pub at either end of the street, a church in the middle of it, and a few small houses and cottages clustered around, plus another couple of pubs and several boarding houses and – the superior, newer phrase – guest houses. A long avenue of birch trees led out of the village, which was half a mile inland, to the large private houses facing the sea. There was a promenade which petered out after a short distance, and became merged with sand dunes. Beyond this promenade, if you drove or walked along the narrow coast road, you reached Parker's Point, the end of the bay that enclosed Clempstone, and the beginning of another bay. Here there was a green field where motorists sometimes stopped to eat sandwiches. In the other direction, past the substantial Victorian or Edwardian houses, was a sprinkling of old coastguard and other cottages dotted along the road that led to the next village, Greystone, a couple of miles away. Hugo Headley's cottage was here, a few hundred yards away from Grandison House, on the way to Greystone.

I had another reason for excitement. The Junior South East Tennis Championship was held at the tennis club, 'junior' meaning under eighteen. Last year I had got into the quarter-

finals, and this year I hoped to win. On the Thursday before this
championship began, Melissa, her mother and myself were
driven down by Father from London. Muriel the cook and a maid
named Daisy had gone down a couple of days earlier. To my
regret I sat in front, instead of in the back with Melissa. Father's
hands on the wheel were large and competent. He never spoke
much when driving, and I was surprised when he asked if I found
it dull at Clempstone. Dull, with Melissa there, and with the
Junior Championship coming up, how could it be? I didn't say
this, only that I liked it, which was true.

'Your mother finds it dull.' I just shook my head at that. 'She'd
like a holiday abroad, but I love England. I could live happily
down there, playing golf, fishing, sailing. I should need nothing
more. That surprises you, I dare say.' I said I didn't know. I was
not used to such conversations with him. 'But Deirdre – it
wouldn't suit her.' I made no reply, and he gave up the
conversation.

When we arrived at five o'clock we were greeted by the
Passloves. Senior touched his cap, rubbed his hands, said we
should find everything in apple-pie order. Junior, who was
wearing a short-sleeved shirt open to show a hairy chest, first
stood with hands on hips, then picked up and carried heavy
suitcases as if they were filled with feathers. There was the
usual chatter about the need for a cup of tea. Hilda Paton felt a
headache coming on, and said she would have tea in her room
and lie down. I unpacked, then went straight up to my tower,
opened the window and leaned out, feeling exhilaration at the
sight of the sea. Below me I saw Melissa come out of the front
door, walk down the gravel drive, cross the road to the promenade and stand looking first left, then right. She turned when I
called to her and recrossed the road when I said I wanted to show
her my room. I took the stairs down two at a time, and led her up.

'I can shut myself away here, be entirely on my own.'

She glanced at the photographs of tennis players, and at the
books. 'What do you do up here?'

'I don't know. Read mostly. And think.' I should have liked to
say I thought about her, but the words would not come. And
now that – so soon, immediately on her arrival – I'd fulfilled the

dream of her entry into my secret room, the idea of kissing her seemed out of the question. She went to the window, leaned out as I had done. She had changed into shorts and a striped shirt, and I saw her lean legs, the muscles tensing a little as she looked out, her hair thick, glossy, curling up slightly at the back. Even as I thought I might join her and put an arm round her waist she turned and asked, smiling slightly, what there was to do. Swimming, I said, walking, playing tennis or golf, going out fishing with Passlove junior in his boat. Then I remembered that she liked riding, and added that there was a stables in the village which rented out horses.

'Not madly exciting.' She stood in the middle of the room, frowning a little. Perhaps I looked disappointed, because she smiled again. 'What about a quick dip?' Ten minutes later we were in the sea, shouting and laughing to each other, and afterwards we went for a walk along the sand dunes. She said she was here partly as a companion to her mother.

'She thinks she's ill, you know. Whenever anything goes wrong she says she's ill.'

'Has something gone wrong?'

'In a way. Not much.'

I started to say something about how wonderful it was to have her there.

'You're going to be a tennis champion, you shouldn't be thinking of girls.' I said boldly that I could do both. 'Oh no, you can't. Aren't you playing in a tournament here? You don't know how demanding girls can be.' She kissed me, not on the cheek but on the lips, and said I was sweet. A couple of years later I might have regarded the kiss and the word as casually dismissive, but at the time I was delighted. My journal note read: 'Showed M tower room, went swimming, she kissed me. Didn't respond, should have done. Next time I shall kiss her first, tell her I love her.'

That wasn't the way things turned out.

At dinner Melissa was very gay, saying what a good swimmer I was, telling Father he'd been cowardly not to come in the water, asking about the stables. He seemed to enjoy what I thought of as chaffing (almost a period word), even boasting in what seemed to me an unsuitable way about being a better swimmer than me, which was true.

'We lead a simple life here, no metropolitan pleasures.' Hilda Paton said that was a good thing, and Melissa that she just adored the simple life. It occurred to me that with a maid and a cook it wasn't so simple, but I didn't say so.

'Onions,' Hilda said suddenly. 'There were onions in the sauce. I should have been told, I shall suffer.' She placed a hand somewhere in the region of her heart.

'Mummy, don't make such a fuss, you must have known.'

'A *fuss*,' Hilda Paton echoed. 'What I know is that when you're unwell it's no use expecting sympathy from your family.' I noticed she had eaten all the onion sauce on her plate.

Father said perhaps she would tell cook other things she should avoid, and she gave him a sufferer's hopeless smile.

'Really it should be nothing but a tomato and a lettuce leaf.' Daisy brought in a fruit trifle loaded with cream. Hilda looked at it, Melissa said of course she mustn't touch it, and she agreed. Then she said that if Harold would excuse her she would sit on the balcony outside her room and enjoy the evening sun. When she had gone he asked if she often suffered like this.

'She's seen four doctors and two specialists. They found nothing wrong except that she eats too many sweets.'

Father's voice was uncharacteristically playful. 'Not spoken like a dutiful daughter.'

Have I mentioned Melissa's eyes? They were deep brown like dark toffee, long-lashed and large, and they seemed to grow larger when she was either pleased or angry. They looked enormous now as she asked, 'What makes you think I am one?' Father laughed but did not comment.

Later I spent half an hour in the tower room reading an article by Fred Perry about developing your forehand drive, then went to bed. My usual room in the front had been given to Hilda and Neil, and Melissa was next to them, the two rooms having a connecting door. I was sleeping in the back of the house, in a room opposite my old one. As I turned the door handle I heard, could not help hearing, Melissa and her mother arguing, although I could not distinguish the words except for a final phrase. This was Melissa's. 'I shall do what I bloody well like,' she said. I heard the slam of the connecting door, then silence.

That was Thursday. On Friday Melissa went out, I met Hugo Headley again, and saw the man with the squint.

The Sixties

Aunt Aggie

Aunt Aggie

On the Saturday after the visit from biographer Duffy I drove down to see Aunt Aggie in her cottage a couple of miles outside Guildford, taking with me a box of Fortnum's chocolates. It is one of the unfair facts of life that some people can stuff themselves with chocolates and rich foods without putting on weight, while others have only to look at a liqueur chocolate to make the scales behave as if Goliath were standing on them. I belong to the latter group, Aunt Aggie to the former. Both of us love chocolates, but only Aunt Aggie eats them.

I had telephoned in advance. 'Can't ask you to lunch,' she said immediately. 'Never eat it now, can't be bothered, and must have my rest afterwards. Come to tea.' I asked if she was sure a cup of tea wouldn't be too much trouble. 'Sarky, are you, young Geoffrey? If I ask you there'll be *tea*, bread and butter, scones and a cake and two sorts of jam. But not home-made, shop bought's better.'

'You mean you're too lazy to make it?'

'Don't be cheeky.' Aunt Aggie liked men to be handsome and dashing like Hugo Headley. In default of dash she was pleased if they were cheeky. When Leila, who had been listening to my end of the conversation, asked how I could be so revoltingly pert, I knew I had struck the right note. I suggested she should come with me, knowing she would refuse. She found that a little of Aunt Aggie went a long way, a sentiment that was reciprocated. 'I always thought you were a bright boy,' Aunt Aggie said to me once. 'I see you need to live with a woman, but did you have to choose one who was quite so *dull*? You have to prod her to make sure she's alive.' When I said Leila's restfulness was the quality I valued most, she said I must be half-dead too.

It was her agent who said Agatha Elder was a hopeless name for an actress, and christened her Mary Storm. He chose well, for her acting style was stormy, and so was her temperament. A critic said once it would be nice if she could ask the time of day on stage without making it sound as if she were waiting for Armageddon, and her rows with producers were legendary. By the acting standards of my day she overacted hopelessly, but in her time, which was a little before World War I to the beginning of World War II, Mary Storm was a name to reckon with, as I knew from spending an hour or two poring over her cuttings books, which said among much other praise that she was the best Mrs Erlynne since Marion Terry originally played the part, and that her Mrs Arbuthnot in *An Ideal Husband* was incomparably the finest ever to 'grace the boards' as the reviewer put it. In a way the heart attack that forced her to give up the stage in 1941 had been a piece of good fortune, for she would never have been able to adapt her acting style to post-war fashion. Not, of course, that she saw things that way. Her contempt for modern acting and modern reviewers was expressed loud and often.

Aunt Aggie was now eighty, but on her good days as lively as a woman twenty years younger. She maddened me, but I was very fond of her. She lived in what had once been a workman's cottage, the end one of a row in a village street, with a neat garden in front, and quite literally roses round the door.

'You've *arrived*.' She held out her arms. 'I thought you were never coming, did your car break down?' She looked at it standing outside the gate. 'Still the same old banger, must be ten years old. I suppose you can't afford anything better.' I said it had brought me down from London in less than an hour and a half, and that if I'd come any earlier she would have said I'd invited myself to lunch. She showed no sign of hearing this.

'How's the Princess of Sloth? Don't answer, shouldn't have said it, come in.'

The little sitting room that looked on to the street was crowded with relics of her past, old theatre programmes framed on the walls, photographs of her with famous and now forgotten actors like Frank Benson and Lyall Sweete, and of an occasion when some play had been visited by the King and Queen Mary, who had been introduced to the cast. The picture showed Aggie typically making a dramatic performance out of her curtsey to the Queen. Nowadays most theatre people would keep such memorabilia tucked away in a drawer, but in Aggie's time actresses were actressy, and liked to remind you of the fact.

Aggie still took the *Stage*, which I looked at while she made a noise with cups and saucers in the kitchen. Tea was just what she had said on the telephone, except that there were crumpets instead of scones. The teacups were Spode, but mine was cracked, and a fine line of grime showed near the rim.

'Eat, eat,' she cried. 'Eat the crumpets while they're hot. You know what my nice po-faced doctor said when I offered them to him? You should avoid crumpets with your heart condition, Miss Elder. Doctor, I said, you're looking pale, as if you could do with some crumpet yourself. He blushed, believe it or not, he blushed.' She shrieked with laughter. I was used to Aunt Aggie's shock tactics, and merely said the doctor was right.

'No, he wasn't, and he wasn't wrong either. You should die the way you live. I like crumpets and I like pink gin – it was a destroyer captain in the war gave me a taste for it – and I'm not going to give them up because some young squirt says I'll drop dead one day holding a large pink gin in my hand. And I like crumpet, and that's something you're never too old for. I said to the young squirt, I shall die knowing I've had the best of everything.' There was something unusually eager and secretive about Aunt Aggie today. She looked at me as if about to spring some extremely naughty and embarrassing joke.

I haven't said what she looked like. She was six years younger than Father, four years younger than his brother Cornelius who I knew had gone off to Australia, and didn't look much like either of them to judge from the family photograph she kept on the mantelpiece. Father would have been perhaps twenty-one when the photograph was taken, and had already a deadpan Keatonish look. Cornelius had one of those round unmade faces that could develop into anything with maturity, and Aggie between them wore the air of a mischievous elf. They were standing, their father and mother sitting, he a grave figure with beard and sidewhiskers, she small and upright, staring at the camera. Aunt Aggie still had those elfin features, with cheeks now highly coloured. Her eyes, deep-set like Father's, were surrounded by a mass of wrinkles. She had always favoured dramatic colours, and on this afternoon wore a bright blue dress with diagonal stripes of lighter blue across it, and sleeves that came down to her wrists. Her hands were reddish and heavily veined, an old woman's hands.

I ate two crumpets, something Leila would never have permitted, then tucked into bread and butter. Aunt Aggie kept pace with me. I thought it likely that she had spoken the truth about not eating lunch. When she poured the second cup of strong Indian tea she paused, pot over cup. 'So what is it you want? No use saying you've come just to see me, that won't wash.'

'All right then, I won't say it. I've talked to Kevin Duffy.' She looked mystified. 'He's writing a biography of Hugo Headley.'

'The bog Irishman.' She shrieked with laughter, her own voice became mock-Irish. 'Begorra, me young feller, I says to him, you'll find all you need to know about the great and sacred poet Hugo Headley in the book of his poetry I gave the world these many years agone.'

'But you didn't say that, Aggie, did you? You sent him up to your attic and said he could take away anything he found there.'

She waved the rough red hand. 'Ah, it's only a little attic.'

'But you did do that? And didn't bother to look at what he took.'

'I was very tired. He was a bore. And I had another visitor coming, I wanted to get rid of him.' She looked at me roguishly, let her head drop back against the cushion of the chair. 'What business is it of yours anyway?'

'Have you any idea what he took?'

'Ah, what does it matter? Do you know that poem of Emily Dickinson's, "My life closed twice before it closed"? I know the meaning of that, that was when my life closed, when Hugo died all those years ago. Nothing has been the same since.' Her eyes had closed, tears rolled down her cheeks. She wiped them away, opened her eyes again. 'When I gathered his poems, and saw them published and wrote my little bit about them and him I meant what I said, it was the end of something. He was the love of my life.'

I didn't know whether to be moved or to applaud, whether it was Agatha Elder speaking or Mary Storm acting out a scene. Or, as often happens with stage people, a bit of both. When she had

64

made the speech she gave me another of those mischievous glances, as if something important remained unsaid. I told her of the letters Duffy had taken away, and what he was trying to make of them. She listened attentively, her little eyes sharp.

When I'd done, she asked again why I had come to see her, and I hardly knew what answer to make. The mystery of Headley's disappearance had been pushed to the back of my mind for years, why should I bother with it now? Because Melissa had been involved with him, and I had thought myself in love with her? Surely not. Because I felt I should have known Father better, and in some way had failed him? That would be nearer the mark, or even painfully on it. 'Aggie,' I said, 'tell me about the family.'

'The family,' she echoed, as if I were using an unknown word.

'Father never talked about it. Where you were brought up, what family life was like, what schools you went to, that sort of thing. All I know is that my grandfather was an ironmonger in Newcastle.'

'Not true.'

'He wasn't an ironmonger?'

'It wasn't in the city, but a few miles outside in one of the suburbs, though it was separate then, a place called Plashet. If you lived there you went to the District School and then into Corbyns, a factory that made rubber goods, not the kind you're thinking of, rubberised raincoats, rubber boots, bands and so on. You worked in the factory, and that was the end of you. It was a place to get away from, and we all got away in the end, all the family.'

'But it's right about him being an ironmonger?'

'Our father kept a shop, that's right, Silas Elder, Ironmongers and General Store. Harry and Corny worked in it too for a while when they left school, and that was when they were twelve years old, it wasn't the way it is now, I can tell you. But they were both bright lads and before long they found work in Newcastle, Harry in a solicitor's office, Corny with a building contractor. Father was fit to be tied, expected them to take over the shop when he retired. It was the biggest disappointment of his life, maybe the only one. Most things happened the way he wanted.' A different note had entered her voice, the distant echo of a Geordie accent. 'It was a place to get away from, Plashet, and a home to get away from too, I can tell you. Our father thought all boys and girls had a bit of the devil in them, and you could get rid of it with the strap.'

'He beat you? All of you?' She nodded. 'What did your mother say?'

'*What did Mother say?*' She laughed, an old woman's cackle. 'She said nothing, my innocent young Geoffrey, our father's word was law. It was all like something out of Dickens, Mr Murdstone was his name? He ruled the roost and knew what was best for everybody, our father. You know we had family prayers at every meal, not that there was anything so unusual in that, but if one of us was late he missed tea or dinner. That was when we were at school, mind, but even when the boys got jobs they had to be home by nine each night.'

'What about your friends? They must have thought it was an odd household.'

'Friends? You don't understand what it was like, how could you? We didn't have any friends, anyone we brought home our father ran the rule over them as he called it, to make sure they wouldn't lead us into sinful ways, so we all learned not to bring anybody home. Only one exception, Cissy Young, she was my great friend at school, her father was a manager at Corbyns, and for some reason our father took to her, used to let her cheek him in a way none of us would dare, and seemed to like it. She'd come to tea once or twice a week. She had pigtails and he used to pretend to pull them, tell her she was a naughty girl. All very Barretts of Wimpole Street, with Cissy playing Elizabeth except that she wasn't an invalid but full of bounce. She used to write to me after I left home and came to London, talked about coming down to join me but never did. Married one of the directors at Corbyns instead and died in childbirth, which was something that used to happen in those days. But Cissy was the only one. Corny never brought boys home that I can remember, knew they'd be told off for something or other and then he'd get a taste of the strap later on, and Harry never made friends at school anyway, he was always a loner. But it was no life for anyone, and I don't know why they stuck it. Well, they didn't, not for ever.

Harry got the job with the estate agents in London, and Corny went off to Australia.'

'He kept in touch?'

'He used to write to Harry, once or twice to me. He had a hard time at first, worked in the Sydney docks.'

'He never came back to England?'

She shook her head. 'Got out of the docks, started up some business of his own, doing rather well, then he died in a train crash. Still in his twenties. I cried my eyes out.' There was something glib about the way she said this. Then she went on, 'So he never saw me on the stage, poor old Corny,' and the remark was so true to her egotistical character that I felt she must be telling the truth. I asked when she had left home.

'I stuck it till I was sixteen, then skedaddled, ran away to London. Soon after that our mother died. I never went back for the funeral, I was sorry about that, but our father said he wouldn't let me in the house. Mind you, her death broke him up, he died himself not so many years after.' I asked if she had any photographs of her parents. 'Never kept them, why should I? Just that family picture you've seen, and I kept that for us, not them.'

'I can understand why Father didn't talk about it. What was he like in those days?'

'Marvellous, just marvellous. He was the oldest, you see, and our father held him responsible for everything. He was supposed to look after us, see we got to school and straight home from it, didn't stop to play with other kids. If Corny got into a fight, or I splashed home through puddles and got my shoes and stockings dirty, Harry took the blame. Our mother used to try and hush any trouble up and sometimes she did, but he usually found out in the end, and then he used the strap. We all got it, but Harry took the brunt.'

'I wonder he didn't leave as soon as he got out of school.'

She glared at me. 'I could shake you, Geoffrey Elder, you're so thick. Boys and girls just didn't leave home in those days, and the way we'd been brought up to believe everything our father did was right we wouldn't have done anyway. We respected him, don't you understand, and so did everybody else. He was a shopkeeper maybe, but he was still a big man in Plashet. People looked up to him. Our mother worshipped him.'

'But you got away.'

'That's right. Once I left school I was always in trouble, seeing boys along with Cissy, and staying out late. The boys were different, under his thumb even after they got jobs in the city. Corny could do silly things, but Harry was always the dutiful son. They didn't get away until our mother died. And there was trouble when they did.'

'What trouble?'

She sat brooding, head forward and looking what she was, a very old woman. 'I should leave it.'

'What do you mean?'

'Just drop it, let O'Muffy O'Duffy say anything he likes, what does it matter, who cares, it's water under the bridge and stale water at that. Mind you, if I'd known those letters were upstairs I might have put a match to them.'

'I don't understand why they weren't in Hugo's cottage. He must have had the notes from Father just before coming down to Clempstone, and those from Melissa when he was actually there.'

'I'll tell you why. After Hugo disappeared the police looked over the cottage. Then they came to see me in London, I was doing a Maugham, *Lady Frederick* I think, can't remember. I told them what was true, that our affair had finished two or three months back, and what wasn't true, that I hadn't seen him since we broke up. I saw no reason why I should give those nosy parkers every detail of my private life. And then a little alarm bell rang up here.' A hand went to her head, as if the bell were ringing there still. 'I'd written letters to him – I told you he'd been the love of my life, and when you're passionate about somebody you don't care what you say or do.' I thought she was going to say I wouldn't understand her emotions, and she might have been right, but she forbore. 'There were things I wouldn't have wanted people to read. So I went down – of course I had a key – and there I found Headley ma and pa. A dismal pair of wetfish they were too, I can tell you, the father canting on all the time about Hugo's way of life and how he was bound to come to a bad end, the mother with her lips padlocked tight but agreeing with every miserable word. Of course they were certain he'd drowned, never had any doubt about it, and didn't seem particularly sorry. I think they'd only come down to make sure there was nothing around that would besmirch the family name. I told them they should be honoured to have been the parents of a genius, but snivelling little bourgeois that they were, they thought nothing of that. I don't mind theft and cheating and malice, you get used to them in the theatre, but I can't stand cant. When I came to do the book they insisted on seeing what I'd said in the introduction, and took out one or two references, wouldn't let me say more than that he'd lived a bohemian life. Bohemian life nothing, he was a villain, it was why I loved him. When a villain's a genius, how can you help loving him?'

I didn't try to answer that question, but asked one that cast back to what she'd been saying. 'What about Father? Did you see him when he came to London?'

'Of course I did. And he gave me money when I was on my beam ends, which was often enough in those days.'

'But he can't have approved of you, can he? He was respectable and solemn, one of your snivelling bourgeois, isn't that right?'

'Approval, disapproval, what does it mean when you love somebody? There was no cant about Harry, he was a fine man. You never understood him, that was your loss. He had a gift for choosing the wrong women, that's all. Lily was just a stuck-up prig, and your mother was a bitch. Do you see anything of her?' I shook my head. After the war Deirdre had married the vice-president of an American advertising agency and gone to live in New York. She wrote to me twice a year, and sent an expensive present at Christmas. 'Lucky you.'

'Did you find the letters in the cottage?'

'Nope.' Aunt Aggie occasionally made descents into outdated American slang. 'The wretch can't have kept them, but I didn't know that at the time. I didn't want to go searching for them with mère and père around, and they were only too happy for me to take away any papers connected with Hugo rather than having to go through them and find out things they'd sooner not know. This was about a month after he disappeared. The police had been through everything, and they'd pretty well lost interest, or so I thought. So I bundled up a lot of stuff, including some unpublished poems, took it back to London and went through it. Or most of it.'

'You don't remember the letters from Melissa, or those Father wrote to him?'

'Can't remember, but if I'd seen them I wouldn't have paid much attention. I made a bonfire of some stuff and couldn't tell you why I didn't put them in too, didn't notice them I suppose. Maybe I shouldn't have let O'Duffy take them away, but it's all a long time ago and I won't be badgered about it.'

'What did you mean, there was trouble at home? What was it about?'

'Some girl or other, I never knew the rights and wrongs of it.' She closed her eyes again and put her head back, so that she looked like a highly coloured doll dropped into the chair.

'Who was the girl? Was the trouble to do with Father?'

'It might have been, I don't remember. I'd flown the coop. And I told you, I won't be badgered.' Eyes still closed, she said, 'What are you doing now, I forget who your agent is, is he doing his stuff?'

This was an evasion. She knew perfectly well the name of my agent, that he was somebody who hadn't been on the scene in her day. She'd recommended me to approach her own agent, and I'd said I doubted if he'd want me, or could do much for me. However, we went through the routine of naming my agent again, she with eyes still closed. I knew from her tone that it was no use pursuing the matter of the mysterious girl, and asked whether she had heard from Hugo since his disappearance. At that her eyes opened, as those of a doll do when you move it from a lying to a sitting position. She snapped at me, saying Hugo had drowned, and of course she hadn't heard from him.

'What's the matter with you, Geoffrey Elder? What kind of nonsense have you got in your head? You've nothing to do and fancy yourself as a detective, is that it?'

I found it hard to say why I wanted to revive the memory of those days at Clempstone long ago. The teasing sense that she was telling me less than she knew had prompted the question about Hugo. It was no more than a piece of shock tactics to make her understand I was not to be fobbed off by chat about my agent. All this passed through my mind, but I said simply that I wanted to find out what Father's notes referred to, and who 'M' was.

'If you dig in the earth you'll turn up dirt.'

'You mean you know, and it's something discreditable?'

'Nothing of the sort. What I'm saying is that Hugo did a lot of things he shouldn't.'

'Was he blackmailing Father? That's the way the notes to him read.'

'Possibly.'

'What about?'

'I've no idea.' Her piercing little eyes looked directly at me. I was not sure whether to believe her. 'If I tell you one or two things about Hugo you'll understand, but I want them to go no further. You don't tell them to that bog Irishman.' I said of course I shouldn't do that. 'All right, then. I told you I'd broken with Hugo, and it was because I couldn't stand the way he went on. I'm not talking about other women, but he'd take money from your purse, forge your name on a cheque – he did that so badly the bank rang up, and I had to say I'd sprained my wrist so that I couldn't write properly. But I had a Fabergé watch an Italian count had given me after seeing my Mother in *Six Characters*, something I kept locked away and only brought out to show visitors. When it went missing I knew Hugo had taken it, and he didn't deny it. What do you think he said? What does it matter, darling, it's insured, of course I'd never have taken it otherwise.' She shook her head, smiling. 'That was the end for me. We'd had rows before, I like a good row, but this time I was very calm and quite serious as I told him what he'd done was unforgivable, and I never wanted to see him again.'

'But you did.'

'Once. If I tell you about *that*, it's to put the detective nonsense out of your head, you understand? And again, it mustn't go any further.'

I took a leaf out of her own conversational book. 'Aunt Aggie, who would I tell it to? As you said yourself it's so long ago, who'd be interested?'

71

The little raw red hand clenched, and for a moment I thought Aunt Aggie would turn into Mary Storm. Then she said I was an impertinent brat, and told me of the visit Hugo Headley had paid her in the last week of July.

He had come to borrow money, and he was frightened. His desperation might be measured (Aunt Aggie said) by his coming to her after the affair of the watch. Why did he want the money, who was he frightened of? Hugo liked to gamble, had lost a lot of money he hadn't got at a club called the Five Aces. Similar things had happened before, and Hugo's usual tactic was to give any such club a wide berth for a few weeks or even months, leave London and stay at his Clempstone cottage, the final result being the fairly harmless one that he was barred from the club. Unfortunately the Five Aces was owned by a man Hugo had bilked before, a man named Dusty Hegarty who decided that enough was enough. He had sold the debt to somebody called Lucky Lambert.

'A debt collector?'

'Not exactly. You don't know about selling debts?' Her dress had ridden up a little, and the raw beefy fingers pulled it down.

'Aunt Aggie, you know much more about the wicked ways of the world than I do.'

'You meet people, you hear things. When you sell a debt you do it for perhaps twenty-five per cent of the total amount. The buyer pays you that. Then he tries to collect.'

'By threats? How much did Hugo owe?'

'I don't know. He asked if I could lend him a thousand pounds, and you can guess what I said. Then he told me half that would help, I said that was still impossible and asked what it was for. This man Lambert had been to see him, said he'd taken over the debt from Hegarty, and if Hugo didn't pay up within a week he could get himself measured for a wooden overcoat.'

'It sounds like a bad thriller. You're sure Hugo wasn't putting you on?'

'I can tell when somebody's acting, I do it myself. He was frightened, I'd never seen him like it, and I couldn't bear that. I gave him a hundred pounds. It was the last time I saw him.' She brooded on it for a few moments. 'Something else, he was excited too. Danger excited him. You'd have had to know him to understand, and you were just a boy.'

'But he was frightened.'

'That was physical. He was afraid of having his legs broken or his face slashed, of course he was. But danger, losing money he hadn't got and trying to find ways of raising it that might land him the wrong side of the law, he loved all that. When he took my watch, that was a kind of gamble. I might have told the police and he'd have been charged with theft, but he gambled I wouldn't. It was the sort of risk he liked to take.'

'You mean he might have hoped to get money from Father that would pay off Lambert?'

'Perhaps. Or more likely he hoped to fiddle things somehow so that he ended up showing a profit.'

'So what do you think happened?'

'I think whatever plan he had didn't work, and he was desperate. From what he told me he took this man Lambert seriously. He thought he might end up a cripple, and it terrified him. So he went for that swim, and never meant to come back, that's why he didn't need a towel.' She looked at me. 'You don't believe me?'

'I'm not sure.'

'You think he shows up badly.' She must have seen from my face that this was an understatement. 'You don't understand. He wasn't mercenary.'

'You could have fooled me.'

She slapped a hand on the tea table. The cups rattled. 'You're an idiot, you understand nothing.' She stood up, bent but imperious, Mary Storm in person. 'You've tired me out, Geoffrey Elder. Go away.'

I said I was sorry to have upset her. She replied that she was not upset, but so, so tired. I asked again if she knew of anything that might have given Hugo a hold over Father and she turned on me, her voice high, the red spots on her cheeks accentuated.

'What's wrong with you is you're a bad actor, you have no *feeling* for the stage, you can't make a living from it and never will, and so you try to find petty little things to occupy your time. To try to dig up things in your father's life is *infamous*, and you'll regret it.' I began to say I intended nothing of the sort, but she did not listen. 'I've told you to leave it, and if you have any thought for the family you will.'

I had a distinct feeling that some of this was adapted from a speech made by Mary Storm in a play, perhaps Edwardian, brought up to date. I said again I was sorry, thanked her for tea, and went.

That evening I told Leila about the visit, omitting the phrase about the Princess of Sloth. She listened, feet up on an old sofa. At the end she said Aunt Aggie had a point.

'Whatever you learn won't be very nice, will it?' *Nice* is one of Leila's words, part of her gift for understatement. Friends have a nice or not very nice house, the same applies to meals eaten out, to plays and clothes, and pretty well everything else you can think of. If the last trump sounded she would say it was not very nice of the authorities to give us such short notice. All this is part of the placidity I find so soothing. I said I supposed I had some feelings of guilt about my father, and anyway I wanted to know the meaning of the letters. I asked if she didn't have similar guilt feelings sometimes. She considered, then shook her head.

'I just never think about things like that. Anyway, surely what your aunt said explains it.'

'Of course it doesn't. Don't you see, if Headley was in such a difficult spot, likely to be beaten up or even killed, and if he managed to get money out of my father, it makes a staged disappearance much more likely. He'd have a strong incentive to disappear.'

'I suppose so. I don't see what you can do about it.'

'I could go and see Melissa.' Leila raised her eyebrows. 'No need to look like that. I haven't seen her for years.'

'You used to think she was rather nice. So you told me.'

'I doubt if she ever thought I was, looking back at it. And I could try to find out if those figures with names out of old gangster films, Dusty Hegarty and Lucky Lambert, are still around, and if Aunt Aggie was telling the truth or just inventing a story.'

'Would she do that?'

'Making up tales comes naturally to her. I'm sure she didn't tell me all she knew.'

'If you don't mind my saying so, I don't see how anything any of them tells you is going to help in finding out why your father wrote those letters.'

She was right, of course. Leila's common sense sometimes depresses me.

'I could go to see Dodo Everard. He goes back a long way with Father, I don't know how long. If there was a secret in Father's past he might know it.'

'There's a spot on your jacket, it looks like food. Take it off, and I'll see if I can get it out.'

Good mother Leila!

The Thirties

(i) Talking to Hugo

I've already said that in my memory it was always fine at Clempstone, but the journal shows how wrong this was. The entry for Friday says: 'Rotten day, raining at first then very windy. Practice for tournament. Lot of stuff about foreign politics at breakfast, M knew about it, felt ignorant. Afterwards she went out on her own, hardly saw her all day. Saw Father with funny man in village. Met Hugo H, who said he was going abroad. Miserable.' So much for the truthfulness of memory, which says all days at Clempstone were undilutedly blissful.

There as in London Father always read the paper before breakfast, and in both places we had two, delivered by a boy from the village, *The Times* and the *Banner*. Father read *The Times* carefully, then looked quickly through the popular paper which he dismissed as rubbish. Deirdre, however, read the *Banner* thoroughly, lingering particularly over a gossip column called 'Man in the Know', and on any feature to do with fashion. I used to read the sports pages in both papers, but not much else.

It was Father's reading of the papers, or rather his comments on what he had read, that prompted the breakfast skirmish. He said that the Olympic Games, which had been opened a week earlier in Berlin, seemed to be tremendously successful. Hilda, who was nibbling at a fragment of dry toast, paid no attention, but I saw Melissa's head raised from her plate as he went on.

'Apparently the organisation has been wonderful. That's what's lacking in this country. We could learn a lot from the Germans.'

Melissa put down her knife and fork in what I can only call a decisive manner. 'It's easy to organise things if you put everybody who disagrees with you in prison.'

Father looked startled for a moment, then smiled. 'I think on reflection you'll agree that's an overstatement. If you read the stories in *The Times* you'll see that there have been crowds of a hundred thousand every day, all tremendously enthusiastic for the games and for their Führer. I don't think there's any reason to doubt that the enthusiasm is genuine.'

'What about the Jews?'

He buttered a piece of toast carefully, took a small spoonful of marmalade. 'What about them? I have nothing against them as a people, but I don't think it can be denied that they have gained a disproportionate amount of influence over the commercial and industrial life of the country. That's being corrected, and I don't doubt there are injustices that should be put right. I hope they will be.' Melissa stared at him, her toffee-coloured eyes enormous. 'But when I compare those injustices with other news in the paper, like the story that there is Red rule in Barcelona, with churches being burnt and priests murdered, I'm bound to say that seems to me more important than the imprisonment of some unfortunate Jews in Germany.'

That, as near as I can remember, is what Father said, and the deliberate long-windedness – it wasn't exactly pomposity – with which he said it. It sounds awful today but lots of people said similar things then, when persecution of the Jews was mostly confined to depriving them of their business power, closing down shops, banning them from any important jobs and forcing them into exile. I read recently a book about the 1936 Olympic Games which contained comments by many foreign visitors who saw no sign of persecution and, like Father, admired the smoothness with which the Games were run.

I think he was as little prepared as Hilda or myself for Melissa's reaction. She stood up and fairly shrieked at him. 'How can you be so stupid, don't you know that's just propaganda? Haven't you read *anything* about what's going on in Germany?'

Father's tone remained what must have been maddeningly calm and reasonable. 'When you say reports by people who have the advantage of being on the spot are untruthful propaganda, I can't agree with you. And these other things you mention, may they not be propaganda too?'

He said this with a slight smile, and it may have been the smile that she found unbearable. She cried out something about being bloody stupid, and left the room. Hilda, abandoning her toast and muttering something apologetic, went after her.

Father sat staring ahead of him, the smile seemingly fixed on his face, then he too left the table. I was left to finish my eggs and bacon. I was aware of course that Hitler had come to power a few years earlier in Germany, and that there was some sort of trouble going on in Spain, but about the rights and wrongs of the argument I knew nothing at all, and cared nothing either. I was amazed and impressed that Melissa took an interest in such things, and of course I was on her side, if for no other reason than because she was young and Father was old.

That was a bad start to the day. And then? Then I must reconstruct, writing as I am so many years later, and with this vision of the sea at Clempstone always present, a vision in which it is invariably calm and a soft blue, less brilliant than the Mediterranean but more delicate to my eye, with often a deepening haze clouding the vision a couple of hundred yards out from shore, and within the haze the muffled putt-putt of an engine and occasional stray words and phrases from unseen fishermen sounding across the water. I remember swimming often in that still sea, out into the mist that looked impenetrable from the shore, but when one was immersed in it seemed not to exist. Wrapped in my cloak of invisibility I looked back at the shoreline, the sand dunes and beyond them the row of grey Victorian houses along the front and the less decorous outlines of the various examples of English marine architecture, with their fretted balconies and verandahs and mock-Tudor timbering – and in the case of Grandison House modest towers. None of the other houses had towers.

It is such days I remember, but that Friday was not one of them. The argument at breakfast had affected me. I had never heard anybody speak to my father as Melissa did, or for that matter heard any young person call an older one stupid. I was astonished by her daring and her passion, and longed to talk to her, although worried that she would be as impatient with me as she had been with Father because of my ignorance. I must have gone up to the tower room and lingered there in the hope that she might come to find me, for the next thing I recall is looking out from the window and seeing her striding along the promenade wearing a red mackintosh. I watched until she turned down the avenue leading to the village.

I contemplated setting out after her, and meeting her in the village by apparent chance, but as is often the case in youth I remained undecided. Then Daisy came up and said my father wanted to speak to me. He was in the drawing room, back to me, looking out of the window at the sea. When he turned he spoke abruptly, and with the breakfast argument in mind I thought he might be angry, but this proved wide of the mark.

'I have to go out, and may not be back for lunch. I rely on you to – ah – keep Melissa and her mother amused.' I said yes, without asking how this might be done, or remarking that Melissa had already gone out and that nothing I suggested or said was likely to amuse Hilda Paton. 'Your mother will be here tomorrow. And Neil. And Dodo Everard is coming. Things will be livelier at the weekend, it's dull for you I'm afraid. Then there is the tournament, you'll be getting in some practice for that, no doubt.' I said yes. He coughed and said he hoped I would do well this year, then coughed again. 'That little affair at breakfast, I don't want you to think I—' The sentence stayed uncompleted. 'Melissa is a headstrong girl, I fear, very ready to express her opinions. Or somebody else's opinions.' He seemed to expect a comment, but I was incapable of making one. He essayed a smile, patted my shoulder and left. I see this now as one of the inconclusive gestures of affection he was always trying to make, and to which I was unable to respond. I went round to the tennis club, but found nobody there who wanted to knock up, and wandered along the front in the direction of Greystone.

I have said already that memory, treacherous memory, won't summon up the weather on that Friday, but the rain must have stopped and been succeeded by the strong wind mentioned in my journal. And the wind did blow strongly there, raising little clouds of sand among the dunes, lashing the sea into breakers that creamed and gave off a fine spray as they ran up the shore. This must have been such a day, for I recall pausing as I watched a swimmer bobbing among the waves, and thinking it was foolish to be out in such a sea. At moments the swimmer seemed to be drifting out, then with a few strokes he would get nearer to shore, then struggle to maintain his position. As I watched a hand was raised, then lowered. He looked in trouble. I moved out of the sand dunes down the beach towards him.

I don't think I've mentioned that I am a good swimmer, not fast but powerful, and able to swim quite a distance. As I approached the swimmer waved again, and shouted something I could not hear. I took off shoes, socks, jacket, trousers and shirt, so that I was standing in vest and pants. The waves crashed down menacingly. It was a rough sea but I knew I could swim in it, although I wouldn't have done so for pleasure. An image entered my mind, of Melissa walking beside the dunes. She saw me plunge into the sea, the battle with the breakers, clapped her hands as I reached the exhausted swimmer and brought him back to shore, looked at me with love in those toffee-brown eyes. I dived into the breakers, felt the exhilarating blows of the sea. Then I put up my head to see what progress I was making, and found the swimmer I had come in to save just beside me.

'Bit rough,' he said. 'Had enough myself.'

In another couple of minutes we were back on the sand. When I said he had been asking for help he shook his wet head.

'Misunderstanding I'm afraid, just saying come on in, the water's lovely. But you're shivering, came in without a towel, use this old one of mine, bit grubby I'm afraid.' He shook his long hair, from which water dripped, then towelled it and his body vigorously. I knew very well that he had called for help, not because he needed it but for the pleasure of seeing me strip off and make a fool of myself by going in the sea, but of course I couldn't say so.

'Come up to my cottage and I'll give you a cup of coffee. You're Geoffrey Elder, isn't that right?' I had recognised him already as Hugo Headley.

He had called the cottage a tumbledown shack, and that was true. There were slates off the roof, two broken window panes had been replaced by cardboard, paint had peeled off the front door. At the side a battered, rust-spotted Austin 7 stood in a gravelled space. Beyond it was a field with the grass a foot or more high, and a wooden shed with the door hanging off it. The living room contained a sofa which had one missing leg replaced by a pile of magazines, and two armchairs with springs sticking up out of them. A pair of socks lay on the floor beside an enormous jigsaw, empty beer bottles stood beside the door, and two dirty glasses were on a rickety table beside a pile of manuscript. There was, I learned later, a kitchen where Hugo ate, the sink usually stacked with dirty plates and cups, and upstairs a bedroom with a large double bed in it and not much else, and another room containing all sorts of junk. There was no bathroom, something less unusual then than it would be today. When Hugo wanted to wash or shave he did so in the kitchen sink, when he wanted a bath he went in the sea.

Some of this I saw later, after Hugo had disappeared. At the time I was aware chiefly of surprise that anybody could live like this. Since then I have known actors, some of them successful, whose houses or flats were marked by a similar dingy untidiness, but nothing in my small experience had prepared me for it. When Hugo returned with mugs of coffee he noticed my wondering gaze.

'Fair old tip, isn't it? Needs the loving hand of a good woman. Trouble is I don't know any.' I sipped the coffee, aware that modesty, the inadequacy of the towel, and the necessary discarding of vest and shorts, had left me slightly damp. My trousers felt as if they were sticking to my skin.

'So you're down for the summer. And how's everybody at Grandison House? Don't answer, silly question. How am I, that's the thing we should all be asking ourselves all the time, how's my immortal soul getting on in its mortal body, that's always the question. Not just for me but for you too, and all the family.'

I hardly knew what to say to this, but it proved unnecessary to say anything. Hugo was quite capable of maintaining a conversation that was essentially a monologue. I know actors who do the same thing, and even when they are witty tend to find them rather a bore. Very likely Hugo's self-absorbed monologue would bore me now, but I was sixteen and was fascinated. I should add that on this occasion the self-absorption was not absolute. He approached the subject of his own activities via me, as it were, and there may have been an ulterior motive in what he said, he was perhaps fishing for a response which he didn't get. I put down what he said as nearly as I remember it, omitting my monosyllabic or inane comments.

'What are you going to do with your immortal soul, my young Elder, when you leave the shades of the academy? I'll tell you what you shouldn't do, and that's go up to one of those places where they turn out cardboard dummies who wear the right clothes and go into the civil service or the law or a stockbroker's office or any other place where they can say hallo old boy, I say old boy, didn't we meet when we fagged for old Pisspot at Eton or weren't we at the House old boy, or didn't we meet at Lady Pisspot's reception last year old boy, when you were with Bingo Bigbore's party? Don't go in for any of that, my young Elder or old younger, not if you want to preserve your immortal soul alive. Remember, life's the thing, get into it as fast as you can, paint yourself with it, slosh it all over you, in the destructive element immerse. That's what I was doing just now, kidding you into immersion in the destructive element.' I said I knew that.

'And you don't resent it? Or perhaps you do, doesn't matter, what you have to do is make things happen, understand? I saw you out there, thought there's a prissy-looking lad, let's shake him up a bit, and I did. I didn't know how you'd react, ignore the drowning man, punch me on the jaw afterwards, never mind, I was making something happen. Why want to do that? Because I'm a poet, and that's what poetry is, making something happen in words, something that hasn't happened before. So remember, life's the thing. Life and poetry and making things happen, and suffering when they don't go right, and fucking as many women as you can.' He flung back his head and laughed. 'And I'll bet those are things your ma and pa never told you. And how are they, your ma and pa?'

I have said I was both fascinated and repelled by him. The repulsion may be easy to understand, especially when I add that even now when he had just come out of the sea there was an aroma about him, a smell of flesh and sweat and dirt. Yet the

85

fascination was there too, for me as for others. He was exuberant and open, even though the openness was obviously untrustworthy, in a way I'd never known. I sometimes think, thirty years later, that untrustworthiness is deeply attractive to the respectable, who long for the irrational actions they never commit.

But that's hindsight. It is hindsight too that tells me he had come round to the question with which he had begun, about my parents. I said I didn't know he'd met them. It was unimaginable to me that this figure with his long hair, fisherman's jersey and espadrilles covering grubby feet, could ever have crossed the threshold of Manfield Terrace or even of Grandison House.

'In a manner of speaking I do.' He gave me his monkey smile. 'I met your ma at some party or other in her flower shop. And I know your brother Justin.'

'Half-brother.'

'Brother, half-brother, you had the same sire but a different dam. Justin sees your ma occasionally, or so he tells me. I know your aunt, that great actress Mary Storm, oh yes I know her. And your dad, we've corresponded. He can be a bit of an awkward cuss, your dad, don't you find?' I shook my head. 'Ah well, you're his son, apple of his eye no doubt, it's different for you. For the matter of that this country's full of awkward cusses, people who don't appreciate the divine right of poets to live the way they want to. Money doesn't matter, what are a lot of banknotes compared to a poem? But still, you can't cash a sonnet at your local Barclays branch. And some people won't let you alone.' He sat looking down at an old worn rug beneath his espadrilles. 'I'd like to get out of this bloody country.'

I asked if he meant he wanted to leave and not come back.

'The way I feel at this moment, yes. I want to be somewhere hot and harsh, a different landscape, different people. I might write a different sort of poetry.' He gave me the monkey grin. 'But there'd be the same people in that other country even though they had different faces, people saying you signed an agreement for this, you owe me money for that, blah blah.' He got up. 'Nice to talk to you, young Elder, say hallo to your dad for me. And don't forget, life's the thing. It'll get you in an awful lot of trouble and maybe do for you in the end, but it's better than saying hallo old boy to the fat-faced fools at Lady Pisspot's.'

Bits of this conversation took on some importance after he disappeared. Thinking back, I'm not sure whether or not I took his advice. I didn't go to university and have never been part of an old-boy network, but nor have I behaved as if life, in the sense that Hugo Headley used the word, was the thing.

After leaving him I went along again to the tennis club in the hope of finding somebody I could practise with, but found only holiday-makers patting the ball over the net to each other. I wandered disconsolately back to the house in case Melissa might have returned, but saw only Hilda, sitting in the drawing room with a striped shawl round her shoulders. I asked if she knew where Melissa had gone.

'She said she was going to the riding stables, and just left me here on my own. Children can be cruel, and neglectful. But you're too young to understand that, and I'm sure you would never be cruel to your mother or father.' I had no idea what she was talking about, the idea being inconceivable to me. Her lower lip trembled, and for a moment I feared she might be about to cry. Then she asked, with the voice of an adult indulging a child, how my tennis was getting on and whether I'd won any cups lately. I told her I had entered the Junior Tournament here at Clempstone and would be playing in the first round tomorrow, and escaped. The conversation with Hugo had left me dissatisfied, uneasy. I wanted to see Melissa, and with that in mind walked to the village.

When I write that the avenue was attractive, with its birch trees on either side and solid, stolid houses interspersed with bungalows along its length, the attraction owed in part to the wide grass verges in front of the houses and the rambling gardens behind them, those are latterday feelings. They are based on a recent visit, when the verges had vanished in the cause of widening the road, and most of the Victorian houses had gone, replaced by perky little affairs in red brick, interspersed with small shops calling themselves General Stores or

Ye Clempstone Tea Shoppe or The Seaside Emporium. In the Thirties the avenue was just the road that led to the village, with a few houses that did bed and breakfast, and I walked up it blind to trees, verges and houses, thinking of Melissa and that moment in the tower room.

I didn't see her in the village. I went to the riding school, just off the village street, and was told nobody resembling her had taken out a horse that morning, or even paid them a visit. I left the village and took a narrow road that led out to Parker's Point. From there the walk back along the coast road, on the beach or between the dunes was pleasant enough, but still why didn't I go straight back along the avenue? No doubt because I hoped to meet Melissa.

The road was a country lane, with fields on either side. Halfway along it, at a sharp turn, was a pub called the Jolly Fisherman, a small place which I had been into once or twice on earlier holidays with Father or Dodo Everard, the landlord winking an eye at the fact that I was obviously under age. At one side of the pub was a bit of ground that served as a car park, and there I saw Father's Armstrong Siddeley. The discreet black body might have belonged to many Armstrongs, but I knew the number. I was surprised because I thought he had been going further afield, but I assumed he must have finished his business and stopped for a pint of beer on his way back. In London he would not have gone into such a pub, perhaps not into any pub, but as I have said he behaved differently in Clempstone.

I pushed open the door, entered the public bar and found it empty. There was no saloon bar, but at one end of the public bar a door led to a small snug. There I found Father. He looked up, saw me, and for a moment his expression was one of dismay. Then his features settled back into their usual impassivity.

He was not alone. The man with him was not the kind of person I would ever have expected to see in Father's company. To my teenage eyes he was old, by which I mean something over forty. He had a thin face, and a complexion so dark that it looked as though his face had been stained. A few strands of hair were plastered over his scalp. He wore a very old and shabby blue blazer with some sort of insignia on the breast pocket, a greyish shirt with a frayed collar, and a striped tie that looked as if it might be that of some school or regiment. The tie too was a little frayed, and when he stretched forward to the glass of whisky in front of him I saw that his jacket sleeves were short. Hugo Headley dressed carelessly, and lived in what I would have called squalor, but that was to some extent a matter of choice. This man had about him a mock-smartness, expressed in the blazer and the tie, that spoke of a real poverty not quite kept at bay.

Father looked at me, apparently lost for words. The other man smiled, revealing as he looked at me a strong squint, so that only one eye inspected me, the other straying to my right and fixing its attention on the bar. He stood up, revealing a body out of keeping with the thin face. His voice was deep and somehow oily, his manner oozed familiarity.

'The name's Bill Bentall, Major Bentall as was. And you're a chip off the old block if I'm not mistaken. Very pleased to make your acquaintance.' A hand, hard and horny, clasped mine.

Now Father spoke, but not to me. He bent his customary deadpan look on the stranger and said, 'I don't think I need detain you longer.'

Bentall ignored this. 'We go back a long way in a manner of speaking, your father and me. Running into him like this was what you might call a real funny coincidence.' I asked whether they had known each other in the war. 'Oh no, we go further back than that, to when I was a kid. We knew each other although we didn't, in a manner of speaking, isn't that so?' The straying eye swivelled alarmingly, shifting about from bar to ceiling and window, then back again. All the while he smiled. Father said nothing. 'I could use another. My round, I think. And one for the young spark, whatever he fancies.' Father seemed to hesitate, then rose. 'Don't say no, we're friends, I hope.'

'I'm sorry. We have to go.'

The smile stayed fixed on the other's brown face. 'If you're in that much of a hurry, all right.' As we approached the door he called, 'Good to see you again, I'll be in touch.'

We walked together to the car in silence. He got in and pulled the self-starter. I longed to ask where he had met this old acquaintance fallen on hard times, and what had been meant by that phrase about knowing and not knowing each other, but didn't dare to do so. Father stayed completely silent on the journey back along the coast road, and we were at the house in a few minutes. Daisy, who saw us come in, said something pert about not expecting him back to lunch. Father glared at her, said she should tell cook he was here, and went straight up to his room. Daisy tossed her head and pranced out to the kitchen.

Melissa was a little late back, and when I said I had looked for her at the riding stables said she had changed her mind and gone for a long walk. Afterwards Father retired to a little room he used as a study, Hilda said she would lie down, and Melissa rejected my suggestion that we should look for mussels, which were sometimes to be found just beyond Parker's Point. Later I heard her voice raised in argument with her mother, though the words remained indiscernible. I went up to the tower room and read another article by Fred Perry, in which he said he had developed his tennis forehand by playing table tennis.

Then I went round again to the club, to find the scene altogether changed, every court now occupied by those of about my own age who had come for the tournament. Some I recognised, others were new to me. I was watching a boy named Nowell, whom I had beaten last year, when I felt a tap on my arm. A lank red-haired boy wearing spectacles said he would be next on this court, and asked if I would like a game. When Nowell came off he grinned at me, asked if I saw how his service had come on, and said he looked forward to caning me if we met in the final. I asked the red-haired boy if he was down for the tournament and he said yes, but he didn't expect to get far.

From the way he played it seemed certain he was right. When we practised serving he found difficulty in returning a service I'd developed recently which went straight down the centre line, and his own service was no more than a means of propelling the ball over the net. He was a useful retriever but seemed to have no attacking strokes, and I found myself spraying my forehand drives with delightful accuracy to within inches of the sidelines, and even succeeding in top-spinning balls on my weak backhand. When we played a set I won the first four games and then let up, so that the result was six-two. Afterwards he thanked me, shook hands and said it had been very helpful. I went back feeling cheerful for the first time that day.

(ii) The Weekend Begins

And then the weekend. If some of Friday remains vague to me, I remember perfectly the weekend that might be called the first and worst of my adult life, the last weekend of happiness at Clempstone. I almost wrote 'the last weekend of happiness I ever knew', but that would be ridiculous. I am happy enough with Leila, and there have been times on the stage when I have known my performance to be not just adequate or good, but have felt myself reaching out into dimensions of intelligence and understanding I never knew I possessed. Was I not happy then? Yes, surely, but it was not the emotion I felt when swimming with Melissa early on that Saturday morning. If there is such a thing as pure, innocent happiness, I knew it then.

I woke early that day, to a shaft of sunlight coming through the curtains, and when I looked out saw blue sky. A swim before breakfast, I thought, why not? When I got to the beach I saw that Melissa was already in the sea. She waved to me and I swam out to her, using the breast stroke instead of my usual overarm. I have bathed often since then on Mediterranean beaches where the water was warm and not breathtakingly cold like that of the English Channel, but I can remember nothing so fine as the sea at Clempstone, the gasp at the bite of the water's chill, then the spreading warmth as the body became accustomed to it. We called a few words to each other, but mostly gave ourselves to the pleasure of swimming in the calm sea, kicking up fountains as we floated, racing each other to a buoy several yards out. Back on the beach afterwards she peeled off her orange cap, towelled herself, and said it had been wonderful. I told her of my dash into the sea to help, or even save (as I thought) Hugo Headley.

91

'Just the sort of trick he would play.'

'You know him, then?'

'Of course.' She explained that he had been brought to the house by Justin. 'He's rather ghastly. Do you know, the second time he came he tried to touch Daddy for money?'

'I believe he's very hard up, his cottage is an awful mess. But he's an extraordinary chap, reads his poems very well.' I didn't say where I had heard him read them, because it would have emphasised that I was a schoolboy. 'He told me he's thinking of living abroad.'

'I am too. I'll probably go to Spain.' She checked herself as if thinking she might have said too much. 'Don't talk about that, will you? Not to anybody.' She put a finger to her lips, then to mine. 'It's our secret.'

'Our secret,' I echoed happily.

She drew me to her, so that I felt the warmth of her body through the thin dark blue robe she wore, and kissed me firmly on the mouth. As we walked up the beach I saw on the promenade the figure of Passlove junior, arms folded, staring at us. He turned as we approached, and when we got to the house had disappeared.

So the weekend that was to end catastrophically began with Melissa's kiss, a touch I felt on my lips throughout the morning. The times when we are positively happy are few, or so it seems to me, but this was one of them. Those standard clichés of metaphor about walking on air and having a song in the heart – yes, I can endorse them when I remember my feelings that morning. I could have swum to France, jumped out of the tower window and landed soft as a feather, run a mile in record time, blasted Fred Perry off the centre court at Wimbledon. I went round to the club, saw the list of the tournament draw posted up, and noted that I was down to play rather late, at six o'clock, somebody named S. Goldstube of whom I had never heard. Nowell was in the other half of the draw, and I looked forward to beating him in the final.

What happened next? Dodo Everard arrived in his old Daimler, a car specially enlarged and adapted at the back so that it would hold any small items of furniture he bought on the road in his occupation of antique dealer. His name was Cyrus, but I had known him for ever as an old friend of the family and had always called him Dodo. When I was a child he had charmed me by producing eggs from under his arm, a stream of coloured ribbons from his shoe, a glass eye out of his real one. Later we had gone to visit him and his wife Bella in the large house outside York where they entertained on a scale and with a zestful informality unknown to Manfield Terrace. I can remember Dodo wearing a chef's hat, carving away at a large ham and a gigantic turkey, calling out, 'Come along now, any more for any more, just step up and be served.' Bella, wearing a striped butcher's apron, stood beaming by his side, piling up plates with slices of meat and stuffing until the guests cried for mercy. The cries were not uttered quickly, for most of them were local business people cast in the same large physical mould as their hosts, men with apoplectic complexions and straining waistcoat buttons, women with powerful arms and massive breasts. Dodo did not look as if about to suffer an apoplectic fit, but he was a big man, over six foot tall and extremely broad, with powerful arms and legs and a mass of curly grey hair.

I have said he was Father's friend. There were obscure jokes they shared, words and phrases they used that I never heard in any other mouths. One was 'underconstumble', which I have just found, to my surprise, in the dictionary as a jocular dialect version of 'understand'. I can remember the two of them singing together at Manfield Terrace, Dodo at the piano, a bit of nonsense that went

> 'I underconstumble
> And so I don't grumble
> I'm ever so humble
> When big bullies tumble
> Although I may mumble
> "He's just like Hugh Trumble"
> *He got what he deserved.*'

The two of them belted out the last line, sweat on Dodo's brow, Father's face alight with pleasure, while Bella looked on benevolently and Deirdre with a pained expression. I laughed too, as children often do at something incomprehensible that amuses the adults. I once asked Dodo what it meant.

'Hugh Trumble was a great Australian cricketer.' I nodded and waited. 'And he got what he deserved. So the song says.'

'But what does it mean, what did he deserve?'

'Why, I don't know, to be hit for six most likely. That's what most of us deserve, but if we're lucky it doesn't happen.'

So I was no wiser. There were other songs and phrases just as meaningless, 'Bobby the Big Bad Bangbang' was one that I remember, and they also sang sentimental Victorian ditties.

Dodo's arrival brightened up the emotional atmosphere. Melissa, who vanished after breakfast to reappear just before lunch looking positively radiant, was obviously delighted by his stories of deals done during his early days in Canada with dubious characters, like the man in Vancouver who tried to sell him Napoleon's cocked hat, and another in Montreal who had produced letters testifying that a blood-stained naval jacket was the very one Nelson had worn at Trafalgar. Even Hilda managed a wan smile at his stories. Father, who had been silent at breakfast, took Dodo straight off to his study, and they came out half an hour later laughing over another preposterous story about Napoleon. This concerned a schoolboy who was asked if he could tell the class the Emperor's nationality, played for time by saying, 'Of course I can,' and was amazed to find the answer correct. Dodo saw my straight face.

'What's wrong, young Geoffrey? You're looking a bit umpish.' I said I couldn't see why they thought it funny. 'You don't underconstumble? Never mind. How's tennis, Dennis?'

Greatly daring, I answered in his own kind of language. 'Where's Bella, feller?'

He flung up his hands. 'Very good. Your father and I have been kidding each other with that sort of double talk and double rhyme ever since we were at school. Then I went to find a fortune in Canada but never did, and we met again – when was it? My memory's a sieve, but I think it was soon after your father came down to London. Harry had landed this job with the firm that now bears his name—' he made a mock bow to Father '—and I was at an auction rooms. Have I got it right, Harry?' Father said he thought so. 'But you were asking about Bella. She's stayed at home. This is what you might call a flying visit, and somebody's got to mind the shop.'

He laughed at this and so did I, because of course Dodo had half-a-dozen shops up north, and people looking after all of them. I remember, as a child, being taken to a shop that was more like a warehouse, and getting lost there, running about in rooms full of wardrobes, tables and desks, and then becoming frightened when I found myself in a room full of animals' heads and skins, some on the walls but others piled up round the room, so that the intelligent eyes of a buck stared at me from one corner, next to the yellow curved horns of some gigantic creature that may have been a bull moose. Near to them was a tiger's head over which I stumbled and fell, so that I found myself just beside the menacing horns. I screamed, Dodo came in and found me, and said with a laugh that I'd landed in the zoo.

Neil Paton arrived before lunch. I see I haven't described him. Neil was short and dark with a ready smile, very quick in movement around the court when he played tennis, a clever player without much power in his strokes – but I'm writing about his tennis, not his character. Neil was always cheerful, avoided arguments if possible, and was extremely attentive to women. When he entered a room and saw a woman he knew he would be likely to go over at once and talk to her, about her activities rather than his own. He would be particularly strong in recalling remote members of her family whom he had met once or twice, distant cousins who had gone out to farm in Kenya say, and would ask about them with every appearance of interest. This was typical of his approach to women of a mature age, but he was equally attentive to those of his own generation, ready instantly to admire their new dress and then go on to discussion of the latest play or novel, which he seemed always to have read. There are men who prefer the company of women to that of their own sex, and Neil was one of them. Only in the presence of the young was he not quite at ease, so that at the

Patons' tennis parties he was more likely to be found talking to a matron than her daughter.

I told him that Melissa and I had been swimming before breakfast, and Neil was characteristically enthusiastic.

'You'll be a champion swimmer next, as well as a tennis player. What with swimming and riding, Melissa's keeping herself fully occupied.' I said she hadn't been riding, and told him how I knew. 'She hasn't? I must have misunderstood what she said.'

Hilda did not come down to lunch. Neil said she had one of her migraines, and that when she suffered them there was nothing to do but rest in a darkened room. At lunch he was unusually silent, and as I've said Melissa laughed a lot at Dodo's jokes. I've mentioned Daisy's pertness, and this was enhanced by the way she walked, almost bouncing from step to step, setting dishes on the table with an air that was somehow provocative. When she left the room Dodo laughed, glanced at Father and shook his head. Father's face stayed Keatonishly grave.

(iii) At the Clanders'

Afterwards Melissa sat on the verandah talking to her father. I had decided to ask her if she would come out for a walk to Parker's Point. On the walk I was going to mention casually that I was playing my first round match at six, and suggest equally casually that she might care to watch it. Accordingly I hung about in the drawing room reading, or pretending to read, the daily paper. The door was open and their voices, which had been no more than a murmur, suddenly became audible, or at least the words spoken by Melissa did.

'For God's sake, it's none of your business.' To that her father made a reply I could not hear. 'All this hypocrisy makes me sick. You know Mother—' At that point, feeling awkward and probably looking shy or silly, I coughed and made my appearance. To my surprise Melissa took my arm. 'There you are, I've been waiting. You haven't forgotten we're going to the Clanders'.'

I echoed the name feebly. Neil looked from one of us to the other. 'Oh well, if that's what you've arranged.'

Melissa glared at him, eyes sparkling. 'Why not see how Mummy feels? Since you're not otherwise occupied.' She strode off towards the gate and I followed, without the least idea why she should be so angry or her father so hangdog. She turned left along the road towards Parker's Point, walking rapidly.

'I say, are we really going to the Clanders'?' Even I, with my lack of interest in current affairs, knew of Professor Claude Clanders, star of the wireless programme 'What Do *You* Think?' Clanders – he died during the war years and his name, so well-known in the Thirties, is now forgotten – was a Professor of Economics who had become famous as a know-all ready to express an opinion about absolutely any subject, from the proper way to make a bed to the unlikelihood of a European war. He had a high piping voice, and this combined with the fact that his views never admitted the possibility of doubt, left the rest of the panel and many listeners in a state of real or synthetic indignation. 'Let's consult Claude,' the genial retired Brigadier who acted as chairman of the programme would say, and the phrase became a catchword when any problem arose, one used by thousands of people who had never listened to 'What Do *You* Think?'. I knew Clanders had a house at Clempstone in the direction of Parker's Point, a place we called the Swiss House because it resembled a Swiss chalet in appearance, but had never seen him in the village.

'Why on earth did you tell Daddy I hadn't gone riding?' I might have said it was the truth, but just shook my head. 'Never mind, it doesn't matter.'

She stopped. On our left were the links, to our right sand dunes and beyond them the sea. I thought of being among those dunes with her, naked or almost naked (I was modest then), warm sand beneath us, bodies entwined, saying 'I love you' or something like it, unworried about consulting Claude or whether she had or hadn't gone riding. But all that was a vision, a mirage. I could see it was no use suggesting a siesta in the sand dunes.

She looked at me, seemed to come to a decision. 'Yes, we'll go and see them, it can be fun though he's a fearful old bore. But not now.' She tapped my lips with her finger, as she had that morning.

'Another secret?'

'Another secret.'

'To do with your going to Spain?'

'Perhaps. I'll meet you at the Clanders' around four o'clock, tea time, though we'll be lucky if we get any tea. All right?' I nodded. 'But if anybody asks at home, we've been there since lunch, understand?' Her lips replaced her finger on my lips for no more than a moment, then she crossed the road and was lost among the dunes. Five minutes later I remembered I had said nothing about my tennis match, but reflected that since I should see her at tea there was plenty of time.

So it was that at exactly four o'clock by my wrist-watch I walked up the wooden steps of the Swiss chalet and went in the open front door. The place stood on its own in an unkempt sandy garden, where the only flowers to be seen were clumps of marigolds. I could hear voices from behind the house, but it seemed polite to enter by the front door, on which I rapped gently before going in.

The room I entered was long and wide, and there was something odd about it, although it took me a few moments to realise that the nature of the oddity was a complete absence of chairs and sofas. At the far end there was a long low table made from variously coloured woods, and there were what looked like home-made bookshelves round the walls with masses of books piled anyhow on them, but chairs had been replaced by cushions. There must have been thirty or more large cushions, most of them beside the table, but others grouped nearer the door. Big ashtrays stood on the floor, with all sorts of things in them from cigar and cigarette ends to peach and plum stones, and bits of coloured ribbon. The cushions also were bright, ranging from scarlet and acid yellow to emerald green and a peculiarly vivid blue. As I stood staring at them I said 'Hallo,' and the word came back like an echo.

But it was not an echo. Framed in the doorway that led to some inner part of the house was Professor Clanders, his face familiar to me from newspaper photographs. Those, of course, were in black and white, and he was now revealed as having a slight thatch of gingerish hair, a red face with little eyes that twinkled behind large light-rimmed spectacles, and full red lips surrounded by a scrubby ginger beard. The colouring was not especially surprising. What made me goggle at him was the fact that, except for a pair of loose sandals on his feet, the Professor wore no clothes. As he advanced into the room I perhaps retreated a step or two, far enough to make him snigger. The sound, something less than a laugh, rather as though a piece of machinery in his nose and throat had been put into operation and then suddenly stopped, was, so far as my experience goes, unique to Professor Clanders.

'And hallo again,' he piped. 'And who are you, young man? And why are you staring? I thought nowadays the young knew about the facts of life.'

I stammered something about looking for Melissa Paton, and he sniggered again.

'It must be plain to you that you will not find her here, she is not secreted about my person.' I learned later that this facetiousness was typical of him, it was another side of the knowingness that had made him famous on the wireless. 'If the young lady is here you will find her disporting herself in the garden with other guests. But you have not told me your name, or why you should expect to find the no doubt fair Melissa here.' When I identified myself he nodded. 'My daughter Erato is friendly with – can it be your elder brother? – his name at least is Elder, a lively young man.' I said he was my half-brother. 'Is that so? Well well.' He looked at me as I moved uneasily from foot to foot, trying to avoid the sight of his reddish paunch and the appendage beneath it. 'I see you are a victim of the national pudeur, or do you perhaps think these scattered cushions signify an orgy? Not so, I assure you. They symbolise a rejection of the stiff ceremonies represented by Western furniture. The Japanese sit always on cushions and make their beds on the floor, and they are among the best adjusted and most civilised of peoples. As furniture becomes lower, so the humans who use it are more relaxed. Damn braces, bless relaxes, who said that?' In his high voice the question ended as a squeak. I shook my head. 'William Blake. Let us join the others, and see what's to do.'

The garden was no more kempt behind the house than before it. A rambler rose straggled along a wooden fence at the back, a feeble hawthorn hedge protected those in the garden from the eyes of any passer-by. Among the longish grass, in an area flattened by the impact of their bodies, a man, three women and two children sat or lay on rugs and cushions. The children were naked, but I saw with relief that the adults all wore clothing, although my heart sank as I remarked that Melissa was not there. Behind me Professor Clanders, his disdain for pudeur apparently not extending outdoors, had assumed a pair of shorts. One of the women was speaking as we walked towards them, and raised a hand in greeting without checking the flow of her speech.

'Be a good animal, Lawrence said, be a good animal, be true to our animal instincts. If only we obeyed that rule, if we were true to our animal instincts we should live full, happy and creative lives. If we were true to our deepest feelings men and women would live at peace in the world, Claude has often said so.' Mrs Clanders, as I rightly guessed her to be, had a face as red as her husband's, with thick arms and legs. She wore a blue and white sleeveless dress of some intractable material that rustled as she moved, and sandals like her husband's. He nodded agreement and piped, almost on a note of surprise, 'Yes, I have said that, that is quite true. I say, let the animal out.'

'*Let the animal out*,' his wife repeated emphatically.

'But supposing he rapes or murders,' the man asked. He lay on his stomach, and as he raised his head I saw it was Justin. Beside him sat, cross-legged, a girl of about my own age whom I guessed, again rightly, to be Erato. She was twisting grass stalks into a chain.

'That is not animal but human behaviour. Animals mate but do not rape, and they kill for food, not from malice. Claude knows what I say is true.'

Claude, the court of last appeal, nodded. 'Prunella is right, social anthropologists have often remarked it. Animals kill, man murders.'

'Not if he has joined the Peace Pledge Union.' The other woman, who said this, had iron-grey hair pulled up in a bun, a pale face and agonised ascetic features. She was perhaps the same age as Prunella Clanders, that is around forty, but something about her manner, and her long plain grey dress, made her look older.

The Professor plumped down beside her, and gave his snigger. 'Now Ellen, don't talk to me about the PPU. I mean, really, don't talk about it.'

'And why shouldn't I talk about a movement for peace that has seven hundred groups and more than a hundred thousand members?'

'Because, my dear Ellen, peace must come from within, not without.' A plump finger wagged before her face. 'The PPU suits Mr Hitler very nicely, thank you. He just loves the idea that we should stop making guns and aeroplanes and rely on his good nature. He is not a good animal, Mr Hitler, he is a human being, but still he has a lot of sense. There will be no war in Europe, because it doesn't suit Mr Hitler or Mr Baldwin to have one, *not* because a lot of nice ladies and gentlemen say they renounce the use of arms. I had a little something to say about all that two weeks ago—'

'Three,' Prunella said.

'—and really I think it settled the question. At least, nobody tried to answer me.' Another snigger. The agonised lady's face remained firmly turned away from him.

While this conversation went on nobody took the slightest notice of me, except that Justin raised a hand in greeting. The Professor had not told them my name, nor did anybody ask it. I wanted to leave but hardly liked to walk out of the garden, or to say something about their rudeness in ignoring me. Now, however, there was an interruption in the form of a wail from one of the children, who ran to her mother saying that Donny had been throwing sand in her eyes. Prunella removed herself unwillingly from the discussion.

'Don't be a baby, Clytie. Just forget it, and it will soon be better.'

'I want some tea,' the boy shouted from the sandpit. The Professor detached himself from conversation with Ellen and looked round.

'And so say all of us. This young man came here for tea. He was invited by Melissa Paton, who is not here. He seemed to think I was concealing her about my person. He is—'

He paused and I told them my name, which evoked no response. The Professor put hands to mouth and called, in the manner of a man using a megaphone, 'Donny and I want some tea.'

Prunella was now talking to Ellen about peace, war and human motives, and seemed not to hear. Clytie kept a hand on her mother's rustling dress and went on wailing. Justin lay on his rug, face invisible. Erato remained absorbed with her grass stalks.

The Professor threw up his head like a mooing cow. 'I want some tea.' He lowered his head. 'Erato.'

The girl got up. 'Why does it always have to be me?' The question seemed unheard. As she passed me she said, 'Come on, you may as well help since you're here.'

We went into a large untidy kitchen. Erato put a kettle on to boil, found a stained wooden tray, pointed to a row of mugs. I put some of them on the tray. She cut great doorsteps of bread and buttered them, found a dingy-looking cake and put it on the tray. Then she stood with her back against the sink, looked at me critically, and asked, 'Cat got your tongue?' I said something about nobody speaking to me. 'If you wait for any of them to talk to you, you'll stay dumb. They all like the sound of their own voices, nobody else's. I'm getting out.'

'Leaving home?'

'What do you think I mean? I finish school this year, then they won't see me for dust.'

102

'Won't your father and mother mind?'

'Old Piss and Wind will hardly notice, and Mum's all for women living their own lives, or so she says. I can look after myself, don't you worry.' She pulled at her lower lip. 'You're staying with Melissa?'

'No, she's a guest in our house.'

'I wish I looked like her. Do you think I'm attractive?'

She was short like her parents, rather plump, with a broad ruddy face. 'Sort of.'

'Sort of,' she mimicked, then came over and kissed me hard, her mouth squelching against mine. It was my day for being kissed.

Behind me a voice shouted, 'I want my tea.' It was Donny. 'Are you going to seduce him, E?'

'Not while you're around listening at keyholes or looking through them. If you want tea, take it out yourself.' She went further into the house, banging the door behind her. Donny snatched a doorstep, stuffed it into his mouth and went back into the garden. I took out the tray.

'Tea,' the Professor said in a voice of utmost surprise. 'I say, this young man has made tea, and he has brought *cake*. A slice of cake will be just the thing.'

I put the tray on a rug and said their daughter had made the tea. The remark, like the tea, went unheeded. Prunella and Ellen continued their discussion, which now seemed to be concerned with the peacefulness or otherwise of Mohammedanism. Clytie rushed to the tray, picked up a doorstep and wandered away with it. Not until the Professor called, 'Prunella, I say, what about tea?' did his wife uncoil herself from Mohammedan religion, pour tea into mugs and cut the cake. She then took two mugs and two pieces of cake, one for herself and the other for Ellen, and went back to her discussion. Professor Clanders poured his own tea and cut his own cake, listening to the discussion with an abstracted air. I took the tray across to Justin and sat down beside him. He rolled over, sat up, took a mug, asked how I liked his new family, and laughed at my look of surprise.

'Not exactly my family. Claude's writing his memoirs and

I've been engaged as his amanuensis, or general dogsbody. Live as family, take down the great man's thoughts when he has them, then polish them up with him at the end of the day.'

'I didn't know you were a secretary.'

'I'll let you in on a secret, I'm anything that pays money. I take it the old b's down here?'

I said yes. 'And Neil Paton. And Dodo, Mr Everard, do you know him?' Justin shook his head. 'And Melissa. She said she'd meet me here, but she hasn't come.'

'You can't rely on Melissa.'

'She said she might go to Spain.'

'She says a lot of things she doesn't exactly mean. And what she says isn't always what she does.' He looked at me with a smile that implied he could say more if he felt like it. ''E's been after you. Lipstick.' I took a handkerchief, wiped it off. Perhaps I blushed. 'Nothing unusual, she's a frustrated girl. Wouldn't you be if you were called Erato? Know what the others are called? Clytemnestra and Adonis. Claude says the names will encourage them to lead full artistic lives, Prunella says it too, with knobs on. Prunella says everything Claude says with knobs on.'

'Do you like working for him?'

'Sufficient to the day are the cash blessings thereof, as you'll discover when you're a bit older. If anything better turns up I'll be up and away in a trice or a jiffy. Did you tell the old b we'd met?' I said a hesitant yes. 'And no doubt he mentioned I'd been inside?' I said yes again, then asked what had happened. 'I started a mail order firm with another man. We ran out of credit and he vanished leaving us owing lots of money. Muggins was left holding the can. If I could have got hold of enough cash to pay two or three of the people making most noise we'd have pulled through, but the old b refused to stump up. So yours truly went inside for what they called fraud. Can't recommend it, though the porridge in Wandsworth is very good.'

At that moment there were screams from Clytie, who rushed from the far end of the garden apparently covered in blood. She had fallen heavily on some bits of rusty agricultural machinery that had been lying there for a long time, and cut her face and hands. Reactions varied. The Professor rushed indoors and telephoned the nearest hospital, Prunella retired saying she could not bear the sight of blood, Ellen Corliss went down the garden to look at the rusty machinery. Justin shouted Erato's name, and very soon she came out with bandages, cottonwool, iodine and water, bathed the cuts and bound up Clytie's arm. As before, nobody remarked on my presence, and there was no sign of Melissa. It was five o'clock, and my match came on in an hour's time. I left.

Reading what I have written about this encounter with the Clanders family, I wonder if I have exaggerated, made them seem impossibly comic. In fact, apart from Claude's celebrity, they were no more than a slightly unusual group in a decade when progressive parents sent their children to mixed-sex schools like Dartington, Bedales, or if they were a little more daring A. S. Neill's Summerhill. The Clanders were not exceptional. The impact they made on me almost as of creatures from another planet marked only my lack of sophistication.

(iv) The Catastrophes

When I got back I knew Deirdre had arrived, because the house was full of flowers which she had brought down from the shop. There were red and yellow roses in the dining room, an elaborate arrangement of exotic lilies at one end of the drawing room, carnations and some purplish daisies on the piano. Deirdre herself came down a few minutes after I returned, looked at me, and said with a slight air of surprise that I was growing up.

'People will soon be saying, with a boy as old as that she must really be middle-aged, though for a woman of her age she is *well-preserved*. Aren't they two of the most ghastly words you've ever heard, "middle-aged" and "well-preserved"?' I said nobody could possibly use such words about her, and she laughed.

'I do believe my son has learned to pay compliments.' It was a warm day, but she looked wonderfully cool in a sleeveless dress that almost matched the green of her eyes. She stretched out one arm, examining its delicate whiteness almost wonderingly. 'Where is everybody? Fled from this boring place apparently. I'm not surprised.'

I told her Father and Dodo had gone to make a tour of the local antique shops, Hilda had a migraine, Neil and Melissa were somewhere around. She heard me out, then asked whether I knew about the party arranged for that evening. It was not unusual for us to give a supper party at some time during the holiday, to which other summer visitors we knew were invited, but I had not known it was to be on this Saturday evening. I learned later that Father had arranged it for this day in part to welcome Dodo and Neil, in part because it was the opening of the tournament and I should have played my first round match.

'According to cook she's been asked to prepare for several extra guests. You don't know about it? Well, whoever they are, they're bound to liven things up. I love a party. What do you think of the flowers?' In the course of this conversation we had been wandering round within and then outside the house, and were now at the back looking at the garden where Passlove junior was cutting the grass, while his father sat at the door of the garden hut, mug of tea in hand. As we stood there Passlove junior turned and pushed the mower back towards us. He came within two or three yards, touched hand to forehead, then turned away. Deirdre looked after him, stroking her left arm with her right hand. I told her I was playing my first round match in less than an hour. She seemed not to hear me, although she had heard because as we turned back into the house she said, 'I must come to watch, would you like that?' I said I should like it very much.

(Again, as I put this down three decades later, I am aware not of falsity but of inexactness. This is a sixteen-year-old boy talking to his mother – who, however, has to be called not Mother, Ma or Mummy, but Deirdre. What words did I actually use? Not, I'm sure, 'I should like that very much,' nor what might now be conventional, 'I'd love that,' possibly just a simple 'Yes.' I was pleased – more than pleased, delighted – yet I cannot catch the phrase I used.)

She went back into the house. I hung about on the verandah waiting for Melissa's return, and at last saw her coming back from the Greystone direction, head down. I went to meet her, and reminded her that she was supposed to come to the Clanders'.

'Yes. I got held up.'

'I didn't know anybody. It was beastly for me.'

'I'm sorry.' She looked directly at me, and I saw a bruise on one cheek. I asked if she had been in an accident.

'A car went by, a stone flew up and hit me.' She made to walk past, and I stood in front of her and said something about how mean she had been to leave me alone at the Clanders'. At that she turned on me as she had on Father at breakfast a day earlier.

'I'm sick of this. First you tell tales about me not going riding, then you come moaning about being left alone, as if people like the Clanders care whether you knew them or not. Anyway, wasn't Justin there, couldn't you talk to him?'

I said yes, I had talked to Justin, then foolishly added that he had said she wasn't going to Spain.

She stared at me. 'You said that? You told Justin I was going to Spain?'

'Not exactly. It was just that he told me you often said things you didn't mean.'

Her body quivered with an emotion that, I realised miserably as she spoke, was anger. The bruise on her cheek stood out, a livid mark. Her voice was controlled and low. 'What I do and where I go are nothing to do with you, am I making that clear? And when I tell you something I don't expect you to repeat it to the first person you meet. But since apparently you have to blab out everything that's said to you, we'll just say hallo and goodbye in future. And please don't follow me around, I'm sick of it.' With that she went into the house.

I went in too, up to the tower room, and wept. I might have stayed up there for hours, reading the gloomier and bloodier bits of Webster and Tourneur, if there had not been a tennis match to play. As it was, however, the thought of the match and of a comfortable win against S. Goldstube cheered me as I changed into flannels and selected my best racquet. In adolescence all things seem possible, and my imagination played around a scene in which I won the final with triumphant ease and went up to receive the Riverton Cup watched by my family and of course by Melissa, who said nothing afterwards but gave me an embrace more eloquent than words. Buoyed by this vision I went downstairs to find that the whole household, with the exception of Hilda Paton, was coming round to watch. Father and Dodo Everard had returned, Dodo in particularly good spirits, saying they'd been round and about, he'd bought one or two nice pieces, and had been impressed by seeing how widespread were the interests of Branksome and Elder, when they went to look at the progress of a new estate along the coast. Deirdre had changed into another sleeveless dress, this one smoke-blue in colour. Neil patted my shoulder, and said I only had to play half as well as I did against him to be sure of winning the tournament. And Melissa was there too. She did not speak to me, or even look at me, as we walked round to the club, but she was there.

Let me put the occasion into context. The Junior South East Championships were important to local young players, but no more than a dot in the whole tennis spectrum. No Davis Cup selectors were hovering round thinking, 'My word, the boy's brilliant, we might try him in the singles instead of Bunny Austin,' there were no stands for spectators and no need of them. The umpiring of the early rounds was done by club members, the few people who came to watch used the club deck chairs, and it was in them that the Grandison House contingent settled themselves. The umpire, who for this match happened to be the club secretary, introduced me to my opponent, an introduction that gave me a small shock of surprise. S. Goldstube was the lank red-haired boy with whom I had practised for an hour on Friday afternoon. I was not only surprised but pleased. I had played against Goldstube, knew his limitations, and looked forward to coasting comfortably into the second round.

Five minutes after the match began I realised my mistake. No doubt Goldstube had looked at the draw, discovered my identity, and deliberately sought me out to see the strengths and weaknesses of my game. He had also concealed some of his own skills. The service that had been only a means of getting the ball into play was replaced by an awkward kicking serve which had little power behind it, but was difficult to take because of his height. And although he certainly was basically a retriever, without any real forehand drive, he now unveiled a looping topspin stroke that I found hard to hit. By the time I had mastered it I was down four-love, and although I pulled back one game on his service I lost the set six-three.

Goldstube seemed to have no supporters, and mine had found little to applaud, but when the set was over Father came across, said he thought I had got the measure of him now, advised me to use my forehand more, and said there was no need to worry, I could do it. I took a few risks, came up to the net and volleyed, and won the first two games. Then Goldstube used the knowledge he had gained about my backhand weakness, and began to play slow looped shots on to that wing. It was an obvious enough tactic, his looping was not consistent and I should have been able to counter it, but the misery I felt at having fallen out with Melissa combined with the almost greater misery of knowing I was putting up a wretched display in front of her, wrecked me completely. When I tried to slice my backhand returns I either sent the ball into the net or high in the air for an easy kill, when I ran round and played the ball on my forehand I was hopelessly out of position. I looked despairingly at the watchers, but got no help from them. Father sat with folded arms, Deirdre looked bored, Dodo baffled, Neil sympathetic. And Melissa? Her attention seemed to have wandered, she appeared to be watching a game on another court.

I lost the second set six-two, and with it the match.

What did anybody, could anybody, say? I have blotted it from my mind, with the exception of Goldstube's damp handshake, and Father telling me that I'd played below my best, but it was not the end of the world. And the rest of the evening exists for me not as a whole, but in flashes. I know I went straight up to the tower room on my return, and said I wanted to have supper there and not join the party, and I remember that Dodo came up and with a mixture of sympathy and jovial bullying persuaded me otherwise. 'You're a man, not a schoolboy now . . . the school of life is the school of hard knocks . . . the man who never lost anything never did anything either . . .' With these and similar clichés, along with the observation that nobody got anywhere by being umpish, Dodo lured me downstairs.

He must have been up in the tower room with me for some time, since when we came down most of the guests had arrived. There was a couple named Ellerby who came down to Clempstone every year, an accountant called Minchin whom I had seen at our London dinner parties, with his wife and sister-in-law – and the Clanders, whose unexpected presence added to a feeling of unreality, as if I were seeing people and events while in the grip of fever. Throughout the evening I was conscious of viewing everything through, as it might be said, two ends of a telescope, one which showed things as they were while the other exaggerated or diminished them, so that a voice would change from its normal tones to a screech or sinister whisper, a face that was three feet away appear suddenly almost to touch mine, then recede into the middle distance. There is a medical name for this condition, although I have forgotten it.

This feeling of unreality was such that I saw the Clanders – invited, I learned later, at Melissa's request – without surprise, and there seemed nothing strange in encountering Hugo Headley, a glass of something or other in his hand, long hair lustrous and carefully combed, a dark blue cravat at his neck and a brightly coloured belt round his waist. When I came down people were in the drawing room and on the verandah, glasses were filled with white wine and red, whisky and soda and gin and lime. Deirdre was at the piano playing Cole Porter, and a group round her sang 'You're the Cream in My Coffee' and 'My Heart Belongs to Daddy'. Claude Clanders, sweating red face turned upwards as when he mooed for tea, piped, 'Oh, my heart belongs to Daddy, though I think you're perfectly swell.' The face seemed alarmingly close, veins and pores visible, then it receded.

Later Deirdre was replaced at the piano by Dodo, who vamped inaccurately but with gusto while he played sentimental songs. Father, beside him, sang in a fine deep baritone:

110

'When you are happy, friend of mine,
And all your skies are blue,
Tell me your luck, your fortune fine,
And let me joy with you.'

And Dodo at the piano joined in lustily:

'But when the night falls tremulous
And the last lamp burns low
And one of us or both of us
The long lone road must go,
Look with your dear old eyes in mine,
Give me your handshake true,
Whatever fate our souls await
Let me be there – let me be there – with you.'

As they finished the song Dodo collapsed over the keys with laughter, and Father was laughing too. Dodo slapped him on the back, said he needed another drink. A refilled glass seemed often in his hand that night.

Father spoke to me, his face seeming thrust into mine, huge. I tried to blink it further away. Glad you came down, he said, know what it meant to you, have to face up to things in life, rough with the smooth, things don't just go away. Then I was clasped in Deirdre's embrace, smelled the scent I remembered from childhood, light but faintly sharp, she cooed consoling words. Neil came up, said things I can't recall, sympathetic things. It may sound as if I was affected by drink, but in the whole evening I drank only a single glass of wine.

What else do I remember before the terrible end? The food, of course, laid out in the dining room and eaten buffet fashion, something less usual then than now, at tables, standing, or sitting out on the verandah. Dodo carving a ham, Father carving chicken and beef, jellied veal, something or other in aspic, potato salad and Russian salad, Daisy handing things round, Prunella with plate piled high talking to Father about something called the public ethic while she ate, his face a wooden image, Hugo with glass full then empty, Daisy refilling it, Erato saying best meal we've had for a month, calls for cook who appeared beaming, clapping and glasses raised, Father and Hugo going out of the door, female Minchin saying understand you're a tennis champion, turning away and the whole wretchedness coming back, a vision of the strokes I could have played, the open spaces into which they could have gone, running round on the forehand to hit a winner, then puddings, huge trifle, fruit salad, wobbly charlotte russe, Daisy saying you're not eating Mr Geoffrey cook will be upset must have some, Hugo brushing past me muttering something holding out glass for a refill, Daisy's face almost touching mine, feeling her breath, breasts touching me, moved back and away, trod on a foot, knocked glass out of an Ellerby hand, broken, apologies, Daisy sweeping up. Then later the piano being played, not Deirdre not Dodo but Claude, wagging his ginger head and singing something, dancing, Melissa in Dodo's arms why not in mine, Erato close to me saying come on, come on, then when I said no, speaking words clear and loud: 'Know what you are, a silly sulky *prick*.'

From all this I fled, noise, dancing, Erato, fled into the dark garden where there would be no distortions of vision. I walked round the side of the house and leaned against the scullery wall gulping air, grateful for the silence broken only by the faint susurrus of the sea. But standing in dense darkness I became aware of another sound than the sea's sibilance, a human sound, perhaps a voice, perhaps two voices, an exclamation quickly muffled perhaps, perhaps a shoe striking against a stone. I moved in the direction of this real or imagined sound, away from the house and the reassurance of a touched wall, into the empty darkness.

The sounds ceased, or I heard them no longer. I stopped and stood, then on an impulse knelt in the dew-damp grass, placed my hand on it, rubbed the wet hand over my face, sucked the damp fingers.

Darkness was broken by a strong beam of light. It came from a torch and was focused on the gardener's hut, outside which a few hours earlier Passlove senior had sat with his mug of tea. Its door was flung open and a voice shouted with the power of an Old Testament prophet, a voice I barely recognised as Father's: '*Whore.*'

What I saw in the torchbeam will remain with me until the end of my life. A rug had been put down on the floor of the hut and there a woman knelt on all fours, dress pulled over her head, body naked from the waist down. A man was behind her, trousers around his ankles, his prick (yes, I repeat the word Erato had spoken to me only minutes before) driving in and out of her. Neither face was visible, but even as I looked the tableau collapsed, the man rolled off the woman and began to pull up his trousers, the woman pulled her dress over her buttocks, then turned and put her hands across her face. I could see them both.

The man was Neil Paton. The woman was Deirdre, whom I no longer called Mother.

That single word Father uttered was succeeded by a strangled cry, like the sound made by a wounded animal, and that by grunts, shouts, sounds cut short like something heard through an imperfect address system. The torch flashed off, on, off again. I caught glimpses of Father wrestling with Deirdre, punching Neil. Then I turned and ran, not back to the piano and the dancing, but up to my tower room. I don't know what solace I had hoped to find in it, but there was none. I picked up the racquet that had failed me and smashed it again and again over a chair until some strings were broken, then held it in the door jamb and bent it back so that the frame cracked.

While I did this I saw, as I have seen over and over again during the years, the image of my rutting mother on all fours. It was as if I had been presented with the reality of the rhetoric I loved in the Elizabethan playwrights.

With the racquet broken I was somehow sated. I went down to my bedroom, drew the curtains, locked the door, turned off the light, went to bed knowing I should not sleep. I did not wake till morning.

113

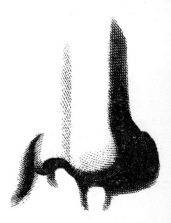

The Sixties

(i) Lucky Lambert

The appointment with Lucky Lambert had been made for me by
Jack Davey, crime reporter on the *Banner*. Before I became a
moderately successful actor I had been a less successful
newspaperman, and I still knew people in Fleet Street, Jack
among them. He remembered the Headley disappearance, and
fixed an interview for me on the basis that there might be some
sort of story in what came out of it. The pretext was that I
wanted to write an article about Lambert for *Big People*, a
monthly magazine that specialised in articles about those who
had recently become famous or notorious. *Big People* was not a
scandal sheet like the recently founded *Private Eye*, the articles
it contained often being admiring to the point of adulation.
They had run a series of pieces on the Beatles, a long profile of
Harold Wilson when he became leader of the Labour Party,
another about the Cliveden Set at the time of the Profumo affair.

Lambert was now Joseph Lambert, the sobriquet Lucky discarded. He had become a property owner on a large scale, with
an interest in a firm of building contractors, and so was a
reasonable enough subject for interview. Leila, however, said I
should never be able to carry it through successfully. I pointed
out that I was, after all, an actor, and tapped the half-dozen
sheets summarising Lambert's career that Jack had given me.

'That won't help you to talk about Hugo Headley, will it? I
think he'll throw you out on your neck.'

I said she underrated my persuasiveness, and she shrugged
and promised to have bandages ready for my return. A fine
August morning found me sitting in the reception room of
Lambert and Lambert, Contractors and Consultants. My
appointment was for eleven thirty, and the clock above the
secretary's head said precisely that when a buzzer on her desk
sounded, she switched a smile on and off, and said Mr Lambert
would see me now.

The man who came round a large desk to shake my hand
didn't look as if he had once collected debts by force or threats.
Wings of grey hair framed the face of an ageing character actor

playing Man of Distinction rôles, a top civil servant perhaps or, if one dropped a little in the social scale, the manager of a good restaurant. His voice modified this impression a little. It was quiet and pleasant, but with a Cockney East End accent audible in the vowels when he asked me to tell him something about the kind of article I had in mind. I went into my prepared spiel, which linked the rise of what I called the Lambert empire with the new spirit of the Sixties, and said what interested me particularly was how the enterprise had begun. He heard me out patiently, then said 'Yes,' picked up a nail file on the desk and began to clean his nails. I waited.

'Very well done.' He put down the nail file. 'But what do you really want?' I stared at him. 'You don't work for *Big People*, and they don't want to run a profile on me.' I cursed Jack Davey, who said he'd arranged a cover in case of any check-up. 'I know the editor, saw him at a conference a couple of days back, thought it was odd he hadn't mentioned anything and checked with him. Now your cover's blown, you might as well tell me what scandal sheet you work for before I ask you to leave.'

The words were said quietly, almost gently. I hesitated, unsure how to reply.

'If you're thinking up another fairy tale I shouldn't do it. I have a sense of humour, but I don't like being kidded.'

There was menace in the manner, though not in the words. Or so I thought. In any case I gave up the pretence of being a reporter, and told him what I was trying to find out. He heard me through without interruption, his hands still on the desk before him. Then, to my relief, he smiled.

'I like it. Maybe it isn't true, but I like it. I told you I had a sense of humour.' He looked at his watch, perhaps to show the elegance of his cuff-links, then came round the desk. 'Stand up a moment.' I stood and quickly, deftly, his hands went over me. Then he nodded and said, 'You're clean. All right, I'll give you ten minutes. Ask questions, but you don't make any notes, right?' I said yes, and he went back behind the desk and began to talk. As he spoke, voice and language almost imperceptibly changed, as if thinking of the past implied some kind of return to it.

'What you got to understand is buying a debt and then collecting is a chancy business. Often as not you find the man who owes has skipped the country, or he's hired a minder with a bit of a reputation for looking after people, or he's genuinely skint so there's really no way of collecting. I once bought a debt for twenty pence in the pound, businessman who'd had a bad run at blackjack, said the dealer had fiddled the game and refused to pay. Seemed straightforward enough, had a nice wife, nice house, couple of kids. But Dusty, I bought it off him, Dusty knew something I didn't, because within a couple of weeks the man had skipped the country with some bird he had in tow, and that was the end of it.'

'You lost the whole debt? You got nothing back from Hegarty?'

The Man of Distinction smiled. 'You must be joking.'

'You must have been angry at being tricked?'

'Angry, what for? Dusty put one over on me, that's all. Times I did the same to him, and it did him no good in the end. He moved into drugs, hash, speed, nose powder, you name it, got hooked himself, died a few years back. What you deal in you don't touch, it's a golden rule.'

'You bought Hugo Headley's debt from him. How much was it?'

'Not a lot. Fifteen hundred perhaps, two thousand. I don't exactly remember, it was a long way back. Another world, you might say.'

'And then—' I didn't know quite how to put it. 'Did you try to collect? He had no money.'

'Correct. And I knew that. I probably gave Dusty ten per cent on the paper value, maybe only five. It was taking a chance, I've never minded that. Then when I met Headley I could see it wasn't twenty to one, it was a hundred to one against collecting.'

'What was your impression of him?'

'I don't go in much for impressions, but I can tell you after talking to him for five minutes I knew there'd be no way of getting any readies without putting the screws on.'

'So you approached his parents?'

'Did I say so?'

'You talked about putting the screws on.'

'Who says I did? You want to listen a bit closer. I said there was no way of getting at him unless I put the screws on, that's all. I never did anything out of line, never threatened anybody.' He stared at me, eyes unblinking. 'I never saw Headley except that one time.'

'I'm told he was frightened. He said he'd been threatened that if he didn't pay up in a week he'd be hurt. Or killed.' I couldn't bring myself to use the term 'wooden overcoat'. 'Perhaps you sent someone to see him.' He made no reply. 'Did you?'

'I don't recollect. What I'll tell you is this. If somebody representing me saw Headley they had no authority to make any kind of threat, and I'd be surprised if they did. In any case he slipped off abroad.'

'He disappeared. He may have drowned. Or committed suicide.'

'You think?' I said it was what I was trying to find out. 'I'd say he liked himself too much to do anything like that. But you can think what you like, and no doubt you will.' He looked at his watch. 'Mr Elder, your time is up.'

(ii) *Wer Wer Conquers All*

That weekend we went down to see Leila's father, the Canon, who lived in a large rambling house a few miles from Oxford. When we arrived I had the immediate impression that the house had been taken over for a village fête, an event by no means unlikely. A field opposite the house was being used as a car park, there was a tent on the lawn, some dozens of people were milling about, and a lop-sided banner in red and gold hung from the first floor windows of the house which said WER WER CONQUERS ALL.

'I rang Daddy. He said nothing special was happening this

weekend,' Leila said as we got out of our Ford Prefect. It was apparent from the clothes and manners of the mini-skirted girls and long-haired young men lying on the grass and drifting in and out of the tent that they were not villagers. Apparent also from their colour, which was by no means universally white, but included yellow, two or three shades of brown, and black. A figure wearing a magician's conical hat and dressed like Harlequin walked along the ledge where the banner hung, and somebody cheered. The Canon approached us, beaming, with Leila's elder sister Olivia beside him. Leila's father was small and round, and wore gold-rimmed spectacles that slipped down his nose. Olivia was a taller, thinner version of Leila. Although she was thin her clothes always seemed a size too small for her, and she walked in a flat-footed awkward way suggesting that the sensible shoes she wore were too tight.

'Leila, my dear, wonderful.' The Canon folded his younger daughter in an embrace. 'And Gordon. What a surprise.'

'Daddy, I rang and told you. And it's Geoffrey, not Gordon.'

'You weren't expected,' Olivia said severely.

'But are *very* welcome. This whole thing is the most tremendous success. Look there – television.' And indeed a TV crew and camera, under the control of a woman with cropped hair above a Hollywood-style eyeshade, moved among the crowd taking pictures. A cheer went up, and the TV crew turned their attention to the ledge, where Harlequin had reached the cords that held the banner, at which he was tugging. Somebody shouted, 'What about a double somersault?' Harlequin waved, gave another tug at the cords, and they unravelled so that the banner now said FLOWER POWER CONQUERS ALL.

'Very true.' The Canon nodded admiringly, and made no reply when Leila asked what it was all in aid of. She appealed to her sister.

'It's a meeting of Weflap. West and East For Love and Peace.' Olivia's expression was that of one under torture.

The Canon gave Leila his full attention. 'You must have heard of it. And you too, Gor— Geoffrey.' I shook my head. Leila said she'd heard it was a fringe group that believed in love. Her father beamed again. 'A universal appeal, don't you think? Weflap is spreading like a forest fire through the Home Counties, and it seemed right to help. One must always do what one can, don't you feel? I could wish there were more of my parishioners here, but it's a splendid turn-out.' With a touch of reproach he said, 'You've missed the speeches. Swami Ramcharand was splendid, and a Tibetan Lama led us in a most unusual form of prayer.'

Olivia said vengefully to her sister, 'They've had prayers and they're waiting for tea. And we're short-handed. You may as well help, now you're here.'

Leila followed her obediently. One of the engaging things about Leila, although at times one of the most infuriating, is her compliant nature. She always does what comes easiest, what she thinks other people would like, even – as in Olivia's case – what she may be almost ordered to do. I once told her she was like a cushion, waiting to be sat on.

'Dear girls, dear girls,' the Canon said as he watched their departing backs. 'Olivia is my prop, my mainstay. But Leila . . . ' He let the sentence drop, and tried another. 'It is difficult to be a woman in this world.' I hardly knew what to say to that. 'People say marriage is a sacrament, and of course that's true. But how many of these young people are married, and does it matter? You'll say that's an odd question to come from a clergyman, is he a Benthamite you'll ask yourself, can he be a Benthamite?'

I nodded, not sure what a Benthamite was. 'You're very liberal-minded.'

'I do hope so. What about marriage, though?'

'How do you mean?'

'What are the prospects of you and Leila—' his delicate little hand pawed the air in search of a phrase '—getting hitched?'

'I'm not sure either of us feels the need for it.'

The Canon took a fine half-hunter from the recesses of his cassock. 'Time's getting on.' Was this an indirect reference to our marriage prospects? As if summoned by the watch a girl appeared beside him, her shirt revealing flesh between it and her jeans, her small face lost in a forest of hair. 'Ratty says she's ready for the Zig-Zags any time.' Muttering acknowledgement of this the Canon walked quickly, almost trotted, towards the house. The girl said, 'He's round the twist, isn't he? Mind you, got some of the right ideas. Come over, get in one of the groups, you might be on the telly.'

I looked inside the tent, where a band was playing some immensely loud but unintelligible song, a young man bellowing words into the microphone, couples clutching each other in a parody of dancing. A glimpse was enough. There was no sign of Leila, who was presumably cutting bread or buttering scones. I walked in the direction of the TV crew. The jeans of the cropped-haired woman with the eyeshade were tucked into high, well-polished black boots, and she was stamping impatiently as a horse. She said to the cameraman, 'We've got all we want of this shower, where are those fucking Zig-Zags?' Her gaze rested on me, flicked away, came back. 'Who are you?' I told her my name. 'You're an actor, right?'

'Right. And who are you?'

She did not reply, but took off the eyeshade revealing a broad hard face, the sort of face one used to see in pictures of Russian women agricultural workers who had over-fulfilled their production quota, and a wide mouth turned down in discontent. Memory is a never-ending series of rooms and passages down which one wanders, seeing many known yet still unrecognisable figures. Why should we recall these people, met only once or twice, who said nothing memorable, made no particular impression? They wake no echo in the mind, we pass them by. But once in a hundred times some connecting link is made, a face seen ten, twenty, thirty years ago can be placed like a photofit police picture over the present features, and the act of recognition takes place. What lit the spark in this case? The turned-down mouth, perhaps, and then the phrase used by Olivia to Leila came into my mind, 'You may as well help, now you're here.' That phrase, or something like it, had been spoken to me many years ago. It summoned up Clempstone, the smell of the sea and its salt taste on my lips, a tea party where Melissa had not appeared, long-dead Professor Clanders, an untidy kitchen. I said, 'Erato.'

'Ratty. Nobody's called me by that other bloody stupid name for years. So what are you doing here, Geoffrey Elder? Don't tell me you belong to Weflap.' I said a friend had brought me. She

nodded. 'I tell you why I'm here, because everyone's saying
"Peace, it's wonderful," doesn't matter how crazy the group is,
as long as they say peace people love them. This lot have got an
international collection of singers and dancers called the Zig-
Zags who're supposed to do a song and dance routine. They
haven't turned up yet, and without them it's pretty much of a
waste of time. I nearly got in touch with you a couple of months
back.'

'For a TV film? I wish you had.'

'Nothing like that. I only do documentaries. What we're
shooting today is part of a sixty-minute film about peace movements in Britain. It was about Hugo Headley, remember him?
Let's get a beer, we've got our own supply. Chet, if anything
happens I'll be in the van.'

The van was in the field, among cars which had flowers and
slogans painted on them. We sat in the front seats. Ratty found a
plastic glass for me, but drank her beer from the tin.

'You remember he disappeared, never turned up, and all the
kerfuffle about it? Of course you do, you were in the middle of it.
Well, I met some prat at a party who thought Headley was the
bee's knees. He was a publisher, the prat I mean, firm called
Oceanic, and when I told him I'd been around when Headley
vanished he almost wet himself. He was thinking of doing a
book, wanted me to make a documentary about Headley leading
up to the disappearance, and – this is the interesting bit – said he
was in touch with a man who had some fresh info. The name
was Morgan, the man's name. Mean anything to you? Me
neither. Thing is, the info this Morgan claimed to have seemed
to be connected to your family. That ring a bell?'

'No. Except that my father was considering some kind of deal
with Headley about selling his cottage.'

'Yeah, I remember something said about that, but from what I
could gather this went further back. A long way back. The prat
was half-cut – his name was Trelawney – and I'd had a drop
myself. His idea was I'd make this documentary about the
Headley mystery, as he called it, and build up to Morgan's
revelations as the climax. And he'd publish it all as a book.'

'What revelations?'

'I dunno. I saw this Morgan, he's caretaker at some school in South London. Around sixty, struck me as an unreliable character, and you might say I'm an expert on unreliable characters. Not just that, but he seemed to me as if he wasn't all there. But that's not it either. Fixated, that's it. He was fixated.' She nodded, apparently satisfied.

'About Headley?'

'No, about your family, your father specially. But when I saw him he was full of dope, not making a lot of sense. He had this guy with him, very big, head shaved, funny voice, who called him Morgy and acted like he owned him, Morgy was some sort of property. And he was talking money, a lot of money. I told them that was ridiculous, the only hope of seeing big money would be if there was a book and it sold for newspaper serial, a TV company would want the whole story before we coughed up a penny, and then it would be pennies, not what they were talking about. Trelawney took the same line, Morgan wouldn't show us anything, wouldn't or couldn't, and it all faded away. At some point I thought of getting in touch with you, but in the end it seemed like a waste of time.'

'How long ago was this?'

'Early part of this year, I was editing a film about blacks and the police. Surprised you're interested. Skeletons in the family closet?'

'Perhaps. You say this story wasn't to do with Hugo.'

'Never mentioned him. It was about some sort of dirty trick your family had played on him, he wouldn't say what. In the end I told him to put up or shut up, stop wasting our time. Not sure he took it in, but the bald ape didn't like it.'

We went on talking for another couple of minutes. She told me that, as she'd said to me when we met, she had cut free from her family as soon as she left school. Her parents were both dead, and Clytie had gone to South Africa and married a farmer. Back in the garden we saw Leila, who had escaped from duties on the basis of concern for me, and I introduced them. The camera crew stood around chatting up girls. Even in the open I caught a whiff of grass. When Ratty asked Chet about the Zig-Zags she was told again that they'd been held up.

'So when will they get here?'

'Nobody seems to know.'

Ratty slapped her thigh. 'That's it then, no use hanging around any longer. I'll tell old fuddy-duddy we're off.' She turned to Leila. 'Sorry, forgot he was your dad.'

Leila said it was all right. When we left the Canon was on the telephone still trying to locate the Zig-Zags. He embraced Leila with one arm while holding the receiver with the other, and said goodbye Gordon to me. On the way back to Pimlico I told her how Erato Clanders had turned into Ratty. I also mentioned Morgan, and said I might go down to see him.

'Whatever for? I should have thought you'd had enough with Mr Lambert.' I said again that if there was a mystery involving my father I wanted to clear it up, which was true even though the reasons for that wish were obscure to me. Leila made no comment on that, but asked if I thought Ratty was attractive. I told her I didn't have any taste for butch lesbians, and she said she thought Ratty seemed very nice. Back in the flat, over an omelette and a glass of white wine, she said I was obsessed with Hugo Headley.

'You should blame that ginger-haired biographer. But yes, I do want to know why my father wrote those notes to Headley, if that's an obsession.'

'It's not good to worry about the past, it gets you nowhere.' She sipped wine. 'And unhealthy. You should be more in touch with Shoestring, ask him to dinner.'

Shoestring is my agent. His name of course is not Shoestring, but he tells so many hard-luck stories about lucrative engagements just missed, and is so insistent that he has to run his office on a shoestring, that Leila gave him the name. I could see no point in asking Shoestring to dinner. I knew he would drink two or three large gins before he ate, plus all the wine offered to him at dinner, and tell ever more improbable stories about famous figures who had been on his books when they were unknown, and then left him because of natural ingratitude or unethical behaviour by rival agents. I said some of this. Leila replied that I was unreasonable. I ought to stir my stumps, she said, and to talk about my agent like that was not very nice. A day out usually ended with what Leila called home comforts. 'It will be nice to get home and have some comforts,' she would say, and at times I found her desire for home comforts quite exhausting. But on this evening a certain coolness was in the air, and home comforts remained unmentioned.

(iii) Morgan, a Missing Link

On the following morning the cool air had become almost icy. Leila said before she went to work that there were jobs about the place that needed doing. She indicated a lamp socket that made only intermittent contact, so that the light flickered on and off. I said she knew I was no handyman, and might give myself a shock.

'Sometimes I think a shock might do you no end of good. But all right then, ring the electrician. And don't forget Shoestring.' This was no longer Leila the little mother, but businesswoman Leila, who found the casual life of an actor extremely irritating, and was making the fact plain. Was this connected with abstention from home comforts? I shied away from the thought.

So I rang Shoestring, and listened to him for twenty minutes. He told me how difficult times were, and the efforts he was making to persuade Jake Johnson, an American producing a series of revivals, to get me the part of Yslaev, the landowner in Turgenev's *A Month in the Country*. It was touch and go, Shoestring said. If that didn't come off, what did I think about a tour with an excellent company doing Shakespeare's tragedies, early in the New Year? Where would it be? Africa. And where in Africa? Zambia for certain, possibly Kenya, maybe other countries. I said the thought of playing *Othello* in Zambia didn't stir my blood, and he said he'd let me know about the Turgenev. Yslaev is not a particularly interesting part, although he has a good scene in the last act.

Duty done, I rang Oceanic Publishers, and asked for Mr

127

Trelawney. A voice of ineffable stuffiness said it was Reginald Trelawney, and even on the telephone I could understand why Ratty had called him a prat. He, or anyway his voice, would have been perfect casting for Lord Peter Wimsey in an amateur production. When I told him who I was he became quite excited.

'That's really offly interestin',' he said. 'Of course me own feelin' is Headley was a genius, but even allowin' for a chap's excitement when he gets that old thrill Housman talked about, the whole story was fascinatin'. If you think you could offer a new view of it I'd be jolly interested to have a talk. No harm in talkin', is there?' What sounded like a series of muffled pistol shots came down the line, Trelawney laughs. The pistol shots stopped when I mentioned Morgan.

'Morgan, yes, I'd have to call him one of the awkward squad. I dare say Miss – ah—'

'Clanders, Ratty Clanders.'

'She may have told you, he was talkin' about a quite absurd sum of money. I had to tell him Oceanic was not a charity, I really got shirty with him, you produce some evidence I said, and we'll talk about the money side of it. But he never showed us anything, it was all talk.'

'What about?'

'Himself and his hard life, it seemed to be, and some bad deal he'd had from your family. I asked him about Headley, and he said he could tell me somethin' about the connection between Harold Elder – your father – and Headley's disappearance. But he never did, and most of the time he seemed to be only half there, if you take my meanin'. A word of warnin' if you do see him. He got twenty quid out of me one day with a hard-luck story about bein' turned out of his rooms.' He gave me the address of the school where Morgan was a caretaker willingly enough, and said he would love to talk about Hugo Headley over a drink at the In and Out any time.

The Cralkin Junior School was in a South London borough, and the good old Prefect got me there in less than half an hour. The place was deserted except for a few boys kicking a football about in the playground, and I belatedly realised that these were the summer holidays. I asked one of the boys where I might find the caretaker, and he jerked a thumb at a little red brick house just down the street.

I rang the bell. The door was opened by a girl perhaps ten years old. I asked if I could speak to her father, Mr Morgan. She stared at me, said nothing, ran back inside. A large man appeared, shirtsleeves rolled up, arms thick with black hair, an arrow through a heart tattooed on one of them. He said, 'Yes?'

I addressed him by name, and he advanced threateningly on me. I retreated a step.

'What you after, eh?'

'Look, Mr Morgan—'

'I'm not Morgan, who told you I was that bastard?'

'I'm sorry.' I sounded to myself like prat Trelawney. 'But you're the school caretaker?'

'So I bleeding am. I asked you, why are you creeping round looking for bleeding Morgan? One of his lot, eh, is that it?' I had no idea what he was talking about, and said I simply wanted to ask Morgan some questions. 'Ah, you're from the meejah.' His manner softened. 'Doing an article about it, are you? And there's a lot of it about, believe you me. I thought you was one of 'em, see. But anyways, you're too late, mate. You want to see him, you'll have to pay a visit.'

'Where to, what's the address?'

He showed me a fine set of false teeth. 'That's a good one. The address is the Scrubs, mate, where the filthy little sod got what's coming to him, I shouldn't wonder.' He glared at me. ''Ere, who're you kidding? You're from the meejah, you ought to know that.'

What exactly had happened to Morgan? The obvious next step seemed to be the local paper, the *South London Borough News*. There I found a full report in the files of the case heard in the Magistrates' Court of Edward Morgan, age sixty-two, caretaker at Cralkin Junior School, on the charge of indecently assaulting two boys and two girls, between the ages of ten and thirteen. They had gone round to the flat he occupied as caretaker, been given sweets and sometimes small sums of money, and then assaulted in a manner not described. Morgan had pleaded guilty. He had three previous convictions for indecent assault, and the magistrate said it was astonishing that the authorities had not investigated his background. He bore in mind that Morgan had pleaded guilty, and that there was indication that the two girls might have been willing partners in what occurred. He was therefore minded to be lenient, and passed a sentence of four months' imprisonment, while warning Morgan that a further offence would be considered much more seriously.

That had been April and this was August, so Morgan would be out by now, even if he got no remission. I went to look for the probation officer.

As I knew from my days as a journalist, nobody concerned with justice comes out of a Magistrates' Court more cheerful than when they went in. This Court was presided over by two women and a man, and they got through the usual run of cases – driving without due care and attention, street affrays, husband and wife battles, indecent exposures, quarrels between neighbours – at lightning speed, the two women doing a lot of conferring while the man sucked lozenges, nodding occasionally. I sat through several cases while the usher located Mr Pettigrew the probation officer, and took me to the small room at the back of the Court where he sat with files stacked high beside him. He had fluffy white hair, and a nose that twitched like a rabbit's.

'Morgan, yes, certainly I remember him, very well indeed. Did you say your name is Elder? I thought so, yes, what a pity.' Why was it a pity, I asked, and his nose twitched. 'He was anxious to get in touch with you. You *are* Mr Harold Elder?'

'That was my father. He died some years ago.'

'Dear dear, I'm sorry. But I think he would have liked to talk to any member of the family. Morgan is – but perhaps you know him?' I shook my head. 'He is not quite all there, a screw loose, you know what I mean? But only a screw loose, you understand, quite able to look after himself with the exception of his little frailty, which I expect you know about. But emotionally he is a child, reliant on other people. And he has some very undesirable acquaintances.' He sighed. I brought him back to the matter of my family. 'Ah yes. He seemed to have this idea that his life has somehow been affected by Mr Harold Elder, he can become very excited about it. At other times he simply said Mr Elder could help him.'

'You mean give him money?'

'I suppose so. He rambled, you know, he really rambled, and one has only so much time, although of course I was sympathetic.' I said Morgan could talk to me. 'Ah, that's just the thing, you see, I can't put you in touch with him.'

Morgan had been released in June, and advised to report weekly to Mr Pettigrew, who had found him lodgings, and work in a supermarket. After three weeks he gave up the work, saying he had strained his back, and a week later he left the lodgings.

'It's not an unusual story, alas.' With the *alas* his nose twitched again. 'Of course he had served his sentence and was a free agent, but I don't like to think what may happen to him, especially with the kind of friends he has, and the little frailty to which he's inclined. He is easily led astray.' I asked if Morgan had told him anything at all about why he wanted to see my father. 'As I've told you he rambled, and I really didn't pay a great deal of attention. He seemed to think he was in possession of information about your father, and to be quite candid I got the impression that the information might be discreditable. It did occur to me, I hardly like to say it, but do you think it possible that your father may have succumbed at some time to Morgan's little frailty?'

'I should think it most unlikely. You're talking about blackmail?'

'Dear me, perhaps I am.' He ran a hand through the fluffy white thatch. 'Of course he didn't put it like that. He kept repeating that if he could only get in touch with the right people he wouldn't have to worry any more. Perhaps there is something else I should mention. Drugs are widely used round here, and Morgan has friends who are involved, very much so. He is a user himself, although the fact didn't come out when he was charged, and at least one of his friends is a dealer, a man named Sharkey.'

I asked if he knew where any of these friends might be found.

'Dear me, I'm not sure I should tell you. Well, in the unusual circumstances perhaps. There is a pub a couple of streets away, the Dog and Compasses. It is, what should I say, quite a *haunt*, and Sharkey uses it. At one time he took Morgan what I suppose I might call under his wing, not something I could approve of. But then what can one do?' He ran a hand again through his white hair, his nose twitched. I didn't try to answer the question.

The time was just after midday, and there were no more than a dozen people in the Dog and Compasses. I ordered a half of bitter, and told the barman I was looking for Mr Morgan. He glanced at me, then away, adjusted the hairpiece he wore, and began to wipe glasses. I realised I was in a pub for homosexuals. Which is the word I use. In the last year or two I've heard a lot of showbiz people using the word *gay*, but there's nothing particularly gay about what used to be called queers, or when I was young nancies. Americans call them fags, I don't know why, but to me homosexuals, homos for short, seems a good neutral word, and accurate too. There are plenty of homo theatrical pubs, but I hadn't expected to find one here in South London.

The barman said in a light, cultured voice, 'I don't know him, I'm afraid,' and shook his head slightly. I felt a hand on my shoulder, and another voice said, 'Who's asking?'

The hand was big, and the man it belonged to was six inches or more over my height, wide-shouldered, and with a head smooth as a billiard ball. He wore a dazzling check jacket and canary-coloured trousers. Unless the man Ratty talked to had a twin brother, I was meeting him now. I bought him a bitter, and we sat down at a table.

'What do you want with Morgy?' His voice was a piping treble, ludicrous in the great frame. I said just to talk to him, and he glared at me. 'Morgy's dead. Two nights ago he died, my poor Morgy.' He took out a dirty handkerchief, wiped his eyes. A man who had been talking to the barman came across, patted the big man's shoulder, said, 'Don't upset yourself, Billy.' This second man was squat and powerful, with a boxer's ear and a flattened nose. 'What's he want?'

Some bit of elementary good sense told me not to give them my name. I said I had been talking to Mr Pettigrew, and might have a job for Morgan, and asked what had happened to him. The second man answered.

'Fell out of a window at a party when he was on a high, cracked his skull.' Sharkey's shoulders moved, he shook his head. 'You wasn't there, Billy.'

'Bloody Dermot was.'

'I tell you we was all stoned, it was an accident.'

Sharkey looked up at him. 'Who was it went through Morgy's stuff then, took his papers, stuff he'd had for years? If I find that Dermot—' He should have made a menacing gesture. Instead he wept.

The other man said to me, 'I don't know what you're after, strikes me you're nosing round for some paper, but there's nothing for you here. You've upset Billy, and I don't like that. So finish your drink, and do it quick.'

I did what he said. The barman smiled at me as I left, and gave me a delicate wave of the hand.

When I told Leila how my day had been spent, she was not pleased. She never shouted, her approach being one of motherly astonishment at the foolishness of children.

'You really are, you know, Geoff, you really *are*. What do you think is the use of playing these detective games? Suppose you'd found this Morgan, what would you have said to him? Whatever is the purpose of it all?' I repeated what I'd told her before, conscious that she would think it feeble. If I found out something, she reasonably said, it was bound to be upsetting, and why upset myself? As for Headley, he'd obviously got into a mess from which there was no way out, and drowned himself.

'It isn't as straightforward as that. There are odds and ends that don't fit.'

'There always are. Did you ring Shoestring?' I told her about the Turgenev, and the African tour. 'And the electrician?' I think she was pleased I'd forgotten about the electrician, although she didn't say so. In fact, she went on at me for several minutes in a very unLeila-like manner. It ended with her saying that now she knew how I had spent the day she didn't feel like slaving over a hot stove. So we went out and tried a new Italian restaurant in Tachbrook Street. When we came back there were, by mutual agreement, no home comforts.

The Thirties

(i) Neil Paton at Rules

I have said I slept soundly on that Saturday night, but it was a sleep punctured by dreams. I have always wondered at those who, on the psychiatrist's couch, are able to recount incidents of their dreams in exact detail. I dream often, but never recall the people or the incidents with precision. On that night I know I dreamt of Deirdre, of Dodo, of Passlove junior and his father, and I remember that it was a worry dream, in which Passlove senior was telling me something which I tried desperately to understand. There was a phrase he kept repeating which made no sense even though the words were clear, and it seemed that I was prevented from understanding what he said by interventions from the others. I woke with a gasp at seven thirty. The house was silent. I put on swimming things, took towel and dressing gown, and crossed the road to the beach.

The morning was overcast, the tide coming in. Beside the sea, a few feet from lapping waves, Melissa stood looking out across blue-green water. When I called her name, forgetful of the harsh things she had said on the previous afternoon, she turned and even I, not the most observant of adolescents, noticed the extreme pallor of her face and the shadows under her eyes. I said I was going to swim, and asked if she would join me. She shook her head violently and walked, almost ran, back into the house.

Her reaction brought back all the memories I had been trying to suppress, the humiliation of the tennis match, the scene in the garden shed, my father's cry of 'Whore'. I found I no longer wanted to go in the sea, yet felt an extreme reluctance to return to the house. With no purpose except to delay seeing them all again, Father and Deirdre and Neil, I walked away from the house and so, after a few minutes, came to Parker's Point and the car.

It stood just pulled off the road, an old black Austin 7 spotted with rust and with a dented front mudguard. I recognised it at once as Hugo's, and looked through the window. I saw a pair of seaman's trousers and a grubby shirt on the back seat, and a pair of stained plimsolls on the floor. Where was their owner? The sea was calm, the waves only ripples. I looked to left and right, and called his name without result. I tried the door handle, found the car was unlocked, got into the driver's seat and put my hands on the steering wheel, an act later regretted by the police. I looked about in the car for other signs that would indicate where Hugo had gone, but found nothing except cigarette ends and spent matches. Although I rootled about inside, no idea that he might have drowned occurred to me. I thought he must have decided to go for a walk in his swimming things, wearing espadrilles or some other footwear. I stayed around the car for perhaps ten minutes, called his name again, then walked back to Grandison House.

(I was not the first person to notice the car at Parker's Point. Ellen Corliss had seen it there on the previous night, and went to the police when she noticed it there again on Sunday morning.)

Then back to breakfast. I am not sure what I had envisaged as the breakfast scene, but it was certainly not to find all apparently normal, Father at the end of the table in open-necked shirt and flannel trousers, Dodo eyeing Daisy as she brought round eggs and bacon, Neil unusually silent but composed, Melissa now changed into a blue summer dress and looking less hollow-eyed. Only the two wives were missing, but Deirdre rarely came down to breakfast, and Hilda was perhaps suffering one of her headaches. The young always expect that after a crisis, whether emotional or physical, the earth will shudder and the skies fall, and the everyday nature of our breakfasting led me to feel that really nothing had happened, and that what I had seen by torchlight was part of my uneasy dreams. Of course I knew that was not so, but human beings are perfectly able to believe two contradictory things at the same time. It may have been my uncertainty and uneasiness, or a mere wish to make conversation, that led me to mention seeing Hugo Headley's car at Parker's Point, and say that its occupant seemed to be missing.

Dodo put down his coffee cup and said, 'First time I've met him, seemed a queer sort. Gone for a ten-mile walk in his bathing things I shouldn't wonder, wouldn't put anything past him.' Neil made no comment. But Melissa cried out something unintelligible and ran out of the room, and Father's face was drained of colour so that it looked like waxed dough.

Then he turned to Neil. 'You'd better come with me. We have things to talk about.' Neil followed him obediently.

When they were out of the room Dodo said nothing more about Hugo's disappearance, but winked at me. 'Trouble at t'mill. You were there last night, saw it all?' I nodded. 'It reminded me of a party in Melbourne one night that got out of hand, and a couple of men and women put on a show—' I turned my head away, and he stopped abruptly. 'Sorry, lad, I forgot for a moment she's your mother, shouldn't have said that. They must have been crazy, just plain crazy.'

'I don't say Mother. I call her Deirdre.'

'She's a beautiful woman, but she's got the itch.' He put down his napkin. 'Be prepared, my boy. Harry's put up with a lot, but he'll have to do something now. There'll be changes, lad, changes.'

So it was hardly a normal breakfast scene, after all.

It was not until years later that I heard what had happened between Father and Neil Paton, and then it was Neil who told me. In the early Sixties I had a season at the Royal Shakespeare, and was playing Bedauer, the Spanish Ambassador in *Venice Preserv'd* (a smaller part than it may sound), when Neil sent round his card with a note. We had supper together, and he told me something of the background to it all. I knew a little, some I had guessed, but not a word had ever been spoken about it by Father. Neil was not surprised by that.

'I liked him, you know, admired him, but once you'd reached a certain point it was as if a barrier came down, and there was something that prevented him making a real friend of anybody. He loved beauty, physical beauty I mean.' By that time I understood his love of physical beauty very well. 'That must have been why he loved Deirdre, almost worshipped her. Otherwise they had nothing in common. She married him for a decent social position, then got bored with his kind of life in a few months, and looked around. I wasn't the first, you know.

That flower shop, what was it called? Anyway, it was a great place for meeting people, you might almost call it making assignations. Look here, I'm sorry, perhaps this isn't stuff you want to hear.' I said truthfully that I had no strong feelings about it now, and asked what had happened when Father took him off on the morning after the party. 'I'm truly ashamed of it all, we must have been mad. I don't have any excuse, but it was Deirdre who was so keen. I was besotted, simply besotted. You understand what I mean, it must have happened to you.'

'An actor understands everything. If he's a good actor he remains detached.'

'I suppose so,' he said doubtfully. 'But I never managed that with her, don't know that I'd have wanted to. Anyway, it was as if she wanted to see how much her husband would stand. I think he must have known about us, as he knew about some of the others, but that wasn't enough for Deirdre. I think if she could have performed in front of him she would have done, she wanted to see how far she could go and then go a bit further.'

He had taken me to Rules, and we had reached the coffee stage. Neil looked very much the same, the waistline thickened a little, streaks of grey in the black hair, but he was still dapperly handsome, attractive to women no doubt even though approaching or having reached seventy. And still a little uncertain or uneasy in the presence of men, although of course he had a particular reason for unease in my case. I knew Hilda had divorced him and that he had married again, the widow of a rich industrialist who was a pillar of her local Conservative party. Now he brought me up to date. He had started up his own firm after leaving Branksome and Elder, had acquired partners and recently retired with what he called an 18-carat golden handshake. I asked just what had been said to him on that Sunday morning.

'It was comic really, I mean it would have been in other circumstances. He talked about loyalty and all that sort of thing, stuff that goes by the board when you're besotted. Then he changed tack and said suddenly, "She's extravagant, you know, I hope you've thought about that." I tried to tell him there wasn't the least possibility Deirdre and I would set up house together, it was the last thing either of us had in mind, and do you know, I think that shocked him. He glared at me, then said he would expect my resignation from the firm. I said he could have it on the spot, and that was it. I never went back to the office, we arranged the financial details through solicitors, and he took over the work I had on hand, including a new estate in Kent that was rather a pet project of mine. I felt a bit angry at losing it, though you'll say I had no business to be sore about anything. And you'd be right.'

'He said nothing more about Deirdre?'

'Only that she was leaving, and he wanted me out too. So we went, though I talked to that local copper first, if you remember. And it was really the end of our affair, Deirdre's and mine.'

I remembered her leaving. I hung about the house in the morning, waiting uneasily for something to happen, went up to the tower room and tried to read but found I couldn't concentrate on the words, came down again, crossed the road and stood looking at the sea. Then I went into the garden where Passlove junior in his usual shorts and vest was talking to Daisy. He came up to me, grinning.

'You heard the news? That Mr Headley, lives in a cottage Greystone way, he's drowned hisself.' I asked if his body had been found. 'Not yet, but it's what they reckon. Took his car up to Parker's Point, went in the sea and drowned hisself.' I said I'd seen the car, but the rest was nothing more than gossip and guesswork. 'It's what they reckon,' he repeated. 'Why'd he take his car up there and leave it all night if he wasn't going in sea?'

A few minutes later a cab from the station stopped in the drive, and Deirdre came down the stairs wearing a grey town suit and a hat with a veil, Daisy behind her carrying suitcases. She walked with the daintiness of an actress making a dramatic exit, unfortunately seen only by Daisy, me, and the hovering Passlove junior, who seized the cases and put them in the cab. She stopped beside me, lifted the veil.

'Geoffrey, darling. Your father seems to think I should go back to London. You're too young to understand—'

I interrupted her, and said I did understand.

'Oh, very well. In that case you'll know he's being quite absurd. I can't say I mind leaving this ghastly place, but—' Her poise deserted her for a moment, then she said she would see me at home, kissed me on the cheek, got into the cab and was gone.

A few minutes later Father came down and took me into the back room that was called the study, no doubt because there were a couple of shelves of books in it. Whatever had disturbed him when he heard of the disappearance was not obvious now. He spoke crisply, with no apparent emotion.

'No need to go into details about last night, because you were there. I wish you hadn't been. Your mother will not sleep under my roof again.' I made a gesture he may have thought one of dissent. 'What is it?'

'She said she would see me at home.'

He made no reply. Deirdre of course had her keys to the Kensington house and stayed there that night, but he kept to his word as soon as we returned, having the locks changed immediately and giving instructions to the servants that she should not be admitted. He divorced her eighteen months later, citing Neil Paton as co-respondent. The case was not contested. In that period I saw her sometimes, going to the flat she rented off Marylebone High Street. After the divorce I went there to dinner, an occasion alleviated by the presence of Johnjohn and Pat. Deirdre cooked dinner herself and cooked it well – she was competent at anything she put her hand to – but it was an uneasy occasion. I had left school, and Johnjohn and Pat talked encouragingly about the job I'd started as dogsbody on a small weekly paper. Deirdre was scornful.

'What is it, making tea and running errands? I can't imagine how Harry ever let you take it.'

'It's a start,' Johnjohn said. 'Many a millionaire's started as an office boy.'

'And more have ended as clerks adding columns of figures, assistant to the assistant manager. Geoffrey should have gone to Oxford, and been given a decent start in life.' I said I hadn't wanted that, a remark she ignored. 'Your father owed it to you.'

Grandma Pat said I was a lovely boy, and what happened

happened. Deirdre asked what she meant by that, Johnjohn replied that she knew what they thought, and said it was a pity she'd moved out of her class when she married. Deirdre responded that she was sorry they spoke against their own daughter. The evening went on like that, and I was glad when it ended. By this time I was fully conscious of Deirdre's beauty, and aware too that she had what was then known as Oomph, a word associated with the film star Ann Sheridan, who was called the girl with Oomph. No mention was made of a man in her life, but I was also now old enough, or sophisticated enough, to notice a man's razor and an extra toothbrush in the bathroom.

Putting this down, so many years after it happened, I wonder whether it all affected my life. I suppose the answer must be yes. To see your mother copulating with a family friend, and then be told that she wouldn't be allowed into the house where she lived, that must surely be enough to affect any boy's life. When I try to recall my feelings at the time, though, I come up with a blank. I can remember despair at being knocked out of the tennis tournament, and if I close my eyes I can see even now the act shown to me by torchlight, but over my own emotion numbness has supervened. Perhaps a kindly emotional censor has blotted out pain.

When I parted from Neil, with handshakes and good wishes, I think both of us knew we had no wish to meet again. In the successful retired businessman with his 18-carat golden handshake I could recognise nothing of the figure who had encouraged my hopes of being a tennis star. And on his side I dare say Neil was disconcerted to find the promising lad he remembered had become a mere stage player. Life is full of such discoveries.

(ii) The Inspector Calls

When Deirdre had gone the skies darkened and it began to rain, that gentle persistent rain peculiar to English seaside resorts. I had gone up again to the tower room, and was sitting there doing nothing, staring into space, brooding perhaps on the unfair means by which Goldstube had beaten me, when I heard another car draw up before the house. A man in police uniform got out. I went on brooding until I heard my name called, and then went down. At the bottom of the stairs I found Dodo, who said in a low voice, 'Local copper, looking into disappearance of our friend Headley, wants to talk to you.'

In the living room I found Father, all three Patons, and a black-browed jolly-looking man who introduced himself as Inspector Lynton. A constable sat in a corner by the piano, with notebook and fountain pen. The Inspector said he would like to hear about how I found Hugo Headley's car that morning, and listened to my account with occasional approving nods.

'Very clearly put, if I may say so. You got into the car, sat in the driving seat, handled the steering wheel. Why exactly did you do that?' I said truthfully that I didn't know, and he nodded again as if that was a perfectly satisfactory answer. Father asked if they had any idea what had happened.

'Well, Mr Elder, it's a bit of a puzzle. Seems he drove his car from his cottage up to Parker's Point, and went for a midnight dip or something of the sort. This party you had here, can you tell me who was present?' Father, supplemented by Melissa, told him. 'And Mr Headley, was he a friend of yours, Miss Paton?'

'I knew him. Not a particular friend.'

'A friend of Mr and Mrs Clanders, then? You say no to that, Miss Paton. And you hardly knew him, Mr Elder. I'm wondering who invited him to the party.'

'I did,' Father said. 'I had a little business to discuss with him.'

'Ah, that explains it. Except that a party is a bit of a funny place to talk business.'

'He said it was urgent, and we were able to slip away from the party and talk, so it was perfectly convenient.' That was said in his everyday voice, but now he raised it a little. 'I don't understand why you're asking these questions.'

The Inspector's eyebrows went up and down again. 'Maybe I should apologise for asking them, sir. What I reckon is, Mr Headley did go for that midnight dip, and there's some nasty

144

currents just around the Point that can land you in trouble if
you don't know them. Would you know if he was a strong
swimmer?'

'I have no idea. I've said I hardly knew the man.'

I remembered the day he had tricked me into going in, and
told them of it. 'He was quite a strong swimmer.'

'Just so. Thank you. What puzzles me a little is this. Mr
Headley left the party at – when would it be?'

Neil Paton said quickly, 'About ten o'clock. When it broke
up.'

'I asked if he'd like a lift back to his cottage,' Dodo said. 'But it
wasn't far, and he said he'd walk.'

'So he was back there at ten fifteen or thereabouts. Then some
time afterwards, we don't know when, he decides on a dip. That
seems a bit strange to me, but he was an eccentric character, so
they say. But the sea's no more than three or four minutes' walk
away, why did he get out his car and drive to Parker's Point?
That's one thing bothers me. And there's another. His clothes
were in the back of the car all right, but no towel. Mr Headley
had a bit of a reputation for wildness in the village, I know that,
but there's not many go swimming without a towel.'

Silence. Then Dodo said, 'What's in your mind, Inspector?'

'What's in my mind – and I must be careful what I say, I may
be a country copper but I know there's such a thing as the law of
slander – is whether there was some reason why he found it
convenient to disappear.' He looked from one to the other of us.
'Miss Paton, you knew him. Would you say he was worried
about anything?'

'Not to my knowledge.' Melissa's legs were tucked beneath
her, her hands clasped each other. 'Of course he lived in what I
suppose you'd call a bohemian way.'

Another silence. 'Would it be possible, Mr Elder, for you to
tell me the business Mr Headley had with you? If the matter's
confidential, we could go elsewhere—'

'Nothing confidential,' Father said, indeed almost snapped. 'I
am the head of a firm of estate agents. We may be interested in
acquiring some land in this area on behalf of one of our clients,
for building purposes. Headley knew this, and wanted to sell his

cottage and the land that goes with it, a couple of acres. He was very pressing about it.'

'So much so that it couldn't have waited until today?'

'Apparently. The urgency was entirely on his side.'

'And could you tell me the result of your discussion?'

'He wanted far too much money. I told him we weren't interested.'

The constable wrote busily. The Inspector nodded like a mandarin, then said suddenly, 'You're a partner, Mr Paton. Were you consulted?'

Neil jumped as if stung by a wasp. 'I beg your pardon? No, I was not consulted, no reason why I should have been. I really don't think we can help any further, so if you have no more questions—' The Inspector thanked them for their co-operation, Melissa uncoiled herself, the three of them went out. I suppose I could have left too, but I had no wish to go back to brooding in the tower room, and I was curious about Hugo's eagerness to sell his cottage. I told the Inspector what he had said to me about getting out of England, and he was interested, especially in what had been said by Hugo about people not letting him alone. It gave me a sense of importance to see the constable making notes.

Then the Inspector turned to Father once more. 'Would you say Mr Headley was upset when you turned down his suggestion?' With a burst of frankness he added, 'I may say, Mr Elder, that he owed money everywhere in the village, the tradesmen just couldn't get their bills paid.'

Father said Headley had tried to haggle, but their estimates of the value of the land had been too far apart for that. Then he fetched from the study a note written in a dashing hand and signed 'Hugo Headley'. It said he was thinking of selling his cottage and the land around it, and understood Branksome and Elder might be interested on behalf of a client. He understood also that Mr Elder was coming down to Clempstone, and would like to discuss the matter in person. I didn't get a sight of the actual note, but the tone of it struck me even then as untypical of its writer. The Inspector did a little nodding, and asked whether the letter had come out of the blue. Father explained that Hugo had telephoned his office, and he had asked that something should be put in writing. He spoke in his level voice, rather as if he were dictating a memorandum. The Inspector gave a final nod, said he was sorry to have interrupted our holiday, and expressed surprise when Father said we were returning to London. Surely we had only been down for a day or two?

Father glared at him again, and it was Dodo who said Mrs Elder was unwell, had had to return to see her doctor, and that had rather spoilt the holiday. The Inspector did not comment.

When he had gone Father sat looking straight in front of him. It would not be right to say his graven face was a mask of despair, for except at moments of spontaneous enjoyment his face was always a mask. Were the lines deeper than usual? Even in my green youth I realised that he had reason for misery in his betrayal by Deirdre. The misery was evident, for Dodo slapped him on the back and said, 'Cheer up, my lad, that's over.'

Father spoke two words, without looking up. 'Is it?'

(iii) Life with Father

That, as people say, was the end of an era, just as the beginning of the war was the end of an era, or later on the last days of rationing and no more queuing for things in shops. These Sixties in which I am writing are the beginning of another era, so people say, an age of permissiveness and freedom and the destruction of barriers. Is it only because I am now middle-aged that I don't like them? Or am I right in thinking the Beatles' sound is a debasement of music, kitchen sink drama dreadfully overpraised, brutalist buildings an abandonment of responsibility by architects, and the present generation of side-of-the-mouth actors and actresses hardly worthy of the name, but mere creatures of screen and TV directors who are determined that their puppets shall murmur realistically with faces averted, even though this

147

means that the audience can't hear what they are saying? Yes, it's perfectly true that T V directors say I am old-fashioned. True also that I do regard the theatre as the only place in which great acting (to which I do not aspire) can take place, but . . .

But I am indulging in purely personal reflections, unconnected with the quest for Hugo Headley which was also a quest for my father, the real Harold Elder I never knew. I let them stand, but vow not to repeat them.

Of course the war ended an era for everybody, and that fatal weekend was the close of one only for our family. We left Grandison House on Monday, and never returned. It might almost be true to say that we fled, leaving there all sorts of odds and ends including the books and photographs on the wall in the tower room. When the house was put up for sale the Passloves were given the job of clearing it out (the piano, put into a local sale, fetched two pounds), and in due course my bits and pieces reached me. The tennis photographs I threw away, for that defeat by Goldstube marked the end of my aspirations to be a champion, or cured me of boyish illusions it might be said. I went on playing at weekends, but gave up practising. My service never did improve much, and by the time the war came I was nearly twenty years old, and no more than a good club player.

Any thought of becoming more than that would in any case have been ruled out by my asthma attacks. I can remember the first of them vividly. It was my last term at school, and I had returned home after a journey on the top of a crowded bus where several people were smoking. I felt perfectly well when I entered the house, but had taken only a few steps inside the hall when I found myself deprived of breath. It was as if I had been suddenly enclosed in a vacuum, an experience all the more frightening because it was utterly unexpected. I gasped, tried to cry out, pulled my collar open, managed to stagger to a sofa in the drawing room and lay there panting, weeping, choking, feeling as if my lungs would burst.

The attack lasted about half an hour, then gradually subsided. It was succeeded by another, longer one a week later, and I suffered attacks at irregular intervals for another dozen years. Various doctors and specialists agreed I was suffering from asthma, but the remedies they suggested varied from pills to steam baths, breathing exercises, living in a dry climate, and a course of psychotherapy. I tried most of these, although the dry climate was not in the realms of possibility, but none had any effect. Exercise was encouraged so long as it was not strenuous, which meant tennis at gentle club level. There was general medical agreement also that the condition was temporary, and this proved to be right. After some ten years the attacks became less intense, and around the beginning of the Fifties they disappeared.

Were the asthma attacks linked with a subconscious refusal to admit that I should never be more than an ordinary tennis player, were they connected with the break-up of our family life? I am sure this last was true. I put behind me everything to do with Grandison House and what had happened there, my rejection by Melissa, the tennis failure, and the human animals copulating in the shed, although that still recurred in my dreams. In these dreams Deirdre's partner was not Neil but Passlove junior, and one persistent image was that moment in which she had looked at his gleaming brown body while stroking her bare left arm with her right hand.

Our lives were much changed. Father engaged a housekeeper named Mrs Wellstood, a grim, powerfully built woman who called me Mr Geoffrey. She got rid of the existing servants including Daisy, and engaged new ones who seemed lesser versions of her formidable self. She also dismissed the cook, saying that she drank, and replaced her by another who specialised in very plain English cooking, overdone beef and vegetables with taste thoroughly cooked out of them. She ran the house economically and efficiently, every carpet clean, every surface dusted, every piece of furniture polished. She would have done very well as the superintendent of an old people's home.

There were no more dinner parties at home, friends and clients being taken out instead. Occasionally Father took me out to one of the chop-houses he favoured, and over our fillet steaks or Barnsley chops he would make what was obviously difficult conversation, in which I must confess he didn't get much help from me. I would look up from sawing away at my meat to find his deep-set eyes gazing at me with a yearning or pleading expression, as if there was something he wanted me to understand that he could not bring himself to say.

The second time we went out to dinner, he brought himself to mention Deirdre, in the course of saying he knew things at home were not comfortable for me.

'I'm sorry, Geoffrey, very sorry. But after what happened I had no choice.' I asked if he ever saw her. 'No. I shall never see her again.' At this I said I had seen her once or twice – this was before the dinner in the flat off Marylebone High Street – and asked if he minded. 'Of course not, that's a matter for you.' A pause, then more words painfully squeezed out. 'She was very beautiful, and I loved her. There were things I knew about, tried to ignore, but this – this was impossible. I think she wanted to make things impossible for me.' He went on, careful as a man making his way over stepping stones. 'In life we sometimes have to do things that are uncomfortable, distasteful, even things that are wrong. We do them to preserve something that seems to us good, the whole fabric of life as we want it to be lived. Do you understand what I am saying?' I said yes, although I had little idea of what he meant, and asked if he would be getting a divorce.

'Yes. Does the idea upset you?' I said no, lots of people at school had divorced parents. In fact, though I did not say this, it conferred a certain cachet. By the time the divorce came through I had left school and left home, and the people I knew had no interest in whether my parents were divorced, or whether I had any parents at all.

In that dismal time I found I missed Deirdre. She had never taken much interest in me, yet she had infused the house with her personality. The extravagant flower arrangements, the slightly dry pervasive scent she wore, the long laughter-punctuated telephone conversations she had with what she called her girl friends and with clients of A Joy For Ever, all these trivialities seemed important now she had gone. It was not that I missed her as a much-loved mother, for that had never been our relationship, but rather as if a gaudy beautiful bird was no longer there. Perhaps if the house had been run by somebody less intent on the grinding practicalities of life than Mrs Wellstood, I should have missed Deirdre less. If it was like that for me, what must Father have felt? That was something I never thought about.

The question of my taking university entrance examinations came up almost as soon as we returned to Manfield Terrace. Father's view about this remained unchanged, but he no longer had Deirdre to support him, and I found in myself an uncharacteristic rebelliousness. Why was I so set against three more years of education? Perhaps Hugo's warnings about the cardboard dummies who said hallo old boy, didn't we meet at Lady Pisspot's, had something to do with it, but more important was the idea of becoming a famous actor. The stage had replaced tennis in my fantasy world. Father did not go so far as to say that actors led immoral lives, but he had got from somewhere what he said were facts and figures about the amount of unemployment in the theatre and cinema. I replied that the only support I should expect would be for my training at drama school, and after that I would earn my own living. At that the graven features broke up into his smile, and he said of course he would leave me to starve. In the meantime I didn't take the exams, and my report said I seemed to have lost interest in every kind of school activity.

Perhaps in desperation, he called on Aunt Aggie for support. She came to us for a Christmas dinner that also provided a contrast with other years when Deirdre would have invited half-a-dozen friends and neighbours, and Father would have added to them two or three business acquaintances. Last Christmas the Patons had been there, and I remember quite a lot of noise and laughter. This year the company was Aunt Aggie, Johnjohn and Pat, all of them probably invited to convince me of the error of my intentions. Father's Christmas present to me was a tennis racquet of a kind just becoming fashionable, one with an adjustable balance. There was a bit of wire sticking out of the handle, and this could be moved back or forwards until you got the right dispensation of weight. The gift might have been thought ironical in view of my fading tennis ambition, although

151

I am sure it was not ironically meant. I gave him a pipe. Dinner was – I will call it a typical Wellstood meal, without going into details. Then Father gave a toast to 'Next year, and may it be better than this one,' Johnjohn said, 'Hear hear,' and we got down to business.

'And next year's the vital one for Geoffrey, who's got it into his head that he doesn't want to go to Oxford, Cambridge or anywhere else except drama school. Aggie, will you tell him just what that means.'

Aggie was, as often, wearing a dress of many colours, and had perhaps come expecting a party like those of the past. Or perhaps her natural irritability had been exacerbated by the cooking. She looked from one to another of us with a wicked glint in her little eyes.

'You want to know what it's like? There'll be fifty boys and girls all yapping away about how they played Hamlet or Romeo or Lady Teazle or Millamant, and how somebody you've never heard of saw them and said they had a great career ahead. There'll be a lot of old queens and has-beens teaching you, male and female and the male are the worst, who talk about diction and carriage and making entrances and exits, all the things they never learned to do properly themselves, which is why they're teaching and not acting. You'll be indignant when you're the third spearbearer in the show at the end of term, and the star parts have gone to the boys with the profiles and the girls with the figures. When it's all over you'll join the dole queue or get a job in a shop, or if you're lucky manage to get one as ASM at a rep somewhere up in the Midlands where you can't understand half they say, and they think you're a Southern cissy.' She paused. 'And you'll look back on it afterwards and say, "I wouldn't have missed it for worlds, they were the happiest days of my life."'

No doubt this wasn't what Father would have liked to hear, but he took it in good part, saying I should pay attention to the first part of what Aggie had said, and forget the second. Johnjohn weighed in with something about the benefits of a good steady job and the importance of having money come in every week, Aggie said some were cut out for the ups and downs of the life and some weren't. I don't know what response I made, but it can't have been very eloquent.

And that was it. We played a board game Father had bought, in which we were all pirates out to find buried treasure, and then Johnjohn and Pat went home. Nothing was said about Deirdre, but her shadow hung over the evening. Goodness knows why, for she disliked Christmas, which she called the most boring week of the year, but it seemed that something unexpected always happened when she was there. Once she invited the Honourable Something and his wife, two of her best customers at the shop, round for a drink before lunch. They brought his sister and her husband, and the four of them stayed until six o'clock. At the time I disliked such disturbances of what I felt to be proper Christmas routine, but now I missed them.

Did Father miss them too? It was impossible to tell, for he confronted this dull Christmas as he had done the Honourable Something, with that graven calm broken sometimes by his smile. This year, with Deirdre gone, it may be that he found the presence of Johnjohn and Pat irksome, for he relaxed when they had gone, putting on the carpet slippers efficient Mrs Wellstood had put by his chair, and lighting the pipe I had given him. Then he asked whether what I had heard made any difference to my feelings about drama school. I said no.

'Then you'd better go.' I looked at him in astonishment. 'Start next term, I'll make the arrangements.' I said something, I don't know what, and he laughed and patted my shoulder in his way, and said he was all for people doing what they wanted if they wanted it enough. So irrational is the human mind that at the end of this battle which had been going on for weeks, I immediately wondered whether I really wanted to become an actor, and could not think why I had been so set against the exams.

Aggie said sharply that it might not be so easy, there were lots of applicants and not many places, it shouldn't be taken for granted. Then, with no break in her conversation, she said, 'I've had the police pestering me.' She spoke as if they were door-to-door salesmen. 'About Hugo.'

Father was trying to get the new pipe going, tamping down the tobacco, relighting it with a Swan Vesta. He did not comment.

'They seem to think there was some plot by him, and I might have been part of it. I told them it was all rubbish, but they weren't satisfied.' Still he said nothing. The firelight heightened the colour in her cheeks, made her many-coloured dress look like a sheath of flame. 'Why did he come to see you, Harry? That stuff about selling the cottage and the bit of land, that might have done for a country policeman but nobody else would believe it. Or anyway it won't do for me, I knew Hugo.'

In a neutral voice he said, 'Yes, you knew Hugo.'

'Oh, you're all such hypocrites, such bloody sneering superior hypocrites.'

'There are worse things than hypocrisy.' He looked consideringly at the pipe, put it aside, and spoke to me. 'I shall have to break this in some other time. There's no reason why you should be involved in a sordid family squabble.'

'Let him listen,' Aggie cried. 'Let him stay, and hear what fools and hypocrites and villains there are in our family.'

'Watch your tongue,' he said, and now his voice was no longer neutral but commanding. 'Just watch what you're saying, Aggie.'

At that she got up, flung her arms wide, went across and kissed him, and for good measure kissed me too. 'Darlings, forgive me. Harry, you know I always say more than I mean, and Hugo was my one and only love, you know that too. I wanted to sound a word of warning, that's all, in case the nasty policeman called on you as well. You'll be sticking to the story, Harry?'

'The story, as you call it, is the truth.'

'He did want money, I know that.' She paused as if about to say more, perhaps the tale of the Fabergé watch that she told me years later. But what she did in fact was to kiss me, say it was wonderful and she hoped I got to RADA and had a wonderful career. Then she kissed Father again, and said she wished he'd been quite frank with her, but he knew she would help in any way she could. Then she was gone, and we went to bed.

The police did come to see us a few days later, in the shapes of jolly Inspector Lynton and a sergeant. They talked to Father and to me, seeing us separately this time. With me the Inspector went over and over what Hugo had said about possibly leaving

England for good, asking whether he had mentioned a particular place, if I thought he meant it, and so on. Then he became slightly apologetic.

'You see, sir, we've discovered Mr Headley had even more problems than we thought, so that it would have been very convenient for him to disappear, if you take my meaning.' I said I took his meaning. 'This deal he was trying to make with Mr Elder, he didn't mention that to you? Seems odd he shouldn't have done, you might expect he'd have said something like, "This magnificent house and its lovely grounds may shortly become the property of the Elder family" when you were in his cottage.' He laughed heartily, to show this was a joke. I said truthfully that he had said nothing like that to me. Afterwards I asked Father what the Inspector had wanted to know, and he said the man had asked the same questions as before and received the same answers.

And there the mystery of Hugo Headley's disappearance rested, and so far as I was concerned ended.

Early the next year I was accepted at Central, that is the Central School of Speech Training and Dramatic Art, after giving what I suppose must have been acceptable readings of Hamlet's soliloquy, and then of all odd things the prologue to *The Country Wife*. Perhaps Aunt Aggie exercised her vaunted influence, or perhaps I got through the two speeches successfully. Anyway, I found myself among a few young male students and about four times that number of young women, subjected to very much the course of training Aunt Aggie had outlined, although the tutors were nothing like as bad as her description of them, and I didn't get the part of third spearbearer in the end of term public show, but played Deiphobus in *Troilus and Cressida*. As I remember he appears in three scenes, has two lines to speak, and when Cressida sees him she asks, 'What sneaking fellow comes yonder?'

In spite of that obviously low rating of my talents I liked the tutors much better than my fellow students. All the male students were trying to ape Laurence Olivier, who was just then making a formidable impression at the Old Vic, and the girls seemed to be trying to outdo each other in exaggerated speech and style. *Darlings* and *dearests* and *simply angelic* filled the air, along with *really sickmaking* and *absolutely foul*. My dislike of ostentation and self-aggrandisement may well have its origins in the detached relationship I had with my parents, as I'm sure any psychiatrist would tell me in those sessions on the couch to which I have no intention of exposing myself.

The result at Central was that I cordially disliked the flamboyant students who got the best parts, and for the most part turned out to be the most successful players. Some of them, including those who were most boastful about the important people they knew (I shuddered away from the idea of mentioning Aunt Aggie), became well-known, especially in the cinema and later on the small screen, as TV entered almost every home in Britain. I suppose I should have reluctantly to acknowledge that they were among the best of my generation at Central, although to call it a generation is an overstatement, because I was there for only one undistinguished year. My escape was made through the help of Justin, filtered through the person of Zoelle Delano.

Zoelle's father was a first secretary or something of the kind in the Ecuadorian embassy, and she claimed that his influence had secured her place at Central. She was a tall dark heavy girl with raven-black hair that she wore unfashionably long, and a style of acting that might charitably be called emphatic. Her stage whisper was a powerful hiss, her ordinary delivery assaulted the ear, and in any speech calling for emotion she spoke as if summoning the police or the fire brigade. She left Central not long after me, went back to Ecuador, and there married a man who owned several of the country's tin mines. In her days at Central she shared a flat in Fulham with a student named May Pargiter, and gave parties. The rent and the parties were paid for by her handsome father, and there was always plenty to eat and drink, which was itself an attraction for the more impecunious students. Zoelle didn't give the parties to court popularity, but simply because she wanted to have a good time, and liked to see a lot of people. She was a nice friendly galumphing girl, if one could stand the alternate boom and screech of her voice.

The parties were decorous affairs by today's standards. There was no pot smoking or coke sniffing, and nobody went wild on LSD. No doubt there were drug-takers around in the Thirties, but I didn't meet them. Nor was there any dancing, the flat being on the ground floor, with a policeman and his wife in the basement. There was music provided by students who played the guitar, and a good deal of singing, quite often songs in support of the Spanish Republic, which was now firmly in the news. Zoelle and May made things to eat, there was beer or *vin ordinaire* to drink, but no spirits – the diplomat had expressed his disapproval of them, and Zoelle was not one to go against her father's wishes. Sometimes people got drunk, and I suppose a couple may have sneaked off into one of the bedrooms for a quick bash, but I doubt it. I remember one occasion Zoelle ordered a couple out of her room, saying – or rather shouting – 'I will not have focking in my house. You want to do it, you go somewhere else. Here we eat and drink and talk, we do not fock.' Use of the word by women was unusual at that time, and even thought shocking, but Zoelle was only verbally outspoken. When I compare these parties with some I have been to in the Sixties, the change in manners and behaviour astonishes me. Zoelle was having an affair with an American named Randall something or other, but she would never have thought of going into her room with him during a party and leaving the door unlocked, something I have known to happen at parties nowadays, with half the people present high on drugs.

There were usually forty or fifty people present, students, an older actor or two, magazine editors, journalists, an occasional MP or diplomat, anybody Zoelle had happened to meet in the course of an energetic social life. May was very much in the background, installed because Zoelle's father thought it would not be right for his daughter to live in a flat on her own. She paid no rent, and cooked the vol-au-vents, made the canapés and cheese straws, and cut the sandwiches we ate. She also sometimes handed food round (Zoelle, a bottle in each hand, looked after the drinks), and I had just taken a cheese straw when a voice in my ear said, 'Wotcher, my lad, how's the acting lark?'

Justin looked distinctly different. His jauntiness was more

confident, he had less the air of a salesman on the alert for a possible rebuff. Rather, he now exuded prosperity, a look enhanced perhaps by the fact that he was wearing a grey suit with a dark green stripe, and a double-breasted waistcoat. When I asked what progress Claude Clanders was making with his memoirs he laughed.

'Gave that up months ago, too much like slave labour. The old b expected me to be at his beck and call any time of the day or night, whenever he felt inclined to do a bit of dictation, but I got less than some girl typist in an office. I'm in the money now. Milk-bars.'

'Milk-bars?'

'Don't say you haven't seen them about.' It was true that a lot of these bars, a cross between a café and a shop, had sprung up in central London, selling milk shakes, milk and a dash (the dash being coffee) and plain cold milk, along with rolls and sandwiches. There were a couple near the Central, and some of the students had lunch there instead of in a pub. My surprise was that Justin had any connection with them.

'In with a man named Tyler, making pots of cash. MFH Bars, Milk For Health, it's good for you.' He raised his glass of wine, roared with laughter. 'So how's the old man? I hear he's parted company with the tart of Kensington. Beg pardon, I should have remembered that's your mum.'

I should have taken offence, but something about Justin's coarse good humour attracted me, and I said nothing. 'Wish I'd been there that night, Claude and Prunella were full of it, but I was typing away at old let's consult Claude's memoirs, he'd had a sudden burst of activity and wanted to see it all in type straight away. How's the old man bearing up? Parted from our friend Neil, I hear, and can you wonder?' I said Father was well. 'You're a chip off the old block, don't give much away, do you? Now with me, when I think a thing I say it.' Perhaps it was this that prompted me to say I hated life at Central. 'Is that so? Wouldn't have thought you were cut out for it, and that's a fact. What do you want to do then, how about managing a milk-bar? We're setting up a couple of new ones next month.' I said, almost plucking the words out of the air, that I wanted to be a journalist, and can't recall Justin's reply. The bottle-waving Zoelle had moved, and behind her I saw Melissa.

It was a year since we had met. In my mind there was still the image of the Melissa who had leaned out of the tower window, her legs tensed, the outlines of her body visible beneath the striped shirt, and this seemed somebody different. It was not just that on this evening she wore a long dark blue evening dress cut low at the front, with an effect quite different from that of the athletic girl in shorts. She was not less beautiful, but she had a kind of sophistication unknown to the girl I remembered. When I crossed the room to greet her she offered her cheek to kiss, and said, 'Hi, stranger, how's it going?' The greeting, an American style of phrasing uncommon in England in those pre-war days, startled me, and so did the casualness. It seemed to me that we should have renewed our relationship where it had been left at Clempstone, she should have told me the harsh things she said had not been meant, there should have been sighs and explanations.

Instead Melissa told me she had a job in the BBC as a trainee studio manager, asked what I was doing, and said a course at Central sounded really exciting.

'Neil and Hilda have split up, I expect you've heard, it was bound to happen. I thought it would be a good idea if I got out too, so I removed myself to a little flat in Hornsey. Of course I knew what was going on down at Clempstone, it made for a lot of bad feeling. I can't say I altogether blame Neil, though he was an awful fool.'

'You never went to Spain?'

'Spain?'

'You said you might be going there. Perhaps with Hugo Headley.'

'Oh, that.'

'You were annoyed because I mentioned it.'

'Was I? As I say, things were a bit tense all round. Anyway, I never went, and now of course it's pretty well finished.' By this time Franco's victory seemed, and was, assured. 'I don't know what happened to Hugo, don't suppose he's still there.'

'I thought he was dead.'

159

'Is that your guess? I never believed the drowning story, thought it was fishy.' She laughed at the pun. 'I know he was in a pretty tight spot, I think he slipped out of the country and settled down using another name.'

'The police don't seem to believe that. Have you heard from him?'

Before she had time to reply Zoelle took her off to talk to a student who had sent in three ideas for radio plays to the BBC and had no acknowledgement. I wondered who had brought her, a question answered when she and Justin said goodbye to me. Melissa said she looked forward to my Hamlet, Justin winked as he took her by the arm and steered a way towards the door. I felt myself to be cured of Melissa, and perhaps dimly realised even then that I had invented the girl I imagined myself in love with, and the real Melissa was not like that.

(iv) The End of Basher Bentall

A couple of weeks later Justin rang and said there was a man he knew on the *Mid-Kent Weekly News* who was looking for a general assistant, and if I was serious about wanting to leave Central, why not give him a buzz? The man's name was Jerry Wharton, I went down to see him and got the job, in February or March 1938, I can't remember which. Looking back on it, this seems an odd thing to have done, especially since I have ended up as an actor. I think the chief motive, though I didn't realise it at the time, was to get away from Manfield Terrace and life with Father.

I haven't perhaps said enough about my love for the house, a love springing from the fantasies of childhood. The imagined ghosts, the imagined Bussy impaled on the railings outside, and a dozen waking dreams like that of being alone in the house, entering all the rooms, opening wardrobes and looking at Deirdre's clothes, finding a secret drawer in a desk and within it some relic of the past unknown to me, all such absurd imaginings clung to me for years, and were for some reason negated by the end of our family life. And I felt deeply now the lack of communication with Father. We saw each other at breakfast before he went off armed with bowler and umbrella, and met again in the evening, but we didn't talk much. What was there to talk about? I had no interest in the details of his professional life, and only realised much later his bitter disappointment that I not only rejected the idea of going to university but also refused even to consider the thought of entering the family firm. Even tennis, once my asthma attacks began, was a sensitive subject for conversation.

I can find little excuse for the way I behaved, and can only wonder at his forbearance. He didn't reproach me even when I said I'd been offered a job in journalism and wanted to give up the course at Central, but simply asked how much I would be paid. When I told him the pittance Jerry Wharton had offered he coughed, said that would hardly keep me, and told me the size of the allowance he would make. He added with a half-smile that it wouldn't be more than the fees at Central, then gave his little cough again and asked if I was sure that was what I wanted to do. I dare say it was this stilted kindness that made me cry out that I couldn't tell what I wanted until I tried, could I? He accepted the remark as if it were perfectly reasonable, only saying, again with the half-smile, that he hoped I shouldn't have to try too many things.

I may be making him sound like a saint. That would be a long way from the truth.

It was a couple of months before the end of my last term at Central that he took me to see my first Pratterton.

At breakfast one morning he asked me to let him know when I had no classes, and would be free for lunch. We went to one of his chop-houses, and throughout the meal I sensed a bubbling excitement in him that never quite rose to the surface. I had no idea of its origins, or what was meant when he said over coffee that there was something he wanted me to see. We took a taxi to Bury Street, just off Jermyn Street, stopped outside a place called the Victorian Arts Gallery which had two small landscapes in the window, and went in. The gallery was on two floors, and he led the way to the upper one, and to a large picture called, as I learned afterwards, 'A Roman Scene: Nymphs Bathing'. In the background was a villa, in the foreground three women were bathing in a large pool, with behind them an expanse of sky. Or rather, one woman was in the water, another had just come out of it so that drops of moisture gleamed on her body, and the third was wrapped in a flowing gown that revealed one breast. The other nymphs were naked, and their flesh had a pearly creamy sheen so that it almost appeared lighted from within. Years later I saw pictures by Etty and some nudes by Ingres that had something of the same lustre, but at the time these nymphs came as a shock to me. Father stood staring at the painting, his face set in his Buster Keaton mask. I stared too, without knowing what to say. Then he sighed, and spoke.

'A wonderful picture. Don't you think so?' I replied that I had never seen anything like it, and he nodded. 'Classical beauty. He's caught the essence of it.' I asked the name of the artist. 'Pratterton, Nicholas Pratterton. Not one of the most famous Victorian painters, but—' He shook his head. 'I wanted you to see it.'

I said I was glad I had, although in fact I was a little embarrassed, both by the painter's enthusiasm for the texture of flesh, and by Father's interest in it. I did not understand why he had brought me to see it, until he asked where I thought it should go.

'You've bought it.' The pictures on our walls had been chosen by Deirdre, and were either Impressionist reproductions or drawings and watercolours by friends, including one or two done at Clempstone. I don't know what I said to his question, and in any case the answer didn't matter. He hung 'Nymphs Bathing' in the bedroom he had shared with Deirdre, where it replaced a print of Monet's 'Water Lilies'. As we left the gallery he spoke to the woman who sat behind a desk near the entrance, introducing me and saying I had been greatly impressed. She smiled, and said she was glad. At the time I hardly noticed her. Her name was Norma Gayle, and after the war she became Father's third wife.

I don't know how much he paid for 'Nymphs Bathing'. As I

write Victorian paintings are coming back into fashion, but before the war you could buy a small Landseer for a few pounds, and even if Father paid by the square inch the picture can't have cost very much. But this was the first of some twenty Prattertons, almost all of them showing girls and women in various stages of undress, most with a historical background. 'The Rialto: A Princess Disembarks', 'Rome: After the Siege', and 'While Rome Burns' were three of them. At first the Prattertons were confined to Father's bedroom, then they spread to the guest rooms, and finally entered the dining and drawing rooms. 'While Rome Burns', a panoramic affair which showed Nero fiddling in the blazing, collapsing city while two virginal-looking naked women listened to him with rapt attention, hung over the drawing room mantel. As he acquired more Prattertons Father found out a good deal about the painter, and was able to discourse confidently about his place among the artists of the period who favoured classical themes, like Leighton and Alma-Tadema. He probably got some help in this from Norma. The Prattertons became his most cherished possessions, the first and almost the only things he sent away for safe-keeping when bombs fell on London.

On the evening of the day I saw 'Nymphs Bathing' I had an asthma attack, a bad one that left me gasping as usual, and my heart thudding not only in my chest but in my ears. The doctor was called, and gave an injection that quietened me down, although the aftermath of such attacks left me drained of energy for the next twenty-four hours. Probably some psychologists would link the attack to the revelation at Clempstone, and say it was a reaction to the naked flesh in the picture. Certainly I thought at the time that lubricious feelings in Father had prompted its purchase. I am sure now that I was wrong, and that he was prompted by an overwhelming yearning for feminine beauty which he found in these buxom, though not quite Rubensesque ladies.

I stayed three years at the *Mid-Kent Weekly News*, and then during the war got a job in London on the *Daily Record*. The *News* offices were in Faversham, and my duties were at first to make the tea, take messages, learn to type and to use the telephone switchboard. Humble occupations, but I was only eighteen when I joined the paper, and within a few months had become a junior reporter, attending the local Magistrates' Court, writing reports on amateur dramatic shows, interviewing a local brewers' drayman who had retired after forty years' service, and so on. Jerry Wharton, a red-nosed Fleet Street veteran who had settled to a quiet life running a local weekly, found me a room in a boarding house, along with the paper's chief reporter and a junior who wrote up local sport and the smaller news stories. I met girls, took them out to dances, lost my virginity not very enjoyably in a Faversham alleyway (female visitors were not allowed in our rooms at the boarding house), my companion being a girl I had met for the first time at a dance that evening. But this is not an autobiography, and I don't propose to elaborate on my uneventful years at the paper. Only one incident there bore on the brutally abbreviated holiday at Clempstone, on Father, on the disappearance of Hugo Headley.

I still have the cutting as I read it in the paper, the date June 1939:

EX-ARMY MAN'S DEATH AT SEASALTER
POSSIBLE FOUL PLAY

The body of William Bentall, who lived in a caravan outside the village of Seasalter, was found by farmer Desmond Bellinger on Wednesday last. Mr Bellinger rented the caravan to Bentall, who used the washing facilities of the farm. Mr Bellinger suspected something might be wrong when he saw nothing of the man for two days. He investigated, and found the caravan in a state of some disorder, apparently as the result of a quarrel with a visitor. Bentall was on the floor, and had been dead for some hours. Bruises on the body suggest the possibility of foul play, perhaps as the result of a fight, but the police say it is too soon to issue a positive statement.

Bentall had occupied the caravan for some time, and was known in the district as a man of quarrelsome disposition, especially after he had taken drink.

I assumed that this 'ex-Army man' was the stranger I had seen with Father in the Jolly Fisherman, and was naturally curious about him. I told Jerry I thought I had met the man, and asked if I could go down and talk to the farmer and the local police, in case there was an interesting story behind the death. Jerry had been out for a liquid lunch, something that always left him cheerful. He belched, then grinned at me.

'Our cub reporter turns detective, is that it? Discovers lip-stick-stained cigarette stub missed by local coppers, has stub analysed and learns the lipstick is called Come Hither, finds out the only user of Come Hither in Seasalter is Olga the local vamp, arrest of Olga, cub reporter becomes famous as Sherlock Junior.'

Jerry's facetiousness after a few drinks was something we all had to bear. I said I felt sure it was the man I'd met, and repeated that there might be a story in it. He belched again.

'So there might. Talk to the farmer and the copper, Sergeant Tanner it'll probably be, if it is you'll find he's pretty thick. Find out what pubs the man used, and who he quarrelled with. Don't call the farmer in advance, you're more likely to get something out of him if he doesn't know you're coming.' He closed his eyes.

'All right if I go now? We're not busy.'

He opened his eyes again. 'No good, pubs aren't open. Go this evening. Here's the keys, take Daisy.'

Daisy was the office car, a ten-year-old bull-nosed Morris that blew out clouds of smoke, and made protesting noises when going up hills, but had never been known to break down. I had taken a few lessons, and passed the very simple driving test of those days, and it was in Daisy that on a sunny June evening I drove down to Seasalter, which even then belied its pleasant name. It was then separate from Whitstable, a bungaloid village facing the shallow muddy offshore stretch known as the Oaze. After the war the bungaloid growth spread, as more retired people without much money found this to be a cheap area in which to live, and Seasalter became hardly separable from the oyster town.

I went first to Platte's Farm, a mile or more inland from the village. Many Kent farmhouses are pretty, and others have a good nineteenth-century robustness, but Platte's was not one of them. The farmhouse was a gaunt red brick building some twenty or thirty years old, with ramshackle wooden additions at either end. Around were fields that looked reasonably well cultivated, along with others left to grass. In one of these, a couple of hundred yards from the farmhouse, stood a green-and-white caravan. I parked Daisy on the empty road, and went to look at the caravan. I could see nothing through the grimy windows, and tried the door. It opened. I stepped inside.

I could swear that this had not been in my mind when I crossed the field, yet what point would there have been in my looking at the outside of the caravan? There was a bunk bed at one end of it, with the bedclothes jumbled on it, presumably as they had been left. At the other end was a sink, which held dirty plates and cups. Beside it an open cupboard contained pots, saucepans, and a drawer holding cutlery. Beneath the sink was a cardboard box with several empty bottles in it, mostly beer but including an empty wine bottle which bore the label 'Château Fantin-Latour, 1933'. In the centre stood a deal table with a Tilley lamp on it, and there was an oil lamp on a shelf beside the bed. There were two wooden chairs by the table, and an armchair with stuffing coming out of it. A small doorless cupboard by the bed held the blue blazer I remembered, and other clothes put at random on the shelves, shirts, socks, trousers, a cardigan, and beneath them a pair of sturdy boots. Four photographs were on the walls. The light in the caravan was dim, and I opened the door to look at the photographs.

All except one were groups of soldiers, including a much younger but recognisable Bentall. In one he wore a corporal's two stripes, in another a sergeant's three, but in none was he dressed as an officer. One picture showed him with two privates outside a pub, in another several men were looking at a tank on which Bentall rested a proprietorial hand, the third was of a group on parade.

The fourth photograph had nothing to do with the Army. It had as background a row of miserable-looking terrace houses. Before one of them a middle-aged woman looked grimly at the

camera, her hands on the shoulders of a small boy in knicker-
bockers. I turned the snap over and read on the back 'Mum and
me, Chapel Street, '06'.

The place recorded the kind of miserable hand-to-mouth
existence I had expected. I was about to leave it when I saw the
trunk. It was sticking out below the bed, and but for the dim
light I should have seen it earlier, a battered tin trunk with 'WB'
in faded gold letters on the top. I pulled it out and lifted the lid. It
was full of relics connected with the war which, since I had been
born in the year after it ended, seemed to me immensely remote.
There was Bentall's Army registration book, which gave his
home town as Newcastle, said he had been born in 1898 and had
enlisted in the Yorkshire Light Infantry in 1916. There was a
ribbon, a medal, and a scroll which said that Sergeant William
Bentall had been awarded the Distinguished Conduct Medal for
bravery in rescuing a wounded officer under heavy machine-gun
fire at the battle of Passchendaele. There were letters in faded
ink from what were obviously old Army comrades signed with
Christian names, Sid, Bert, Angus, and a typed letter dated 1928
from something called the Old Soldiers' Aid Society, saying
they regretted they could offer no further assistance in view of
the circumstances in which the recipient had lost his last
position. I looked quickly through these letters, but found
nothing connecting Bentall to Father.

And there were the cuttings.

One was from a local paper (I was already sufficiently knowledgeable to be able to distinguish between the typography of
national and local papers), the date November 1910. It said that
Susannah Bentall, of Chapel Street, Newcastle, had pleaded
guilty to procuring abortions for three women whose names
were not mentioned. Her counsel pleaded that she had been led
astray by desire to help the women, and also that her young son
would be left without a parent. In passing sentence the judge
said this was a bad case of a woman who had been under police
surveillance for some time, and that the police evidence had
established that she was a persistent abortionist carrying on her
filthy occupation for profit. She was sentenced to two years'
imprisonment. The other cutting was probably from a national

paper. It showed a photograph of Father, and said Mr Harold Elder had assumed office as President of the Society of Estate Agents and Valuers for the year 1933.

I was still looking at the cuttings when I heard a sound outside, and put them in my pocket. A voice said, 'Put your hands up.'

A man stood in the doorway, a small man with a bristling moustache. He wore a Norfolk jacket and plus-fours, and carried a shotgun casually aimed in my direction. His speech was a kind of bark.

'Come on, out of there. Get your hands over your head.' I stammered something to which he paid no attention, and came out with hands raised. He patted my jacket pockets, then nodded and I put my hands down. I said, 'Mr Bellinger.'

'Course I'm Mr Bellinger. Came out to shoot rabbits, didn't know there were bigger game about. Pity you didn't try something, I'd have given you a good peppering.' A barked laugh. 'Come on then, tell me the old old story before I take you down to Bill Tanner. Knew the deceased when you were a kiddy, did you? Or he owed you a tenner and you thought you'd take it out in old clothing and knives and forks?'

I heard him with dismay. I had visions of a story in the paper headed 'Young Reporter Accused of Breaking and Entering'. I explained, falteringly no doubt but clearly, why I was there, said I had meant only to glance inside the caravan and then come up to the house, mentioned meeting the dead man. He heard me out, tapping his boot with the shotgun occasionally. I thought afterwards he was delighted to play the angry farmer, but that wasn't in my mind at the time. He kept me on the rack.

'So you're telling me it's not one for Bill Tanner. How about a call to your editor, tell him the way his young reporter looks for stories? Wouldn't like that either, eh? So you knew Bill Bentall.' He tapped away at his boot. 'And you were coming up to the house after you'd finished ransacking this place. Right then, better come.' He led the way up to the farmhouse. We passed Daisy on the way. He asked if it was my car, and said it looked ready for the knacker's yard. His own yard as we walked through it seemed in a state of decay. A rusty tractor stood at one end, beside a harrow with a couple of tines missing. Several chickens wandered about, and from the gloom of a shed a pig appeared, and made a rush at them. 'Meg,' the farmer shouted. A big woman appeared in the house doorway. 'Tell Bill pigs are out again.'

'Tell him yourself.' She went back into the house.

'My wife,' Bellinger said, and shouted for Bill. A bent old man materialised from a kind of large lean-to, and began to shoo the pig, along with two companions who had wandered out, back towards what I presumed were their sties. 'Can't get labour. Nobody's ready to do a proper day's work now. This way.'

The room into which he led me was dark, high, and smelled of leather, pigs and whisky. There were hooks and hangers on the distempered walls, a bench with a mass of nuts, screws, hammers, bits of wood and a couple of saws on it, a table and two chairs. At one end of the bench was a meat safe with a wire mesh front. There was a door leading into the rest of the house and he turned the key in this door, saying, 'Got to keep 'em out.' He saw me looking round. 'Used to be the harness room, full of tackle, saddles on the wall, kept a couple of hunters. Now—' He shook his head. 'Only room in the whole damn house where a man can get away from his womenfolk. You know how many of 'em there are?' He counted on his fingers. 'Wife, you saw her. Wife's mother. Wife's sister. My sister. Wife's sister's daughter. I'd like to shoot the lot.'

He went across to the meat safe, and took from it a bottle of whisky, some beer, two pony glasses and two tumblers. He poured whisky into the pony glasses, beer into the tumblers, said, 'Success to temperance,' downed the whisky at a gulp and followed it with half the beer. Then he looked challengingly at me. I had drunk whisky only two or three times, but recognised this as a kind of test, and did my best to follow him. He nodded.

'Only way to drink it, with a chaser. What the Scots do, they ought to know. So what is it you want to find out about the old squinter?' I said I felt there was something strange about Bentall's death, and would like to hear anything he could tell me. 'He never told the truth if he could help it, I can tell you that, and he never looked at you straight, that's something else. He'd have

169

an eye on you and the other sliding about everywhere while he made up his fairy tales. Said he was coming into a fortune, died owing me fifteen pound, and when I looked through his stuff there was nothing worth a brass farthing. Oh yes, I don't mind admitting I had a look, and who had a better right? He owed me the money.'

It would be tedious to try to reproduce a conversation that lasted nearly an hour, during which I managed to drink only two whiskies and a pint of beer, while he put down perhaps four times that amount. I never saw him again, but sometimes a single meeting may be enough to show the course of a life. In the years since then I have never seen anybody so obviously and irredeemably wretched. He had inherited a prosperous farm from his father, who had been a big man in the Whitstable area, turned it into a semi-derelict one, and behind the surface bluster was aware of his failure. He was too grand to spend his time in the local pubs, and so escaped from the recriminations of the regiment of women around him with a crony or two in the harness room. Just before I left Kent for London he died when he drove his car off a bridge into a nearby river. The verdict was accidental death, but I believe he turned the wheel deliberately so that he crashed through the stonework.

This is the gist of what he told me in the course of the drinking session. He had bought the caravan years before, one of several he meant to rent out during the summer season, or perhaps even all the year. Like his other ventures this one had failed, in his view because his wife had not produced the breakfasts and packed lunches included in the rentals. The other caravans had been sold, but this one had a long-term tenant, and when he left they had not bothered to get rid of it. Bentall turned up out of the blue, and Bellinger was delighted to let him the caravan, even though the rent was not always paid on time.

It also became plain that he had liked Bentall, or at least had found the ex-Army Sergeant a congenial drinking companion in the harness room. Bentall had come in the January of that year on a bed and breakfast basis soon discontinued when Meg Bellinger found that he expected a cooked breakfast at any time up to midday. There was an argument, and after that he cooked for himself. Over their drinks in the harness room he told the farmer a good deal about his past life, some of it true like the award for bravery, some false like his claim to have been an officer. He said his mother had died when he was young, and he had been brought up in an orphanage. He had joined the Army as a Regular, but left it in the early Twenties. He had said at times that he was sick of being a peacetime soldier, at others hinted at trouble over the Sergeants' Mess funds. He was vague about what he had done in the last few years, saying he had been down on his luck, but things had looked up lately. And recently, after returning from a trip, he had talked about coming into money.

'Asked me what about becoming my partner here. All the damn place needs is capital. Just haven't got it.'

'And he had?'

'Said so. No, said he was *going* to have it.'

'When did he go on this trip? What did he tell you about it?'

'When? Some time in March or early April, away a couple of days. Began before that though, when he met an old Army pal of his, some Irish name or other, though it was an Aussie accent he had, not an Irish one at all, couldn't understand him half the time. What was the name now, O'Malley? That's not right, but O' something, O'Rourke, that was it. He met this O'Rourke, brought him up for an evening, had a job driving a van for some wholesaler though he seemed pretty much down on his luck. We had a few drinks, and it was after he'd gone that the old Basher got excited. That's what he used to be called, y'know, Basher Bentall. Then Basher went off for this couple of days, and was over the moon when he came back.

'I miss him, I don't mind telling you. Bloody cross-eyed villain I dare say, but he paid his whack. Kind of remittance man, did I tell you that? Used to go down to Seasalter Post Office first Monday every month, collect his money, then spent it in a day or two down at the Crown and Anchor. In the end they put the bar up on him. Could be an awkward cuss when he'd had one or two, told some tall stories, didn't like it if anyone said pull the other leg. We had our up-and-downers, but still.' Bellinger touched his bristling moustache. 'He was a man's man.'

'He never mentioned a wife?'

'Not he. Too fly to get married, wise man.' He shook his head, thinking no doubt of the feminine reception waiting when he left the harness room.

'You were telling me about his trip.'

'Was I? Why should I tell you?' I understood him well enough by now to realise that he would talk if I stayed silent. 'I said to him once, is it money from your family you get each month down at the Post Office, and he laughed and said in a way. Then when he talked about being in the money, I said is this family too? And he said yes, but you might call it a different branch, and nearly split his sides laughing.' He glared at me. 'But I don't pry. All I know is he came back saying he was in the money, but where was the bloody money, eh? Nowhere.'

He looked gloomily at his glass. I have noticed that many hard drinkers reach a stage when they are affected by alcohol, but never move beyond it into complete drunkenness, no matter how much they consume. Bellinger was one of them. At moments he seemed violently angry – with Bentall, me, his wife, perhaps with life – but it all faded away, came to nothing. He went on talking now, for the most part repeating himself. He did not know where Bentall had gone on the trip, only that he had come back talking about providing capital, and about sins always finding you out in the end. When sneaking hypocrites turned out to be bloody villains, he had said, they had to pay for it.

Had Bentall mentioned the name of Elder? Bellinger shook his head. Nor did he know who might have visited Bentall on the night he died. Somebody from Seasalter perhaps? I'd better ask Bill Tanner.

'One more thing. Did Bentall drink wine?'

He gave his barking laugh. 'Drank anything he could lay his hands on, whisky when he was flush, beer when he wasn't. Never saw him drink wine. Why?'

'There was an empty wine bottle in the caravan.'

He shrugged. I got up. 'You're not going? Look here, stay and have some supper. They'll be glad to see you. Don't go.' He looked uneasily at the locked door. I left him at the door of the harness room, staring hopelessly at me as I walked across the farmyard.

I took Daisy down to the village, and found Sergeant Tanner in one of the bungalows, with a blue lamp outside the door that said 'Police'. He was pleased to have a visit from the local press and ready to talk, but as Jerry Wharton had told me he was pretty thick. Or perhaps he just wanted to be discouraging. He said he saw nothing odd about Bentall's death, the man had been notoriously quarrelsome, and more than one publican had told him they could do without his custom. No doubt he'd taken some crony back to the caravan, they'd had a few, and at some time Bentall had fallen down, struck his head on the table and died. Had he discovered the crony? No, he hadn't, and I gathered he hadn't tried too hard.

'Did the pathologist say death was caused by striking his head like that?'

'Said it very well could be.'

'What about a fight, a struggle?'

'Possible. Hard to tell.'

'If he died as the result of a fight that would be manslaughter. Supposing he was hit on the head, didn't just fall?'

'Seems to me, young man, you're trying to make trouble. What was it your newspaper said, "Possible Foul Play"? Well, we've had a coroner's inquest, everything above board, and the verdict was accidental death. Good enough for doctors that was, good enough for coroner, I reckon it's good enough for me.'

'But somebody else was there that night drinking with him.'

'So there was.' A pause before he spoke again. 'You been talking to Mr Bellinger? You have, right. Ever occurred to you it could have been him down there, they had a bit of an argument, then your man slipped and hit his head?'

In fact, odd as it seems now, this hadn't occurred to me, although I didn't say so to the Sergeant. Instead I protested that Bellinger would not have waited more than a day before reporting the death. He nodded.

'I'm not saying that's what happened, not for a minute. I'm telling you we were called in and we found this man whom

173

we're not sorry to be shot of, and we looked into his death and decided it was an accident, and if you think you know better all right, but you be careful just what you print in your paper.' I asked about relatives. 'There were some papers said he came from Newcastle, and we got in touch with the police up there, but they found nobody remembered him.'

In the end we printed nothing except a couple of paragraphs giving an account of the inquest and the verdict. Jerry, who fancied himself as a connoisseur of food and drink, told me Château Fantin-Latour 1933 was a good rather than a remarkable vintage, but certainly one that wouldn't have been bought in Seasalter. And there my investigation, if you can call it that, ended, except that the next time I saw Father I told him of Bentall's death, and asked how they'd met. He said he didn't recall the name, and I reminded him of the man in the Jolly Fisherman. Then he told me he had forgotten the fellow, and that he was a man who mistakenly thought they had met a long time ago, and was trying to sponge on him. Thinking back, remembering the conversation, I knew this to be untrue. It was the first time that, to my knowledge, he had ever lied to me.

The Sixties

(i) 'When years have passed,
is't wise to meet again?'
(ii) The Woman Who Brought
Her Son Up Properly

(i) 'When years have passed, is't wise to meet again?'

All that – Seasalter, Bentall's death, my rushing off in Daisy, talking to Bellinger and the Sergeant – was something I hadn't thought about for years, so that I even had difficulty in remembering the Sergeant's name. It gave me a powerful sense of the difference between that world and this, between the leafy lanes leading down to muddy and featureless but still quietly individual places like Seasalter where Daisy could be parked pretty well anywhere on any road, and if you struck lucky you paid a couple of shillings for a decent meal at a little restaurant in a side street, and – well, the girl in the flat above me, a freelance picture researcher, is thumping out rock music. Since I can hear it distinctly, mustn't it be deafening her? But I know it isn't. If I was asked to name a single difference between the world before the war and this car-packed Beatle-infested era, it would be that the first was quiet, the second noisy. That refers to something more than rock music, even something more than literal noise. Advertisements shriek where they used to persuade, people shout instead of arguing. In the papers, radio, TV, what they've taken to calling 'the media', everything is assessed in terms of 'personalities', manufactured and then discarded. When I say this kind of thing to Leila she tells me I sound as if I'm ninety. She may be right. Is everything worse now, or do I just think it is?

A little more of what I mean is conveyed by a call a few minutes ago from Shoestring, excited by the prospect of my doing some voice-overs for TV advertisements. My ability to use several different accents will be used to express sceptical views about the powers of a new soap powder to housewives in Scotland, Northern Ireland, the Midlands, East Anglia and the West Country. I shall be the invisible local sceptic whose doubts are triumphantly refuted by the housewives as they hold up perfectly clean clothes. In the course of the ads I not only use a variety of accents, but move from bass to alto. Why not employ genuine locals? Because it would take time to find them,

Shoestring says. And it would also cost much more than employing a single run-of-the-mill performer, as Shoestring doesn't say. Isn't this a degradation of the acting profession, an indignity Irving wouldn't have tolerated? If I said *that* to Shoestring, or to Leila, they would say he never had the chance.

Of course I agree. Shoestring is happy, Leila is pleased, I shall be glad to have the cash. My relationship with Leila, however, simmers or bubbles with discontent. She says again that my absorption in the past is unhealthy, and is annoyed because I don't take any interest in what she calls the burgeoning women's movement. I say I have no objection to it, but I am not a woman, and it will be time to talk about the complete equality of the sexes when women grow penises and men bear children. She tells me not to be ridiculous, but in the next breath informs me that medical scientists are saying that in a few years men may be able to produce children. The sexes are converging, women wearing men's clothes, men doing the housework. This silly squabble goes on for an hour, is renewed the next day, and revived at the weekend.

It was during the squabble that I went to see Melissa.

The itch to hear her voice had been raised by Duffy's visit. When I telephoned she sounded just the same, the voice deep, thrilling and youthful. We exchanged polite what-a-long-time-it's-been remarks for a minute or two, then I invented a rehearsal for a TV show near Esher where she lived, and was asked to tea. What did I expect to learn from talking to her, what questions might I reasonably ask? I had no idea, I just longed to see her again.

Esher is not quite the rich business executive's dream of home like Sunningdale, but it is a smugly well-to-do place of wide streets, carefully tended green lawns and large mock-Edwardian and mock-Tudor houses with two-car garages. My seven-year-old Ford Prefect looked out of place in Melissa's drive. Her house was mock-Tudor. The front door was of darkened oak, had a monk's head for a knocker, and a bell-pull which when used created chimes inside. A dog barked. The door opened, and the hound of the Baskervilles leapt at me. At least, that was my first impression of the St Bernard that placed its paws on my lapels and nuzzled me with every appearance of affection. There was a cry of 'Down, Bobby, down,' and his paws were replaced by Melissa's arms, my lips brushed her cheek.

'What a house dog, Bobby, what *shall* we do with you? Lovely to see you, Geoffrey, it must be I don't know how long.' She led the way to a room, all chintz, china ornaments and occasional tables, with a French window leading to a large expanse of lawn. 'Bobby, go and join your friends.' She opened the French window, Bobby bounced out, and two more St Bernards appeared as if from nowhere. 'Don't you just love dogs? Big ones, I mean, not dachshunds and Yorkshire terriers. I breed them, you know. Tell me about the rehearsal, did it go well?'

I said it had been full of stops and starts like most rehearsals, without going into details. Then we sat on the chintz covers that hardly suited the would-be Tudor beamed ceiling, and assessed each other. Or perhaps I should say I assessed Melissa. The girl I remembered was recognisably there, the toffee-brown eyes still as eloquent, the neck unlined, white and fine, but these individual features seemed aspects of another person from the one I had known. The cheeks were fuller and more highly coloured, the shoulders broader, the whole body had filled out so that Melissa was now what is sometimes called a fine figure of a woman. This effect was enhanced by the country tweeds she wore, and her sensible brogues. It would be wrong to say that I was surprised by her appearance, yet the very fact that I could trace within the tweed framework an outline of my Melissa was disconcerting. It was like meeting a distant relative whose speech and gestures remind one of somebody now dead.

A girl brought tea in a silver pot, thin brown bread and butter, china cups and plates. We talked about the problem of making a living in the acting profession, of Melissa's career in the BBC – she had become a studio manager, left during the war to enlist in the WAAF, ended as a Wing Commander, and married Clive at the end of the Forties. We talked about their son Clive junior who was at Rugby, his parents being agreed that you could now get a decent education only as a boarder at a public school, and about the problems and pleasures of breeding St Bernards. She asked if I was married, I replied that I had never got beyond

179

cohabiting, and she said that might be sensible, although I could see she didn't think so. She moved on to the possibility that I played bridge, I told her I didn't, and she said she and Clive spent two evenings a week at the local bridge club. I mentioned having supper with her father, and she said he was keeping wonderfully well. She refrained from looking at the French clock on the mantelpiece. I plunged.

'I had a visit recently from a man who's writing a biography of Hugo Headley.' She showed only polite interest. 'I believe he got in touch with you.'

'I think he did. I didn't much take to him.'

'He's found some letters. From you to Hugo. I think he's going to use them.'

'Indeed he is not.' The fine eyes blazed, as they had done long ago. 'If he tries to print them, he won't know what hit him.'

'I didn't mean he'll print them, only refer to them.' She made an impatient gesture. 'And he's found some other letters – well, notes – from my father. He thinks they involve you.'

'Involve *me*? What *can* you mean?'

I lacked the nerve to ask if she had had a love affair with Father. 'They suggest Hugo was blackmailing Father, or trying to. Do you think that's possible?'

'With him anything was possible.' She looked directly at me, we made what is now called eye-to-eye contact. 'Why do you want to know? I'm not mad to talk about it, the whole scene wasn't very—' She left the sentence unfinished, gestured with a hand that sparkled with rings.

'If Hugo Headley knew something discreditable about my father, I want to know what it was.' She said nothing. 'The last time we met, you said you were sure he was alive. Hugo, I mean. Have you heard from him?'

'Did I say that? If so it was stupid. No, I never heard from him, but then I wouldn't have expected to hear. You know we had an affair, hence those silly letters. He talked about our going to Spain together, then said I was too young, there'd be an awful row, forget it. It upset me at the time, though really he was right. I was very young.'

Her reluctance to talk about Hugo seemed to have melted

away. Those wistful recollections of imagined futures never realised, possible lives that have remained unlived, offer the most tempting self-indulgent thoughts. She shook her head when I asked if Hugo had said anything about selling his cottage and land to Father.

'I think it was a cover for some other arrangement.' She said she didn't know. 'Was he excited or worried when you saw him that weekend, did he tell you anything about his plans?'

'I was mad about him, I'd have done anything he wanted. God, what fools we are when we're young.' Yet even as she spoke the words it was plain she forgave herself that youthful foolishness, and loved the girl who would have done anything for or with Hugo Headley. 'Really he was awful, so unscrupulous. Excited, did you say? I suppose so, and worried too. He'd been up to see his mother and father somewhere in the north, and he'd found something out. He made some joke about the sins of the fathers being visited on the children, and said something else about hypocrisy, some quotation.'

'Shakespeare?'

'I don't know. He was always quoting bits of poetry. This was something about hypocrisy being invisible, except to God. Then he laughed, and said "To God and Hugo Headley", and went on about hypocrisy again.* There were other people he'd seen, friends of his parents who seemed to have something to do with his being so excited. Their name was something unusual, Rocking, Reeking, Rosecliff, something like that. When he was excited he looked like a little boy, a naughty little boy.'

At that the broad tweed shoulders shivered, shook off the past. Melissa Winterbottom reappeared, said I must see the St Bernards before I went, they really were adorable.

I saw the St Bernards, six of them, all extremely amiable if not exactly adorable. She said she hoped the film went well, and I must come and meet Clive some time. Then I left.

And returned to Pimlico.

---

* I found what was probably the quotation. It was from *Paradise Lost*:

> Hypocrisy, the only evil that walks
> Invisible, except to God alone.

Where I had noted Melissa's name and address on the pad beside the telephone.

The sheet on which I had written was torn off, and a thick exclamation mark added to it. Beside it, on the pad, was a note from Leila:

'I believe you really are ninety, can't take it any more, will be in touch. L.'

Was this a farewell note, the sort traditionally placed on the drawing room mantelpiece? I was relieved to see most of Leila's clothes were still in the wardrobe. She had taken nightdress, sponge bag, make-up bag, and not much else. We had had a tiff once before, and she had gone to stay with the Canon, returning after a couple of days. Could she possibly be jealous of Melissa? When I told her about the tweeds and the St Bernards she would understand she had no need to be. With such thoughts I consoled myself.

There were eggs in the refrigerator, ham, mushrooms. I made an omelette, and at supper read *The Cherry Orchard*, and thought how much I should like to play Lopakhin, and how unlikely it was that I should ever get the chance, at least in a London theatre. I thought about Melissa, and wondered whether she would have turned into the same doggy tweedy well-preserved matron if we had married. Leila might have said these were the idle thoughts of an idle fellow, and she would have been right. I contemplated calling the Canon and talking to her, decided against it, went to bed.

In the morning I rang biographer Duffy at the number he had given me and asked whether, when he had spoken to Hugo Headley's mother, she had mentioned some friends named Rocking or Reeking or anything similar. We had not parted on good terms, and he sounded both cautious and curious.

'No, she didn't. Who are they?'

'It's possible Hugo saw them on his last visit.'

'Do you mean they were friends of his? If so I should certainly know about it. I should like you to give me a context.' I saw no reason why I should tell him I had seen Melissa. 'And in view of our last conversation I fail to understand your interest.'

'I'm not thinking of writing anything about him myself, if that's worrying you.' His sniff was audible. 'And I'm sorry if I was a bit hasty when we talked. You can understand I was upset by what you said about my father.' He said unwillingly that he supposed so. 'You've not come across any name like that in your researches? An unusual name, two syllables, beginning with R.'

'I can think of nothing. If you could give me a context it might help.'

I thought but didn't say that if I had any idea of what he called the context it was unlikely I should tell him, and rang off.

I'm not sure what I would have done next but for the intervention of Shoestring, who called me ten minutes later. Panting with enthusiasm, or perhaps in admiration of his own unusual activity on my behalf, he said a TV director was casting for a new crime series based on the exploits of a cat burglar named the Spectre who as far as I could make out would be an up-to-date version of Raffles, or perhaps Robin Hood. It was Raffles, however, that Shoestring mentioned.

'You know he had a sidekick, what's his name, Bertie.'

'Bunny. Silly ass Bunny. But I'd be too old if he wants another Bunny.'

'No no, that's just the thing, he doesn't. This is a wise old bird, Major Percival, always trying to talk the Spectre out of doing things, never manages it, goes along unwillingly, gets in all sorts of trouble. Tremendous part. I said to Scotty, Scotty Scotland, done a lot of *avant-garde* stuff, settled down now to making money but still wants something a little bit way out, I said I know just the man for it, might have been written for him. And he's keen, Geoff, mustard keen.'

'He wants me for the part?'

'Yes, well, that's the way it'll be. He's interviewing, I thought we could fix a date. Just one thing. Did I say Scotty's up in Newcastle? That's it, you see, he's gotta be there to finish up some sci-fi piece he's doing. So he wants to interview in Newcastle. You'd get expenses, of course, might even squeeze a disturbance fee out of him, I don't think you can afford to pass it up.'

Shoestring was probably surprised by my response. Newcastle, which in other circumstances would have been a disincentive, gave me a small electric shock, and a feeling that providence must intend me to make a significant discovery there. I told him to fix a date for the interview, rang Duffy again, and persuaded him to give me Mrs Headley's address, on the understanding that I would pass on anything I found out that might be useful to him.

That evening Leila came round. She rang first, her voice subdued, to ask whether I would be in, saying we had things to talk about. I've called her an earth mother, but mentally Leila is a do-gooder, a consoler of those in trouble, someone who likes to feel she's doing the right thing, the right thing for her being the thing expressing whatever attitude she feels is really up to date. In the past she would have marched with the suffragettes, now she's worried about the coming shortage of food next century, reads Rachel Carson and is keen on women's lib. When she came in carrying a big suitcase, lower lip trembling slightly, I knew she hadn't just taken temporary flight to the Canon. I followed her into the bedroom, where she began to pack clothes neatly into the suitcase, and asked what was wrong. She didn't reply.

'If it's because I went to see Mrs Winterbottom, don't worry, she wears tweeds and breeds dogs. When I think of what she used . . .' I checked myself, realising this was not the right thing to say.

'And you thought she'd be like that, like your memory. Don't you see that's just it, what I can't bear, you just don't live in the real world.' She wailed the last words. I said rather stupidly, I'm a dreamer, aren't we all?

'That's what I *mean*, don't you see? You're here, I can touch you, but really you're dreaming about some play you'll never be in, well I mean some big part in it you'll never get, or it's stuff to do with your father or your mother.' She gave up neatness and threw two dresses into the case. 'You're just not living here and now. Look at the silly things you're always saying about the Beatles, when everyone knows they're great. And about women.

184

I don't know what your father and mother did to you, but they certainly fucked you up.' The lower lip quivered more emphatically. 'I'm so *worried* about you. When I go, what are you going to *do*?'

I said I was capable of looking after myself, and the real problem was what she was going to do, where she would go. I admit her reply rocked me back on my heels.

'I'm staying with Ratty.' I could think of nothing to say. 'She's very nice.'

'But she's a dyke.'

'And what's wrong with that? Perhaps I am too. In any case, the way you've been behaving lately I shouldn't think you'd mind.' I found nothing to say to that either. Now she intoned words that sounded in my ears like the litany of the priests presiding over this unholy decade. 'You have to try to fulfil your emotional potential, otherwise neurosis builds up. What people call nervous breakdowns are just lack of emotional fulfilment, doctors say.' *Doctors say* is for Leila ultimate wisdom, something not to be questioned. I knew that if I asked what doctors, I should be overwhelmed by some variant of 'Everybody knows that . . .' Instead, I wondered whether life with Ratty would fulfil her emotional potential.

'I've told you, perhaps I am a dyke as you call it, though that's a nasty word. Anyway, life with you isn't fulfilling anything.'

'But it used to?'

'Perhaps, I don't know really. I think you were different.'

I told her I was going up for an interview in Newcastle and the flat would be empty, why didn't she stay there for two or three days on her own, and think about it. She asked why I should be away so long, and I mentioned the search for the possible Rockings or Reekings, and said I might look in on Dodo. Even as the words came from my mouth I knew them to be unwise.

'That's it, that is just finally *it*.' She shoved things into the case pell-mell. 'You're not living in the present, Geoffrey, you're like an old man scratching about in the past. Perhaps you have to do it, I don't know, but don't expect me to watch.' A few similar phrases, pitying rather than abrasive, and she had gone.

I felt relief at first, then regret as I thought about the contented years we had spent together. I use *contented* rather than the more strenuous *happy*, and I suppose it was the contentment provided by an earth mother rather than the happiness offered by a lover that I had asked of Leila. Afterwards thoughts of her, and especially of her presumably in Ratty's arms, gave me a sleepless night, but they did not distress me like the idea that my father might long ago have been Melissa's lover. I thought about finding Ratty's number and telephoning, but couldn't think of what words to use. So I didn't telephone, and the next day I entrained for Newcastle.

(ii) The Woman Who Brought Her Son Up Properly

Scotty Scotland was a lunatic pretending to be a genius. Or perhaps he was a genius pretending to be a lunatic. Theatre, cinema and TV breed both kinds. He was a little grinning man who overused the word *fantastic*. The sci-fi saga he was polishing off was fantastic, this idea of the Spectre was quite fantastic and the scripts written by somebody he referred to only as Pongo were with-it, way-out fantastic stuff. It was simply fantastic of me to come up and talk about them.

It turned out, as often with directors, that he did all the talking, about what a fantastic part Major Percival was, how the scripts played off the Major against the Spectre in a way that was funny, dramatic, pathetic, so that a couple of pros like Paul Scofield and myself could play it back and forth like tennis champions at Wimbledon. It was when he mentioned Paul Scofield that I began to suspect he was on what they now call an ego trip. I may improve on the past, as Leila says, but my feet are near enough to the ground to know that Paul Scofield would be very unlikely to look at such a part, and certainly wouldn't be batting verbal exchanges across the net with the likes of me.

After more than an hour with Scotty I was doubtful whether the series would ever be made, and I was right. I got my expenses and that was the end of it.

But I had not come here just to see Scotty Scotland. Duffy had told me Mrs Headley was hazy about some things, but strongly aware of the financial aspects of everything connected with her son's life and work. He had given me a telephone number, and I was surprised when the voice at the other end said, 'Happydays Rest Home, may I help you?' When Mrs Headley came to the telephone I said I was writing an article about her son, and asked if I could talk to her. Her replies were confined to monosyllables, of which the important one was *yes*.

The home was in Gosforth, away from the busy city centre, a district of tree-lined streets peppered at intervals with big, sedate Victorian houses. One of them was the Happydays Rest Home. A sign said visits could be made between 2 and 6 p.m., or at other times by arrangement. The girl at the reception desk gave me a long look when I asked for Mrs Headley, pressed a bell. A woman in a nurse's uniform advanced towards me smiling. She was blonde, plump, slightly reminiscent of a younger Leila. She looked at the roses I was carrying, and said, 'You wanted to see Mrs Headley.'

'Yes. I spoke to her half an hour ago. Is there a problem?'

'She won't thank you for the flowers. She'll think you're trying to get something out of her.'

I held them out to her. 'For you.'

'Thank you. They're nice.' I was reminded again of Leila. 'There's no problem, except – but perhaps you know her.' I shook my head. 'She stays in her room most of the time, thinks the other guests are after her money.'

'Does she have money?'

'Must have, or she wouldn't be here. There's something else. She has good days and bad days. Bad days she sounds all right, but doesn't always make sense. This is a bad day.'

'Thanks for the warning.'

'I'll take you along.' As we walked along a corridor and up a flight of stairs, she went on talking. 'My name's Myra, and I'm called the matron, though this isn't a nursing home, we don't

187

take people who want a lot of medical attention. It's for those who've retired from active life, you might say. Most of them are no trouble, and if they are we get rid of them. Send them on to somewhere more suitable is the way Dr Ginnis puts it. He's the owner.'

'What about Mrs Headley, is she in line for being sent on to somewhere more suitable?'

Another Leila look. 'Oh no, we don't mind a bit of – call it eccentricity. It's when they're ringing bells all the time and falling over and wanting bedpans, and—' she shuddered slightly '—you know. But most of them are bright and chirpy, and love it. Here we are.' She tapped on a door, opened it, said with artificial brightness, 'Mrs Headley, love, your visitor,' and closed the door behind her.

It was a pleasant bed-sitting room, the bed in one corner, a dressing table next to it, a large window looking out on a lawn. The woman sitting in an armchair watching television got up and switched off the set, then turned to face me. With a slight shock of surprise I thought, what a handsome woman. Her hair was iron grey, her features neat and regular, hands small, nails perfectly kept. She wore a grey shirt and jersey, a row of green beads round her neck, matching earrings. She must have been in her late seventies but looked ten years younger. She bore no obvious resemblance to Hugo, yet I could sense something about her that reminded me of him. Then she spoke and her voice, like the screech made by metal scraped over stone, destroyed the effect of her appearance. When she spoke I noticed also the rat-trap thinness of her lips.

'Who are you working for and what do they pay?'

I was unready for such a question, as I had been for her appearance. I said the article had not been commissioned, but I was sure I could sell it. I mentioned that I had known Hugo. She made no immediate reply, simply stared at me. Her eyes were small, almost black, and they glittered, the only eyes I have ever seen that did so. Then she told me to sit down, and I took the chair opposite her. She sat too, still looking at me unblinkingly as if I might disappear if her gaze was diverted.

'You don't look like a fool, but if you're writing about my son for love and not money, you must be one. How do you make a living?' The line of her mouth tightened further when I told her. 'Do you appear on *that*?' She indicated the television's blank face. I said I had done. 'Filth.'

'I beg your pardon?'

'Rubbish and filth, and nowadays more filth than rubbish. You should be ashamed. But you get paid, I suppose. Payment for prostitution. That thing is the corrupter of youth, mocks everything good, works in our lives like a maggot.' I refrained from saying she had been watching when I came in. Now she lowered her voice. 'She is a slut. She opens her legs to any man. What did she tell you?'

'Do you mean Myra?'

'Who do you think I mean? She and Dr Ginnis do disgusting things.'

'I'm surprised you stay here if you think that.'

'I don't *think*, young man, I *know*. What would be the point of moving, another place would be the same, you need not think I'm leaving here. She'd like that. You're a lawyer, is that it, you want to get me out?'

'Mrs Headley, I don't know what you mean. If you're talking about Myra, I must call her that, I don't know her other name—'

'Myra! I'm talking about Nancy.'

I am not inclined to dramatic gestures, but one seemed called for, and after all I am a professional actor. I put a hand on my heart and said, with all the earnestness I could manage, 'I do assure you, with my hand on my heart, that I've not been sent by anybody. I don't even know who Nancy is. My only interest is in your son, in Hugo.'

She seemed impressed, or at least she stopped talking about Myra and Nancy. Her little black eyes looked at me, then away, at the TV, the floor, her hands. 'He broke his father's heart. There was bad blood in him, wicked blood, how else can you explain it?'

'Do you remember the last time he came to see you, not long before he disappeared?'

'I remember everything. I remember a beautiful small boy who always wore his school cap on the back of his head, never did his homework, played truant from school. I remember a boy who lied and lied to me. His father was busy with the shops, it was left to me to see he was brought up properly, and I did my duty. We went to church every Sunday, and to Sunday school, I made sure he went there. And he did go. For a time.'

'He played truant?'

'He was expelled. The Vicar said he must not come again, what he had done was so wicked. It was then I knew there was wickedness in beauty. Rottenness. Filth.'

'What had he done?'

'Too bad to tell. But why not tell it, let the truth be known.' The gleaming eyes looked at me, then away to the TV. 'There were four of them, but he was the leader. When they left Sunday school they urinated on the tombstones. I knew then that I had a devil to contend with, and I fought him, but he was never cast out.'

'You beat him?'

'I did what I had to do. I brought him up properly. His father approved, sometimes helped me. And we forgave him, he could have come into the business, lived a useful life. He could have chosen Jesus, but preferred Satan.'

'What happened to the business?'

'It was sold when Mr Headley died. For a lot of money. Why else do you think they pretend to be concerned about me, fornicating Myra and her doctor, Nancy and her husband, and all the others.'

'The last time Hugo came he asked for money, is that right?'

'He always asked for money.'

'But this was something special, he said he would be in bad trouble if he didn't get it.'

'He always said that.' Her face turned away.

'And then he went to see some friends of yours, do you remember that? Named Rockliff, something like that?' She shook her head. 'That may not have been the name, but they were old friends and they lived near you.'

'I don't remember any of that. Why do you come here and tell me lies?'

Before I could reply the door opened, and a woman came in.

She was tall and thin, with a nose that turned up at the end, and a suspicious look. 'Hello, Aunt Edith,' she said, and then to me, 'Who are you?'

I told her my name. Mrs Headley said, 'You pretend you don't know him, but you do. He's leaving.'

I said I was sorry if I'd upset her, but she ignored the remark. In the entrance hall Myra was saying goodbye to another visitor. She asked how I'd got on, and I said not very well.

'Did she talk about me? Fornication is one of her favourite words.'

'Since you mention it, yes.'

A Leila smile. 'Dr Ginnis and I are getting married as soon as his divorce comes through. In the meantime we share a bedroom. Mrs Headley doesn't approve, there's not much she approves of as you may have gathered. Any remarks about our being after her money? I can see there were. She thinks the same about half the people here, but apart from that she's no trouble. Here's Mrs Fleck. That was a short visit.' The thin woman approached. 'Not in a good mood today, I'm afraid, Mrs Fleck.'

'Couldn't say two words to her without being snapped at.' She said to me accusingly, 'You upset her.'

Myra said she'd been like it all day. I said she'd asked if I was a lawyer representing Nancy, and Mrs Fleck admitted that was her name and agreed to have a cup of tea in the lounge. There tea, sandwiches and buns were being brought round to half-a-dozen residents by a smiling girl. An air of suspicion was natural to Mrs Fleck, but she relaxed a little when I told her what I had hoped to find out. She asked what else her aunt had said, and I told her she seemed to think I was an agent for her niece. She fidgeted with her teaspoon, and became almost friendly.

'We're the nearest flesh and blood relatives she's got, and do you know she's never given a penny piece to help Joe with his cleaning business? It's not gifts we're asking for, I told her, if money was offered I know Joe'd be too proud to take it, but a loan's different. Should I see it back, she says, and then she hasn't got the money, which I know for a fact to be untrue, then she tells me she and her husband had to make their own way with nobody to help them, and we must do the same. I'm sure

I don't know why I go in to see her, she's so disagreeable sometimes. Other times, when she wants something, it's different, I can tell you.'

I began to feel I was involved in dialogue from a soap opera. I mentioned Hugo. She shook her head.

'I was only a kid then, knew him by sight, that's all. Of course she worshipped him, you know that. It was she that wanted him to go in the business, not so much his father. Mind you she was strict, used to try and beat the devil out of him, so my mum said.' I asked, without much hope, if she knew friends of the Headleys called something like Rockliff or Rocking.

'Don't think so.' She nibbled at a biscuit. 'Unless you mean the Rackleys. Bert Rackley had his own little business – well, not exactly a business, tobacconist and sweetshop like Uncle, but never made much of a go of it. They saw a lot of Aunt Edith and Uncle William, through the church and so on. I don't hold with any of that, all hypocrisy. Why do you want to know about them?'

'I think Hugo went to see them on his last visit here, just before he disappeared. I'd like to talk to them.'

'Can't talk to Bert, he's dead and buried years ago. And Dolly's getting on, still looks after herself though, got a little flat on that Wilfred Rhodes estate, though why they should want to name an estate after a cricketer I don't know, I should have thought there were better people . . .'

By the time we parted I had heard all about the Fleck family and especially their health, Joe Fleck's dodgy heart, Nancy's delicate digestion which meant she had to take three different pills every day, and the difficulties Billy and Edgar had at school. It was six o'clock when I found Oldroyd House, negotiated its long walkways, and rang the bell marked thirty-three. The door was opened almost instantly, and a little woman whose head came no higher than my shoulder confronted me.

'I'd given you up,' she said. 'But better late than never, this way.' She led me through a tiny hall into a kitchen not much bigger, and pointed to a cooker. 'It just won't light.'

'I'm afraid I'm not the gasman.'

She looked me up and down, and burst into laughter. 'So

you're not. Silly me. Who are you, then? I hope you're not selling anything, because if you are I can't afford it.'

The tiny living room was filled with framed photographs of all shapes and sizes, on walls, tables and sideboard. The rest of the space was occupied by china figures, boats, jugs and mugs, on which I saw 'A Present from Skegness', 'Beautiful Blackpool' and 'Darling Dolly'. I explained that I was writing something about Hugo Headley, and she said she didn't see how she could help, she hardly knew him. Like Mrs Headley she did not look her age – I worked out later that she must have been in her middle eighties – but her manner could not have been more different. There was an eager expectancy about her, she looked ready to burst out laughing at any moment on being told she had won the pools.

'That last time he came, yes, I do remember. I say the last time, but we hardly ever saw Hugo once he'd gone down south, and Bert said he'd got into bad ways. Mind you, Bert was strict TT, would never have a pack of cards in the house, didn't like work being done on the Sabbath. Me, I always liked boys who cut a bit of a dash.'

'Did Hugo talk about anything in particular, ask any questions?'

'Yes, he seemed interested to know about Morgan.'

'Morgan?'

A bell rang. 'That *must* be the gasman. Back in a couple of minutes.' She was in the room again in less than five. 'Press button lighter on the cooker had gone wrong. If you've got something supposed to work when you press a button, then it ought to work is what I say. Gasman said it's just as easy to put a match to it, and I said maybe it is, but it ought to work.'

'Has he done it?'

'Hasn't got the part, coming back tomorrow. Now, where was I? Morgan, yes, he wanted to know all about Morgan, which was funny because he'd met him. Bert said afterwards I shouldn't have told him so much, but I said why not, where's the harm, we've nothing to be ashamed of, any secrets are nothing to do with us, we did right by the boy.'

The tale she told was strange enough. She had married Bert in

193

1903, and within a few months they had a baby son, Bert had lost his job at a canning factory, money was very short. One night a gentleman came round, said he'd heard they might be prepared to act as foster parents to a baby boy. When they pressed him to know who had given him their name he said Mrs Bentall.

'Course we knew then something was up. This Mrs Bentall, later on she went inside, and quite right too if you ask me.' I said I knew about that. 'So I guessed what had happened, there was a baby born the wrong side of the blanket, and the family wanted nothing to do with it. So Bert and I we told the gentleman we'd have to think it over and he should come back the next day. We talked about it, and Bert he was against it at first, saying it was born in sin, and I argued with him, said it wasn't the poor babe's sin. Anyway he agreed in the end, though I don't know he would have done except we were that badly off. So the next morning the gentleman came back, and we said we'd take the baby, and that was it.'

'What did the gentleman look like?'

'A real gent, you don't see many like him these days. Young he was, dark, with side-whiskers like they still had then, but clean-shaven. He was near out of his mind with worry, and the relief when we said we'd take the boy, I've never seen the like.'

'He didn't tell you his name?'

'No, and we didn't ask. Just said we could call him Mister A. I told him he could trust us to look after the boy, and we did. We brought him up as we said we would, as our own son, Morgan Rackley.'

'Did he get on with your other son, your real son?'

'Charlie? Charlie died when he were eight. He and Morgan they were playing by a canal, and Charlie fell in and was drowned.'

'It was an accident?'

'Bert never believed it was, said Morgan pushed Charlie in and ran off. I said to him, no good going on like that, you're a Christian you must always think the best, isn't that right, Mr Elder? And then Morgan, he wasn't quite like other boys, he'd do something silly and you'd punish him, but he never seemed to understand, he'd do it again. After the accident Bert turned right against Morgan, found fault with everything he did, couldn't bear the sight of him really. Then when he was fourteen and finished school Morgan just left home one night, and we never saw him again. Took some of our savings we kept in a little japanned box in a cupboard. Bert said it was a judgement on us, but I could never see it that way. I loved him as if he'd been my own son, felt as if he was my own, having him when he was that little, only just born.' She said hesitantly, 'Do you know anything about him, sir?'

I said no. It would have been cruel to tell her what I had heard. I asked if they had any further word from Mr A after he left the child, and was surprised by her reply.

'Oh yes, he was very good, very generous. When he left Morgan he said we should be getting a certain amount each quarter for looking after him. He could see Bert was doubtful, for he said, "You have my word, and my word is my bond." It was, too, the money came regular as clockwork in a registered envelope, no letter with it, just the money order to be cashed at the Post Office. Tell the truth, without the money Bert could never have stayed in business. And we saw him again, Mr A, just twice. First time when Morgan was four or five years old, he'd come to see how the boy was getting on, and he gave Morgan a sovereign. Second time was in the war and he was in uniform, ever so smart and handsome he looked. He thanked us for all we'd done for Morgan, and said his responsibility would end when the boy was fourteen, and he hoped he might be able to take up some apprenticeship. Only of course that never happened.'

'You can't tell me any more about what he looked like?'

'Well, I've said, dark and handsome. Wait a minute, there was something, there was a photograph. My sister Alice was round here that day he came in his uniform, she had a little Kodak and was always snapping people. She'd take everybody when they weren't looking, I remember she took me at the washtub one day, I looked a real sight. And she snapped Mr A when he was talking to me. He wasn't pleased, but of course nothing he could do about it, in the end he said it didn't matter, perhaps it wouldn't come out. But it did.'

'And you've got it?'

'Might have, I don't know, I'll have a look.' Having a look meant getting two shoe-boxes full of photographs out of a cupboard, and going through a pile of photographs of the family, of a sullen-looking Morgan, hangdog Bert, jolly Dolly, and demure and tidy Charlie. We were almost at the bottom of the second pile when she said, 'There, that's him, that's Mr A.'

It was a small snap, and the figure in it was taken three-quarters rather than full face, but there was no doubt of his identity. I had seen him wearing uniform long ago in the photographs in Johnjohn and Pat's house. Mr A was my father.

The Forties and Fifties

(i) Wartime at the Record
(ii) Life with May
(iii) And a Life Ended

(i) Wartime at the Record

I have few photographs of Father, none taken at Clempstone, half-a-dozen at Manfield Terrace with Deirdre or at official functions, where the Buster Keaton features are firmly in place, so that it would be wrong to say he looked either happy or sad. He is serious, that is all. There is only one in which he looks utterly relaxed, obviously happy. It was taken in the late Forties after he married Norma, in the tiny garden of the house in Fulham they bought after Manfield Terrace was bombed. He has an arm round her waist, they are looking at each other lovingly, both laughing. I examine this snap minutely, linger over it, wonder whether I have ever looked at any woman like that, and conclude that I probably haven't, except for Melissa long ago.

Proof positive that Leila's right – I don't live in the present? Or that I feel emotion, but like Father for most of his life can't show it? After talking to Mrs Rackley I looked again at this photograph, and thought again how remote we had been from each other. It was difficult to believe in the reality of what she told me. He had fathered a child upon an unknown woman, for some reason it had been impossible for them to marry – or of course either he or she had not wanted to marry – and they had got rid of the baby almost as soon as it was born. Very likely its birth had not been registered, and there was something ruthless about the way in which he had abandoned responsibility for Morgan at the age of fourteen. It occurred to me that the story and the photograph would have given Hugo a basis for trying to black-mail Father, but even as such thoughts occupied my mind I was aware that there was more I should know, even though the knowledge might be distressing. The inadequacies of our own relationship of father and son, the real but stifled affection, the things we never said to each other, the gestures felt but unmade, were no doubt responsible for my desire to find out what I flinched from. The only people who might be able to tell me more about that time were Aggie, and possibly Dodo. Aggie, certainly, must know things she would be reluctant to talk about, and I resolved to be insistent, even brutal, about my right to have this skeleton revealed. Brutality, however, is a matter of temperament, and can't be called up to order. No doubt it is fortunate that I was never called on to attempt it.

There is no doubt at all that Father was happy with Norma, something I admit reluctantly because I never really liked her. I could never get rid of the feeling that she was responsible for his buying all the Prattertons, and that through them she had somehow enticed him into marriage. Even though I believed these thoughts to be unjust I didn't stop thinking them. Norma was several years his junior, dark-haired, a good cook and housewife, what people call a jolly woman. She did her best to make me feel that when we were all together we made a genuine threesome, not a twosome plus a member of the awkward squad. And the Prattertons turned out to have been a good investment, although of course they weren't bought with that in mind. After he died she asked if I would like any of them, and when I said no, told me she would be selling them. 'They were Hal's taste, not mine.' (She was the only person I ever knew who called him Hal.) At Christie's they fetched double or more what he had paid for them. All this I dutifully put down, but the fact remains that I didn't like Norma.

They stayed in London throughout the war, cohabiting in Manfield Terrace where, after my move to the *Daily Record*, I occupied my old room until the V1 wrecked the house. Like most sizeable houses ours became cold, dank, inevitably to some extent neglected, as fuel ran short and central heating boilers grew rusty with disuse, household help disappeared, necessary repairs were left undone. Mrs Wellstood left for a haven in Cornwall when the first bombs fell on London, and household work was done by one or another ancient crone tottering round with dustpan and brush, flicking at tables and chairs with a duster. Branksome and Elder continued to exist in an attenuated form, and with a reduced and ageing staff. There was little buying and selling of houses in London during those years when the continued existence of any property was a matter of chance, but peers and commoners in Northumberland and Cumberland, Devon and Cornwall, still called on Branksome and Elder for advice in maintaining estates and selling houses. Father did not consider his visits to these areas, where rationing was almost unknown and bombs no more than a rumour, as a holiday from the trials and terrors of London in wartime. He was happy to return to Manfield Terrace and to Norma, and often said so. The art gallery where she worked closed down, and she found a job in the Central Office of Information which was to do with the photographic side of the many brochures and pamphlets produced to keep our spirits high. The general free-and-easiness of wartime life was reflected in the number of her friends and acquaintances, including those on leave from the forces, who found a bed for the night on the top floor. Dodo came down occasionally, and once or twice a business acquaintance of Father's stayed the night. He accepted all this with a relaxed joviality that surprised me, and even made a joke or two about the inessential nature of papers like the *Record*. He also said more than once that it was time I settled down.

My move to London came about, again, through Justin. Some time late in the fine summer of 1940, after Dunkirk and when German invasion was expected almost any day, meetings were held in towns all over the country to prepare some organised resistance, although in view of the shortage of weapons it was lucky that the guerrilla warfare in preparation for which we drilled with ancient Lee-Enfields at best and broomsticks at worst, never took place. (Yes, I joined the local Home Guard, having been turned down for military service because of my asthma.) I reported some of these meetings for the paper, including one addressed by a mayor, a retired colonel who was head of the local Home Guard, and a civilian from the Ministry of Defence. After the meeting the man from the Ministry gave me some predictable quotes about putting our shoulders to the wheel and all pulling together, and was then taken aside for a whispered conference by somebody in uniform with a captain's three pips on his shoulder. He raised his head, and I saw that it was Justin at the same moment that he recognised me.

He took me to what he called a place round the corner, a kind of club where youngish men, all civilians, sat in twos and threes at little tables with drinks in front of them, talking in low voices. Some of them looked up and then away, and one man nodded to Justin who nodded back, but otherwise the quiet chatters were undisturbed by the sight of a uniform. We sat at our own little table and drank gin and tonic. I asked what he was doing.

'Just attached here and there, old boy. It's hush-hush, I can't really explain.'

'What happened to MFH?'

'Suspended for the duration. Word is, milk will soon be on the ration. Anyway, there's no future in MFH, not much in anything at the moment, the way things look. How about you?' He didn't actually ask why I was in civvies, but the look did it for him. 'You don't mean to say you're still with old Jerry's lot? Must be like living in a mausoleum. How's the old b, or I should say my esteemed father? Don't suppose you see much of him these days.'

I said he was well, and asked how Justin knew the club we were in. 'Used to have one of our milk-bars in Maidstone, got rid of it within a couple of months after Adolf went into Poland. What you might call foresight. But I've done a bit of business here, know a few people.' He went on to gossip about life in London, told me over-to-you Claude had had a heart attack, and half an hour later caught a train back to town. I saw him off at the station. As he got into a first-class carriage he sketched a mock salute, and gave me a great wink.

A couple of days later he rang me at the office. 'Don Boswell at the *Record* has an opening for a bright vital young reporter, Army reject ideally suitable, must be honourable, fearless, eager, all the things young reporters are. Only those named Geoffrey Elder need apply.' In due course I rang Boswell, got the job, and stayed with the paper through the rest of the war and for a couple of years after it ended.

They were extraordinary years for journalists, and for the papers they served. As country after country fell under Hitler's control newsprint was rationed, and the effect was drastic.

When I joined the *Record* it was down to six pages from its pre-war sixteen or twenty, and shortly after the bombing of London began the six became four. Most of the news was about the war, so what need was there for reporters, what was there for them to write about? And when almost every story not directly concerned with the war was limited to a couple of paragraphs or less, how did we occupy our time? Well, staffs were small and we stayed remarkably busy, with reporters doubling up at times as sub-editors and doing all sorts of other jobs. My activities ranged from sweeping up broken glass after the air raids which punctuated my first year on the paper, to acting as editor for a couple of weeks when Boswell's house received a direct hit and he was killed, together with his wife and son. (His editorial replacement was named Johnson.) And there were stories to be written even in our limited space, snappy pars about the hoarder who accumulated 774 tins of food, and about the oldest inhabitant of the Isle of Wight dying aged a hundred and three. And not only snappy pars, but genuine news stories. I spent a couple of nights in the Underground at the height of the blitz, and wrote what we called a heart-throb about the courage and cheerfulness universally displayed, along with some allegedly factual stuff supplied by the Central Office of Information about the miles of three-tier bunks put up in various stations, and the thousands of gallons of tea served.

And I remember a piece called 'If the Beast Does Invade' (Johnson's headline, not mine) saying that the pikes recently issued to the Home Guard would be extremely useful in the hand-to-hand street fighting that was bound to take place. Of course the pikes were issued because there were no rifles, but did I write that piece tongue in cheek? I doubt it. When bombs are falling daily, buildings being destroyed, people you know being killed, reporters coming back from battlefields talking about the heroic resistance of outgunned and badly led troops, you feel criticism and complaint from those at home would be a stab in the back for those actually fighting. At least, that's how I felt. When the blitz on London ended, and for a year or more we had quiet nights, a sense of disappointment was mixed with natural relief. It seemed one was no longer truly participating in the war. The V1 bombs which began in 1944 were somehow too impersonal to rouse the same feelings. After the war ended I became bored with the *Record*, with newspapers generally, and the hard-drinking girl-bedding life that seemed a natural accompaniment to working in wartime Fleet Street.

Again, though I write 'natural', it was only natural to me. Dozens of editors, reporters, subs, went home each night to wives and families. I had no wife, family or home, and did not want them. When Manfield Terrace was destroyed I moved into a large flat in Mecklenburgh Square which I shared with a reporter on the *Daily Herald* named Roddy something-or-other. (It is typical of my haziness about the period that his last name should escape me.) There we drank what was no doubt weakened gin and whisky supplied by a shady dealer Roddy knew, cooked occasional scrappy meals on a very old cooker, and shared our beds with what seem in retrospect to have been the dozens of girls around at the time, some WAAFs or Wrens on leave, some American girls working for a unit attached to their forces, but most of them French, Polish, Hungarian or Scandinavian, exiles from their own countries who no doubt felt their lives to be more impermanent than ours. Anita, Barbara, Claudette, Estelle . . . I could go through the alphabet and not leave many gaps. Several of them were one-night stands, only one or two lasted longer than a week, and I can hardly recall an individual face or feature, or a single phrase they used. I don't regard myself as a particularly passionate man, and have wondered since then whether I was trying to prove something by this persistent and varied bedding. Was I trying to say I was not by nature homosexual? Was it a reaction to the destruction of the house I grew up in, cancelling part of my life as if it had never been? Or against Father's marriage to Norma, which took place soon after Manfield Terrace had been destroyed, as if he was cutting himself off from an old life and beginning a new one? Was jealousy of him responsible for this uncharacteristic rutting period?

The *Record* years, what I think of as the wartime years though they extended beyond the war, ended when I met May Pargiter again. Shortly after that I became concerned about Father's health.

(ii) Life with May

May Pargiter was the girl who made and handed round the cheese straws and tiny sandwiches at Zoelle's parties, and she turned out to be a friend of Yvonne, another of the Mecklenburgh Square girls, who brought her along to the flat. May was a mousy unmemorable creature, and I did not remember her until she mentioned Zoelle's name. She expressed surprise when I said I was a journalist. I'd been, she said, so good at drama school. I reminded her that I'd given up after a year, and she said she'd assumed I felt I'd learned all I could, and that was why I'd given up. She herself was in a rep at Lee, in the London suburbs, but an important producer had been down to see her play the maid in *Gaslight*, and she was hoping for a West End part soon.

Even then I realised the unlikelihood of a producer coming down specially to see the maid in *Gaslight*, and it turned out that he was interested in the leading lady playing the Diana Wynyard part. Such games of make-believe are what keep dozens of unsuccessful players going in their underpaid jobs at provincial reps, or nowadays in shows at pubs or little private theatres. Of course the dreams might have become reality if May had been any good. In the years immediately after the war the theatre was very open to new talent, because so much of it had been submerged in the services, and Equity hadn't yet achieved its stranglehold over the profession. It wasn't too difficult to get a walk-on part at a rep without an Equity card, establish yourself and then make a case for your acceptance. That was what happened to me. The Lee rep was playing *Ten Little Niggers*, one of the cast fell sick, May said I'd had experience, and I was pushed into playing Tony Marston, who dies pretty early on. I found I enjoyed it, and within a few weeks

I'd said goodbye to the *Record* and was established as a member of the company, supplementing the pittance I was paid with the money I'd saved at the paper. Within eighteen months I was in the West End, playing the small part of Denis Tregoning, described as a 'nice enough young man', in a revival of *The Voysey Inheritance*. It would be right, I suppose, to say I never looked back after what May called my leap into the West End, though almost equally true to say I never looked forward. My talent just about fitted me for the kind of parts I've played over the years in the theatre (the only form of acting I can take seriously), cinema and TV. May's lack of talent fitted *her* for the rep at Lee, and when that packed up after a couple of years, for work in other reps, and occasional bit parts on the magic screen. I also note, as a matter of interest, that asthma never affected me during a stage performance or a rehearsal.

When I gave up the *Record* I also gave up Mecklenburgh Square. May and I lived together for several months in a rent-controlled flat near the Lee theatre. We had bedded down there when I came to see *Gaslight*, and most of the company adjourned after the performance to the nearby Tiger's Head. Nursing her half of bitter May traced shapes with her finger on the damp bar counter, and said, 'I always fancied you.' I was taken aback, not by the phrase which I think had come into fashion in the war years ('I fancy you like mad,' I had said myself to Estelle, or possibly Maria), but by the idea of mousy May fancying any man and saying so – and perhaps even more by being told I was fancied, something no other woman has ever said to me. In bed May was first coy, then ardent, later clinging. 'Up he goes,' she would say at the moment of penetration, then close her eyes and croon gently while shifting about beneath me.

The phrase, which at first I found amusing, soon became an irritant, and the clinging nature of May's affection alarmed me. 'If one of us finds somebody else we'll tell the other, we mustn't be tied down,' she said often at first, and I agreed. But as days became weeks May showed signs of settling into domesticity, even though she would still say earnestly, 'You've got to feel *free*, Geoff, when you love somebody it doesn't mean you're not absolutely free to love somebody else as well, does it?' She began cleaning the flat twice a week, said we needed more furniture, and persuaded me to go down with her to Greenwich and buy two secondhand armchairs. 'One for you and one for me. Then we'll be like an old married couple at home in front of the fire. Except we haven't got any coal,' she added, and giggled. May's giggle, which again at first seemed attractive, soon became like 'Up he goes' almost unbearable. When I told her I was moving out, she nodded. Two tears rolled down, just two.

'I knew you would. You've used me.' What about being absolutely free, I asked? 'That was if we fell in love with somebody else. But you haven't, have you? Just fallen out of love with me, that's all.'

I wanted to say I never had been in love with her and had never said I was, but that would only have made things worse.

'You used me to get into the rep, and now you're known and going to be famous you don't want me any more.'

I protested that this was monstrously wrong, and tried to persuade her that it was my nature to drift about, doing one thing and then another, living with one person and then another, or perhaps with nobody at all. She battered me then with her little fists – but the word is wrong, she meant only to protest, not to hurt.

'Then why can't you stay here with me? I make the flat like a home, don't I? When did I refuse to do anything you wanted?'

Again there was nothing I could say, except *you are not Melissa*, and *I do not feel for you as I do for my father*. The words would have been meaningless to her, and indeed I can't fully explain them to myself. But that was the end of it. I left Lee, and when I got the part in *The Voysey Inheritance* came to live in this Pimlico flat. I have been here nearly twenty years, with no permanent companion before Leila.

This autobiographical excursion seemed necessary to explain some aspects of my character, which must surely in some sense be connected with the need to know the truth about my father. But *this is not an autobiography*. I wrote another twenty pages about life with May (now married to an actor, and to be seen occasionally on TV) and our reactions to each other, but have torn them up.

(iii) And a Life Ended

The marriage of Harold Elder and Norma Gayle took place in the summer of 1946 at a register office in Fulham. I was one of the witnesses and the other was Norma's widowed sister, Margaret Williams. Afterwards we went out to an austerity celebratory lunch at a restaurant nearby. Rationing after the war was more stringent than it had been during it, the five shilling limit that could be spent on a meal was still in force, and the only wine was still Algerian red ink. Then the happy couple went off by train for a honeymoon in Devon. Margaret wept a little as we waved them goodbye, and said Norma would make Hal a wonderful wife. I thought but did not say that in effect she had been his wife for some time.

Nevertheless there was a difference between Norma Gayle and Norma Elder. I went to supper perhaps once a week at the Fulham house, and soon realised that the married housewife felt she had a different status from the live-in mistress. She was still jolly, laughed heartily at her own remarks, performed the miracle of making interesting dried-egg omelettes, and even managed an edible whalemeat stew, but she was now clearly the dominant partner, interrupting Father when he talked about tennis or cricket, and shifting the conversation to the curtains she had been clever enough to buy, what kind of furniture she intended to get for the living room, and so on. Perhaps all this was natural enough, and he seemed not to mind, listening to her with an always indulgent and sometimes adoring look. It may be that I was prejudiced, in part because I inevitably compared the Fulham house with Manfield Terrace. It was in one of the streets between King's Road and Fulham Road which in recent years have become almost fashionable, a commonplace late Victorian terrace house of a kind originally occupied by solicitors' clerks or artisans. Accustomed to the space of Manfield Terrace I found the rooms poky, and didn't share Norma's liking for bijou, 'amusing' bits of furniture. The Prattertons came out of store, and looked monstrously oversize and overbearing in so small a house.

All this Father tolerated, or to be more accurate seemed hardly to notice. Was he bemused by Norma's beauty, was she beautiful? She had a good complexion, splendid teeth, firm strong features, but to me she looked like an advertisement for health salts. Perhaps the difference in their ages lent her enchantment in his eyes, for he was now in his middle sixties. I leave it at that.

We saw each other alone only on sporting occasions. We went together to Lord's, admired the grace of the still youthful Compton, and when the Australians came were astonished by the power and beauty of Lindwall's action and the fading but still brilliant star of Bradman. And we went to the first post-war Wimbledon, and saw Jack Kramer lose to Drobny, and the singles won by tall, gangling Yvon Petra. There he told me some of the things about his marriage to Lily Branksome that I had not dared to ask more than a decade earlier. Before we went he had said he wondered whether I was still interested in watching tennis.

'Of course I am.'

'I thought perhaps – I know you had hopes of becoming a great player.' I said all that was past, forgotten. 'And that you might not want to be reminded of something you'd put behind you. That's the best thing, you know, to put the past behind you. Cross it out, cancel it as if it had never happened.'

'Nobody can do that.'

'I never could. Do you hear from her?'

I knew who he meant. I said I'd had a present from Deirdre at Christmas, and a letter, and that she'd sent food parcels.

'I never hear. Cut out the past, it's the only thing. Glad you'll come to Wimbledon. I shall look forward to it.'

And indeed we spent some long companionable afternoons at

Wimbledon that year, admiring the Australians and Americans and deploring the lack of good English players, something most of the papers were attributing to rationing, which was said to have enfeebled all our young sportsmen. We hardly mentioned my personal affairs – he would have considered questions about them intrusive – but he did express surprise and doubt when I told him I had left the *Record* and was acting in a small repertory company. He said he thought I'd given up the stage.

'I thought so too. But I've had enough of journalism. I liked it when the bombs were falling, but now it's just dull.'

We had taken time out after a long match between two of the women, and were in the tea tent eating strawberries and mock cream, real cream not being back in the shops. He asked about money, and I told him I'd saved quite a lot in my time at the *Record*. 'Good. Is there a woman involved?'

'Not exactly. Somebody I used to know at drama school is in the Lee rep, that's all.'

'I see.' A pause. 'I think we should all manage our own affairs, no interference. But I should like to see you settle down. Decide what you want to do and go on doing it. Not only settle down, get married. You'll find it's the best way.'

I have never liked being told what I should or shouldn't do and said, perhaps more sharply than I intended, 'Did you find it the best way? You tried more than once.'

He turned to look at me, with that sad Keatonic look in his deep-set eyes. 'Lily was a terrible mistake. For both of us. And Deirdre too. They were beautiful, it was the lure of beauty, do you understand?'

A negative reply might have been totally honest, but nobody cares to say they are not tempted by beauty. My next remark was prompted by still-present annoyance about that injunction to settle down. 'Justin says you married his mother for her money, and then put her in a mental home.'

He pushed away the empty plate. 'It is the kind of thing he would say. Do you believe him? But how can you believe or disbelieve, you don't know. Yes, it is true she brought money with her, but I would never have married for that. She was pale, delicately beautiful, fragile, well named. Her hands might have been porcelain, they were so perfect. I loved her, longed for her, and I thought she longed for me. Do you understand what I mean?'

'Sexually, longed sexually?'

'I suppose that would be the word. We did not use it then.' There were fruit stains on his fingers. He stared at them, shook his head, wiped his fingers with a napkin. 'But she hated it, hated the act, found even the idea of it unbearable. At first she tried, I'm sure she did. But the months of pregnancy were terrible for us both. "I don't want it," she said to me about the baby, over and over. "I hate it already, I shall kill it when it comes." When it was born she grew to love it. But she hated me. No, that's wrong, what she hated was touches, caresses. She flinched when I touched her arm, couldn't bear me in the same bed and then not in the same room. I endured it all, Geoffrey, I am a patient man, our doctor said it was post-natal, the aftermath of a difficult birth, if I waited everything would come right. But it didn't come right. One night I insisted, and she screamed and screamed. Then she imagined I had begun an affair with somebody else, rang up the office almost every day to ask my secretary where I was, came in there when I was away and looked through all my papers searching for letters from my mistress, tried to attack Miss Hilder when she refused to let her into my office – oh, it was endless. She began to have delusions, said I was diseased and had given her the disease, you understand? At last she attacked herself with a razor, tried to cut out her womb, when the maid found her the sheet was soaked with blood. What could there be after that but a home?'

'And she stayed there, never improved?'

'Oh yes, she improved, longed to come home, did so at weekends once or twice. Then she went for a maid with a knife, cut her arm badly and marked her face—'

'She thought you were sleeping with the maid?'

'Perhaps. It wasn't true. But there was a lot of trouble, the girl's face was scarred, the family had to be paid to hush up the affair. After that Lily was never let out again.'

'Justin said he was sent to boarding school when he was five.'

'Yes. He was a troubled child, attached to his mother. And

after what had happened I couldn't bear him near me. I paid for his education, and he spent holidays with Lily's mother.'

'I think he did rather well in the war. And he got me the job on the *Record*.'

'So you've told me,' he said coolly. 'Shall we go back to the tennis?'

As he put it, what had happened seemed inevitable, and nothing in it contradicted what Justin had told me. And it answered questions that were no longer so vital to the journalist and actor as they had been to a raw sixteen-year-old. When I heard how similarly he had treated Morgan, disposing of him at birth, paying for his education but keeping him at a distance, it occurred to me that perhaps I had not been a welcome addition to the family. Then I reproached myself, for I had no doubt of his love for me when I was a boy.

Yet marriage to Norma changed him, as surely as it changed her. And his circumstances had changed too, as I discovered when I had the chance of buying the Pimlico flat which I rented. The money saved from my *Record* days had gone, no building society would lend the money to buy the lease to an actor who was out of work more often than in it, and I sent Father a note asking if he would lend me the money. To be truthful, I had expected it to be given rather than lent, but instead he asked me to come and see him. Again, I was surprised that we met in Fulham rather than at the office. There, in the cosy or poky living room, with Pratterton's bathing nymphs looking down on us, he confronted me with an expression more inscrutable than usual. Norma was there too, a momentarily silent but powerful force. A short interrogation about my likely earning power, the imprudence of buying a flat on a short lease like this one, and so on, left me bewildered. I said I was his son, not a client.

'Of course, Geoffrey, of course.' He looked down at the floor, embarrassed. 'But you are now nearly thirty. You've done what you wished, given up a good job in journalism for the risks of a career on the stage.' He paused, and Norma could not refrain from intervening.

'You should be able to stand on your own two feet.'

212

After this she piled clichés one on another, while he listened with an unrevealing face. Cut your coat according to your cloth, neither a borrower nor a lender be, look after the pennies and the pounds will look after themselves, these were only the first of what seemed an inexhaustible stock of ancient saws, delivered with a mother-knows-best amiability that I found hard to bear. When I could endure no more of it I said I would give up the idea of buying the flat. At that he stood up.

'Don't talk like that, Geoffrey. I expect—' he looked at Norma, who shrugged her fine shoulders '—I can arrange it for you. But not through the firm.'

'Not through the firm,' I echoed wonderingly.

'You may as well know now as in a few weeks. These last years haven't been easy, it may be I'm too old-fashioned for what's happening nowadays. I'm selling the firm. There are a couple of young fellows with money who seem to think they can make a go of it, have all sorts of new-fangled ideas. The lawyers are still working out details, but unless there are snags I shall retire at the end of the year.'

It may seem strange that the news should have shocked me. This was a man in his middle sixties, why shouldn't he retire? But the double-breasted suit, the bowler hat, the walk to the office were so much a part of my childhood understanding of what life was like that I had never contemplated the ritual ending. And within what he said I sensed rightly that it was not just a matter of young fellows with money and new ideas, but that Branksome and Elder had lost a lot of business, and had no hope of getting it back. Within *that* there was implicit – or so I thought – the feeling that if I had gone into the business instead of pursuing wayward courses in acting and journalism, the sale might not have been necessary. As it was the bright young men took over, Father was called 'consultant' on the writing paper for a couple of years, the firm's name then became Willis, Frankel, Branksome and Elder, and is now Willis, Frankel and Partners. Father made the loan for the flat out of his private account. I could sense strong waves of disapproval coming from Norma, and knew she thought he would never see the money back. So I was particularly pleased when I had a couple of successful years, and was able to repay the loan sooner than either of us had expected.

After the sale of the firm he had no particular occupation, and of course there was no more buying of Prattertons. I don't know when I realised how much Norma had taken over his life, and that he was not getting enough to eat.

I must not give the impression that she was a 'bad wife', whatever that may be. The phrase could certainly not have been applied to somebody who washed and darned, and kept her little house sparklingly clean, the brass knobs on doors and cupboards brightly burnished. And her husband, too, was always turned out in a way that did her credit (which is how she seemed to me to think of it) when I sent them tickets for the first nights of plays in which I appeared. They would come to my dressing room afterwards and we would go out to supper, sometimes with a couple of other people in the cast. Norma could chat easily about plays and players, as she had about art and artists when working at the gallery. He said little, but seemed to enjoy himself.

But still, she took over his life. It was all, I think in retrospect, a matter of money. She had married a man who appeared to be well-to-do (an extraordinary, ridiculous term, yet no other seems quite right), and now they had enough to live on, but no more than that. For a year or two I did a lot of touring, and had a part in a film epic about Nero that took me to Italy for a couple of months, so that I rarely visited Fulham. When I did, one of Norma's relatives always seemed to be there, either up in London for the day, or paying a visit. She had a sister, a brother, and what seemed an endless supply of cousins and in-laws or near in-laws – as it might be, her sister's husband's brother. Father had become interested in the topography of the area, and went for long walks around Fulham and Chelsea, after which he would make notes about the changes in streets and buildings. I think he had the idea of a book in mind, although he did little more than sketch out chapter headings. Sometimes I accompanied him on these walks, which ranged from the dingier parts around Fulham Broadway and World's End to the fashionable King's Road shops and the streets leading off them, about which he knew a great deal. He startled me once by checking himself when embarked on a verbal history of Stamford Bridge and Chelsea Football Club by saying, 'You don't like her, do you?'

We both knew who he meant. I said she had always been friendly and helpful to me.

'Friendly, helpful.' He repeated the words without emphasis. 'I love her, remember that. I don't know what I should have done if I'd not met her.' We paused to look in the window of a shop filled with bits of old weapons and armour, along with dusty paintings in ornate gilt frames. 'We brought you up wrongly, Deirdre and I. You should have left home, gone to boarding school.'

'I don't think so. I should have hated it.'

'Not important. We were neither of us the right parents for a young boy living at home. D'you like that?' He pointed to a head and shoulders of a woman sniffing a red rose, a yearning expression on her face. She wore an off-the-shoulder gown or perhaps nightdress, which had slipped to reveal a rose-tipped breast.

'Not much.'

'I suppose not.' He continued staring for a moment or two, then turned away. I should not have been surprised to see the painting appear on one of the bedroom walls, but so far as I know he never bought it.

At home he seemed submerged among the relatives, all of whom had loud voices and emphatic laughs. He sat in what became known as his armchair, a comfortable wing-back bought by Norma secondhand, and let the tide of talk about people whose names he hardly knew wash over him. Yet I don't think he was bored. At times I saw him looking at Norma with an expression undoubtedly sensual, yet also wistful and yearning.

The first time I realised that Norma was in effect operating her own rationing system (official food rationing had ended a year or two earlier) was when Dodo and Bella came down to London, and all three of us had supper at Fulham. When we had left Dodo said, 'She doesn't exactly push the boat out, Norma, does she?' My appetite is not large, and I replied that there had been enough to eat. Bella laughed and said, 'Enough for sparrows. He's looking poorly, I think she's starving him.'

I hadn't seen them for a while, not since I'd been touring in Priestley's *Mr Cornelius*, and had a lively evening with them in York. Both had put on weight, and it occurred to me that a few meals suitable for sparrows would do them no harm. But after that I noticed Norma's provision of food was sparse to the point of meanness. Was it that she never fully tuned in to the end of rationing, did she want to keep her weight down, or was she worried about money? I never found the answer, but when in addition she turned vegetarian, and put on the table dishes of lentil, carrot and parsnip stew, I began to time visits for the afternoon or late evening, and the visits themselves became less frequent. It was not until Leila settled in with me, and we invited Father and Norma to dinner that Leila remarked afterwards on the thinness of his wrists, the collar too big for his neck, and the gauntness of his features. She had met him only once before, two or three months earlier, and she was shocked.

'Did you see how he went at that pie, and had a second helping?' Leila had refused to cook a vegetarian meal, providing instead an omelette for Norma and steak and kidney pie for the rest of us. 'She's starving him.'

'Nonsense.'

'Or she gives him stuff he doesn't like, and then he starves himself.'

'Don't be ridiculous.'

Yet I remembered his liking for chop-houses, and felt uneasy. You must do something, Leila said, but I felt a strong disinclination to interfere. At length, prodded by her, I rang up, said there was something I wanted to talk about, and took him to a steak house. We shared a Chateaubriand, but he ate only a little, then pushed it away. He looked frail, his face still Keatonic but the features changed, so that the cheekbones showed markedly, the chin had become definitely pointed, the eyes seemed larger, and sunk in the dark hollows round them. He asked why I wanted to see him alone. I had thought it would be easy to evade the question, but found myself saying, 'Leila thinks you don't get enough to eat.'

216

'Does she?' He looked at the steak on his plate, and smiled. Have I mentioned that his smile, though rare, was youthful, even boyish, and full of charm? 'What does she propose to do about it? Smuggle steak in to me every day?' He said softly, 'There is no need to worry, I am very happy. When you are married, if you ever are, you'll know that happiness isn't a matter of having steak for dinner, however delicious it may be.'

'Of course not.'

'Besides, Norma says eating meat is bad for the digestion.'

I felt the absurdity of the conversation, and did not know how to go on. 'We're both concerned about you.'

'You need not be. There are things I regret in my life, some of them deeply, but marrying Norma is not one of them.'

I am not sure what spurred me to say, 'Is one of them connected with Hugo Headley's death?'

He looked at me out of those sunken eyes. 'One of them is concerned with Hugo Headley, yes.'

I don't have the spirit of the investigative reporter, even though some of this narrative may seem to contradict that, but the events of the Clempstone summer haunted me (this was, of course, long before the visit of that intrusive biographer), and I asked what it was. He shook his head.

'It's nothing you need know. It's best that you don't know. I shan't want a pudding, but I should like coffee.'

It was six weeks later, in late September, that I came home after a day rehearsing a TV sitcom, and Leila said Norma had called to say my father was not well. When I rang her she said perhaps she had been foolish to make a fuss. 'It's just that I felt you should know. We were sitting in the garden last weekend, he was bitten on the neck by a mosquito, and the doctor says it must have got into the bloodstream. Anyway, he's in hospital. I'm going in this evening, and wondered if you'd like to come.'

When we visited him, his condition had deteriorated, and he was delirious, saying to Norma that there were Prattertons coming up at Christie's, and she must buy them. She said she would, but that didn't satisfy him.

'You don't mean it, you didn't ask about a price limit. We're not made of money, what can we go up to? No use going along without settling that.' She was wonderfully composed, said she had money he didn't know about, and could use that.

'You'll buy it, you won't fail?' He had been sitting up, now sank back. 'Beautiful, beautiful, my life has been—' He left the sentence unfinished, began another. 'To *possess* beauty, that's what I always wanted. Geoffrey, where are you? Can't see you properly, you never understood. Give me your hand.' His hand was hot, the grasp so firm it was almost painful. He said in a changed, conversational tone, 'How's the racquet?'

'The racquet?'

'The latest thing, got it for you specially. Beat Fred Perry with it, see you at Wimbledon.' He laughed, let go of my hand, beckoned me closer. The sunken eyes looked at me with apparent intelligence, no madness to be seen in them. 'We got to Wimbledon, didn't we? Centre court?' I said yes, we had got to Wimbledon. He lowered his voice so that I had to bend down to hear him. 'Very good, very good. Only thing I worry about now is Florence. I should never have agreed.'

'Agreed to what?'

'And Headley, that was wrong too. Wrong, wrong. But still ...' His voice faded, he closed his eyes, and I straightened up. But now he sat up with a Jack-in-the-box effect, eyes staring, and shouted, 'Headley, you scoundrel, you rutting piece of filth.' He became incoherent, mixing Headley's name with others, running his words together and blending obscenities into the stream. He tried to get out of bed, displacing one of the tubes strapped to his arm. Norma cried out and a nurse came, then a doctor. The doctor injected him, he collapsed in the bed. When I asked about his condition the doctor said something about the risk of inflammation spreading to the brain.

That was the last time I saw him. Twenty-four hours later he was dead.

Much of what followed has been erased from my mind, as it is said the memory of torture one has suffered cannot be recalled in precise detail, although the face of the torturer may terrify in dreams, and the victim's personality is changed for ever. I remember being told by the doctor afterwards that he was in poor physical shape, and had some obscure blood condition that reduced his resistance to infection. I recall also a stream of Norma's relatives talking animatedly, and Norma in black and weeping. I know that I was surprised by the number of people I had never seen before who came up to sympathise with me after the funeral service. But whether I looked at his face in the coffin, what words were said at the service and what hymns sung, what clothes I wore (I have never owned a black tie, did I borrow one?), and what I did when it was over, all that has been mercifully blotted out.

He had not expected to die (how could one expect death from a mosquito bite?), and had made no will, so that everything went to Norma. I have forgotten the value of the estate for probate, but it cannot have been more than a very few thousands. Norma wrote to say she was selling the Fulham house and going to live with an unmarried sister in Berkshire for a while, and that if there were any mementoes I wanted I was very welcome to them, but I had no need of reminders. Later she sent me a small album, into which he had put photographs of me at every stage of my life. A baby waving a rattle, a little boy staring open-mouthed at the camera, an actor in the school play, a smirking boy wearing his first long trousers, an adolescent shaking hands at the end of a tennis match, and then holding cups and medals won at tournaments – there were some forty pictures in all, every one annotated in his neat hand, with date and place. The last snap was one taken at Clempstone on that final holiday, as if my life or his had ended then. The album seemed the ultimate proof of his love for me, and evidence also of the hopes he entertained, and how I had failed them. I turned the pages over again and again, and wept.

The Sixties

(i) A News Item in the Banner

I returned to my Newcastle hotel room numb with shock, numb as I had been when I heard of Father's death. How could I reconcile Mr A, who put out his child to fostering, with the man whose susceptibilities were deeper than I had ever understood? If Florence was Morgan's mother, what had happened to her? But what chiefly upset me was the evidence Mrs Rackley had provided of a cold uncaring man who had believed everything could be done through the power of money.

When I opened the room door the telephone was ringing. For a few moments my presentiment that I should hear something terrible, some revelation about Father or Morgan, was so great that I could not bring myself to pick it up. When I did so and heard Leila's voice, my relief was so great that I spoke with unusual warmth, wanting her to say she was here in Newcastle, and would be with me in ten minutes.

'I'm at Ratty's. Where did you think I was?'

'I thought—' But I could not tell her what I thought. Instead I said how good it was to hear her, then that I hoped she might have come back.

'You don't sound like yourself. But I suppose you're upset.' I was upset, but how could she know? For a moment I thought wildly that Leila must be clairvoyant. 'I know you were fond of her, though she was never very nice to me.'

'Leila, I don't know what you mean.'

'Don't you read the papers? There's a big obituary in *The Times*. Your Aunt Aggie. She had a heart attack, died on the way to hospital.'

We exchanged a few more sentences. I asked if she was coming back, she said she didn't think so, I thanked her for calling me, she said there were times when a little sympathy was very nice. Then we rang off.

It was true that I'd been so much occupied with Scotty Scotland, Mrs Headley and Mrs Rackley, that I hadn't looked at a paper. In the hotel lobby the porter said he'd done with his copy of the *Banner*. It contained a couple of paragraphs about

223

Mary Storm, by the man who masqueraded as their drama critic, although what he really purveyed was gossipy stories about shows and show people. 'Born Agatha Elder she became Mary Storm, and sure enough she stormed through dozens of parts, and almost as many lovers . . .' Two of the lovers were named, an American impresario and a Greek millionaire, but Hugo Headley stayed unmentioned, the editor or whoever no doubt thinking readers of the paper would be unfamiliar with the name of a minor poet.

As I leafed through the tabloid's pages another short news item caught my eye.

PLANE CRASHES ON KENT HOUSE

A biplane crashed on a house just outside the village of Lightchurch on the Kent coast yesterday afternoon, leaving it in ruins. The pilot, a French businessman named Lecomte, was killed immediately. He had radioed Lydd airport, where he was due to land, moments before the crash to say he had engine trouble, and might be forced to make an emergency landing.

The house is in a small estate of only eight detached houses built between the wars. The owners, Mr and Mrs Evans, were out for a walk when the plane crashed. 'It was amazing luck,' Mr Evans said. 'My wife and I mostly have a nap in the afternoons, but today she said the weather was so fine we mustn't be lazy, and we went out. Silly to call it luck, I suppose, when we've lost our home and most of our belongings, but at least we're alive.'

I read the story only because Lightchurch is five miles from Clempstone, and otherwise thought nothing of it. I rang Dodo, whom I had intended to travel to York to see, and learned that he would be coming down with Bella to Aggie's funeral. I told him I was in Newcastle, and asked if the name Rackley meant anything to him. He said no.

'Or somebody named Florence? Or a man named Morgan?'

'No bells ringing. Who are they?'

I told him what I had learned from Mrs Rackley. 'You knew Father, were at school together, isn't that right?'

'That's so, yes.' There was a leaden note to his voice, he didn't sound like the Dodo I remembered.

'You must know something about it all.' He did not reply. 'Dodo?'

'Yes.'

'I've never asked about these things, but now I am asking. I want to know about them, I think I have a right.'

'We'll talk when I see you,' he said in that same leaden tone.

(ii) Unexpected Visits

When I opened the door of the flat I subconsciously expected to find Leila there, perhaps at the cooker preparing a casserole, saying she knew I would be back some time today and would want a meal. But the place was empty, the newspaper and a couple of letters on the mat, the bed unmade. I looked round without pleasure, shivered slightly. The telephone rang and I picked it up eagerly, expecting it to be Leila. Instead, it was a voice I hadn't heard for years, but instantly recognised.

'Geoffrey. Guess who?'

'Deirdre.'

'You knew me at once, isn't that wonderful.' I asked why she had come over. So far as I knew the last time she crossed the Atlantic had been a dozen years earlier when Pat died, leaving Johnjohn unable to care for himself, and she had arranged for him to enter a home. 'Oh, I've got some odds and ends to see to, but I *long* to talk to you. I've been ringing and ringing. What about lunch today? I'm at the Connaught.'

'Is Langton with you?' The advertising man was named Langton Brady.

'Langton and I have split up, I'm on my own, I'll tell you all about it when we meet. Twelve forty-five at the Connaught.'

It would be wrong to say Deirdre was unchanged in the years since I had seen her, but she was still a beautiful woman. No doubt the red hair remained so only with some artificial aid, but the full figure in the smoke-blue dress retained its curves without being bulky, the white skin was still flawless, the hands she held out to me in greeting were almost unveiled. Her manner was more theatrical than it had been in my youth, something perhaps attributable to the fact that I was no longer a son to be kept out of the way but a man on whom, almost automatically, she tried to cast a spell. She still had about her that sexual magnetism some women never lose, whatever their age. As we drank in her suite (or rather as I drank, for she confined herself to Perrier) she exclaimed about my fame, and her pride in having such a celebrated son.

'You're too modest,' she exclaimed, when I said I was a run-of-the-mill actor. 'You've never pushed yourself as you should have done, but believe me you are *known* in New York, people remember you. What you need is a really good agent.' When I replied that she hadn't asked to see me so that she could advise me about my agent her green eyes opened wide. 'I wanted to see my son, my only child, is that so strange? Have you married Lolly yet?'

'Leila. No, we haven't married.'

'Perhaps you're right to have kept your freedom, I sometimes wish I had. But what you do you do, it's no use harking back. Let's go down to lunch, I'm starving.'

Starvation was appeased by a melon, succeeded by a sole of which she ate a single fillet. When I said I wanted to ask questions about Father she exclaimed, 'Wonderful, I want to talk about him too.'

'When you married him, did he talk about the past?'

'The *past*,' she repeated, as if it was an unfamiliar and almost unintelligible word.

'You knew about Lily, his first wife?'

'Oh yes, he told me about her. She went dotty, had to be put away. And of course I knew about Justin. Harry would never have anything to do with him, couldn't bear the sight of him.'

'Did you know he had another son named Morgan?' She shook her head. 'Not by Lily. I think his mother was named Florence.'

226

'What a ghastly servant's name. Where do you get all this from?' I told her what I had learned from Mrs Rackley, and she shook her head again. 'It's all news to me, news of no interest, it would never have been of any interest. And I don't see why you want to know about it.'

'I didn't know him properly. I want to know more about what he was like. What *was* he like?'

'Oh really, darling, do stop it. Acting in bad plays must have gone to your head. It's no use asking what people are like, as if everyone had some secret personality. He was a man, that's what Harry was like. A very passionate man, if you want to know.'

As she spoke, as I looked at her across the table, I saw that torchlight-illuminated scene, Neil Paton driving into her, and heard again the cry of 'Whore'. Her green eyes looked into mine. She said coolly, 'I don't want to talk about this, you know, and I doubt if you want to hear it. I can't understand why you're asking such questions.'

'I'm sorry, I'll give up. But one more thing. At that time – the time at Clempstone, that last year – do you think he could have been having an affair with Melissa?'

'Melissa, who was – oh, the Paton girl. I shouldn't think so, but I truly don't understand why you want to know.' I told her about the letters. 'Well, you surprise me. Of course with men anything is possible.' She spoke as if they were another species. 'I've said Harry was passionate, but he was very moral too. He tried to be tolerant, I suppose you could say he was as tolerant with me as he could be. In those days – never mind. I think you're a bit like him, and I wouldn't want to shock you. As far as I know, he wasn't sleeping with Neil's daughter, not that I'd have minded particularly if he had been. I can tell you, if he had been he'd have hated himself for doing it.' Her smile, whatever she may have intended, was seductive. 'Now, I've been angelically patient, but I'm not going to answer any more questions. And I've got a favour to ask.'

Was she telling the truth? I was inclined to think so, at least about her ignorance of Morgan and Florence.

227

'Has anyone been asking questions about me? It would probably be an American.' I said they hadn't, American, British or
other. 'Good. I'll tell you what it's about. I told you I'd split up
with Langton. He'd got very tiresome, drank a lot and couldn't
hold his liquor, but that wasn't exactly the reason. It was
because of Garth.'

'Garth?' Americans choose extraordinary names for their
children.

'Garth Cascarino. He's a big figure in New York State, owns
half-a-dozen construction companies, does a lot of government
work. Second generation Italian. Beautiful manners. Langton, I
must say, has behaved well, made no trouble about the divorce
and agreed a settlement.' I said I was pleased to hear it, but she
ignored or did not notice the intended irony. 'The problem is—'
She took a sip of her coffee, apparently uncertain just what to
say next. 'Garth's a bit like Harry, a very moral man. And he has
a bitch of a Mexican wife, Dolores. Half-Mexican,' she said, as if
conceding a point. 'Garth and I want to get married.'

'How old is Garth?'

'I don't ask men's ages, and I don't expect them to ask mine.'
Then, conceding another point, she said, 'Fifty-eight.'

Fifty-eight, I thought, and enchanted by this senior Circe. 'I
don't understand the problem.'

'The problem is Dolores says she doesn't want to let him go.
She's hired some smuthound to dig out all he can about me.
Garth knows I've been married twice, and it hasn't worked out.
But he might be upset if he heard stories – Harry was a difficult
man, you know.'

'You mean if this investigator comes to see me I shouldn't say
anything about Neil. All right, but you'd better speak to Neil as
well.'

'Oh, I have. He understood perfectly. He wouldn't want old
coals raked over, any more than I would.'

'And then there were others, weren't there?' I thought of
Freddie and Toby and Jackie.

'Yes, but that wasn't at all the same. They weren't important.'

'One-night stands? Seven-night stands?'

'You are really disgusting, Geoffrey, as bigoted as your father without his charm. You don't understand that the thing with Neil was serious, really serious. The others were nothing. At least Harry understood that.'

I felt a kind of anger foreign to my nature. 'I can't disgust you any more than you disgust me. When did you ever think there were any responsibilities in being a wife or a mother? You did your best to ruin Father's life and mine, and almost the worst thing is you didn't realise you were doing it. I hope you get what you want, and enjoy being Mrs Cascarino. But if you ask me, Langton Brady's a lucky man.' I left her in the Connaught dining room, green eyes wide in astonishment.

The smuthound never got in touch with me, perhaps finding all that was needed from other sources. In any event, Deirdre never became Mrs Cascarino. She did marry again, however. Eighteen months after that Connaught lunch I received a card inviting me to the wedding and reception of Jackson P. Kranitzer and Deirdre Brady at a hotel in Miami. On the card Deirdre had written, 'Do come, love to see you.' I left it unanswered.

On the way back to Pimlico I read an item in the *Evening Standard*:

PLANE CRASH BONES MYSTERY

Workmen clearing rubble from the house at Lightchurch damaged when a plane crashed on it were surprised to find what are thought to be human bones buried there. Mr Evans, owner of the house, says he has no knowledge of the matter. He confirmed that he and his wife had been the house's only occupants, and can offer no explanation of where the bones may have come from. 'I can only think it was some kind of practical joke,' Mr Evans said. The police are said to be investigating further, but at present the origin of the bones remains a mystery.

They came on the following evening, two men in dark suits. One wore rimless spectacles, and had fair hair cut short. He looked like a stage version of a German professor. That was the Chief Inspector. The other was sharp-nosed, eager, and wore a little badge in his lapel. That was the Sergeant. The Professor was mildly apologetic as he said he was going to ask me to cast my mind back thirty years.

'It's about the bones at Lightchurch. You think they're Hugo Headley's.' He raised thin eyebrows. 'I've read the papers. I can't think why else two CID men would be calling on me.'

'Very quick. And quite right.' His tone suggested he did not quite approve of such quickness. 'Except that we don't think, we know. The bones are Headley's. When he disappeared we had details of his dental chart, so that we could check if or when his body was washed up by the sea. It's come in handy now.'

'And you know the cause of death?'

'He died of a fractured skull. Now of course it's possible he met with an accident, but he certainly didn't transport himself to Cumonholme, and lay himself down there. So we're treating it as a case of murder. I'll just anticipate your question. Cumonholme is the name Mr Evans gave to his house.' A tight professorial smile invited me to share the absurdity of it. The Sergeant smiled too. 'The house that didn't exist at the time.'

'I don't see how you think I can help you.'

'If we may explain, sir. This little enclave, consisting of only eight houses, was put up in 1936.' He cocked an eyebrow, and the Sergeant took up the story, referring occasionally to a file open on his knee.

'The land was purchased in 1935 from a Mr and Mrs Gentry, who were moving up to Scotland. Bought by Branksome and Elder on behalf of a client of theirs named South Eastern Properties. Some delay because of an argument as to the exact siting of the houses, but building began in late July 1936, completed September, houses in occupation October.' The Sergeant closed the file, stopped speaking like a machine switched off. The Chief Inspector nodded. It was evidently his turn.

'The builders have long since been merged in a bigger firm and have no records dating back that far, but we have found a man named McGinty, who worked on the site. He says Cumonholme was one of the last houses to be built. The ground was cleared and the foundations laid early in August. These facts lead us, you'll have gathered, to a conclusion. Headley's body was put among the foundations, probably on the night he disappeared, and then covered over in the knowledge that within a few hours it would be buried completely. But for that plane crash it would never have been found.'

I asked if they would like a drink. The Sergeant looked at the Chief Inspector, who said talking was thirsty work, and a beer made it easier. I got each of them a can of beer and a glass, and said I still didn't see how I could help them.

The Chief Inspector frowned. The Sergeant said sharply, 'When we weren't sure what had happened the file was left open. Now we know he was murdered, and where the body was put. There was a party that night he disappeared at the house you were staying in. Seems reasonable to think one of the people there did it.' He stopped, and the Chief Inspector gave his approving professorial nod before taking up the story again.

'We know a little more than that. Whoever killed Headley knew where to put the body, or in other words knew of the estate being put up at Lightchurch, and that there would be one or two houses where the foundations were being laid. Branksome and Elder, your father's firm, were handling the sale, so he would have known that.' It was part-statement, part-question.

'I suppose so. And his partner Neil Paton, I expect.'

'When your father divorced his wife a short time afterwards it was on the grounds of her adultery with Mr Paton. And this holiday of yours at Clempstone broke up abruptly after the party Headley attended, correct?'

'You've been talking to—' I couldn't remember the name of the Passloves '—the gardener.'

'Never mind who we've talked to, why did the holiday break up?' That was the Sergeant, his voice coarsened, his manner suddenly bristling with hostility. 'Because of trouble with Headley, right? Trouble over him and your mother? He had an eye for the girls and she liked young men, right? So we're told.'

'That's nonsense, just gossip.'

'Is it? Seems to us it makes sense. There's some sort of trouble at the party, Headley disappears, next day Mrs Elder goes home on her own, soon after that the rest of you pack up and leave. Your mother was having it off with Headley, your father found out, and – wham.' He punched a fist into the palm of the other hand. 'But he'd have needed help in shifting the body, or could have done with it anyway. Question is, was it Paton or you?'

'You're out of your mind. You've said yourself Paton was named in the divorce. My mother didn't know Hugo Headley.'

'Couldn't very well name a man who disappeared. But maybe she was having it off with both of them.' His greyhound features broke up in the nastiest grin.

'Sergeant, you're being offensive.' The Chief Inspector was clearly playing soft man in this duet. 'In case you think we're miracle workers, Mr Elder, much of this material had been gathered thirty years ago, but you'll understand it's taken on a different meaning now we know Headley's dead, and where his body was put. And the reason given for his presence at the party, that story about selling his cottage and the land, that always seemed thin. What were your own movements when the party broke up?'

I told them the truth, that I had gone to my room, saying nothing about the scene I had witnessed. It had, I felt sure, no connection with Hugo's death, but in any case I could not have brought myself to discuss it.

'You'll forgive me if I say that doesn't seem satisfactory.' His eyes were severe behind the rimless glasses. I shrugged. 'Why did the holiday end so suddenly? Why did your mother leave on her own?' I said untruthfully that I didn't know, my father had simply said we were cutting short the holiday.

'And you accepted that, without asking questions? Come now, Mr Elder.'

'My father didn't confide in me, if I'd asked he wouldn't have told me. And I was only sixteen.'

'True.' He looked at me thoughtfully, then drained his glass. 'Let me be frank, Mr Elder. I keep my cards on the table, not under it. We've talked to Mr Paton, who has admitted an affair with your mother – he could hardly deny it – but says he knows nothing about Headley's death. We've also spoken on the phone to Mr Everard, who tells us he knows your father was troubled about something, but thinks it was to do with business, not his personal life.' Good old Dodo, I thought, they'll get nothing out of him, and I gave good marks to Neil for stonewalling, although admission of what had happened would have been an embarrassment for him. 'I understand your mother lives in America, but we may ask her for a written statement, or even go over to interview her. This may seem to you like raking over dead ashes, but it's more than that. I have very little doubt that your father killed Hugo Headley and buried his body, but at present I can't prove it, and I wouldn't want to blacken a dead man's name. It may be he had no companion, no accessory. But there's something more to be found out, and I mean to find it. Maybe it's got nothing to do with Headley's death, and if so you'll save time and trouble by telling me. But if I find you or Mr Paton or Mr Everard or anybody else was an accessory to Headley's death I shall have them, never doubt it. Do I make myself plain?'

'You make yourself plain.'

He stood up. 'Thank you for the beer.'

The Sergeant stood too. 'Thank you for the beer.'

They left.

(iii) The Funeral

On the morning of Aggie's funeral I rang Ratty's number, told her who I was, and asked to speak to Leila.

'I don't know if she'll want to talk to you.' There was the sound of voices, then Leila came on. She sounded uncharacteristically flustered.

'It was good of you to take the trouble to let me know about Aggie. I don't think I said thank you properly.'

'That's all right.'

'I'm going to the funeral today. I wondered if you'd like to come.'

A pause. 'I don't think so.'

'Leila, come home.'

Another pause. Then Ratty spoke. 'Look here, I won't have

you bloody well upsetting Leila. Why can't you accept things the way they are? It's just male chauvinism, you think you can whistle and she'll come back. But she's made her decision, opted for something different . . .' She went on like this, and showed no sign of running out of steam when I put the phone down. Five minutes later it rang again. I thought it would be Ratty, but heard another woman's voice, hard and thick. She asked if I was Mr Elder. I said I was.

'I'm speaking for Mr Morgan. Mean anything to you?' I said I knew the name. 'I'm his agent, he's got something to sell.' I said that was odd, because Morgan was dead. Silence on the line. Then she said, 'All right, but there's still his papers. You want to see them? Before anyone else does?'

'I'd like to see them, yes, but not to pay for them.'

'If you don't, someone else will.'

'Perhaps you should go to them first.'

'Don't try to kid me.' I said she had better go back to her client, whoever he was, and say I wasn't interested unless I could talk to him. She sounded surprised and uncertain. 'I'm not sure he'll wear that, but okay I'll talk to him and ring you back.'

I said I was going out, and wouldn't be home again until the evening. She said she would call me at eight o'clock.

When I returned to London from Newcastle I had found a letter from Aunt Aggie's solicitor, who signed himself H. J. Sparrowmate, telling me of her death, saying he had tried to get in touch with me, and asking me to call him as soon as possible. I did so, and said I supposed as her next of kin he would want me to make the funeral arrangements.

'Just what I wanted to speak to you about.' Mr Sparrowmate's voice was deep, rich, altogether unlike the chirping of a sparrow. 'That isn't in fact the case.'

'What isn't the case?'

'I know it must come as a surprise. I told Mrs Peachey she should let you know.'

'I don't understand. Who is Mrs Peachey?'

'I'm sorry,' Mr Sparrowmate rumbled, so happily that he sounded about to burst into laughter. 'Three months ago your aunt was married. I understand the ceremony was completely private. The happy man was Leonard Peachey, who had I believe met Miss Elder long ago. An old flame, one might say.'

Leonard Peachey, how did I know the name? As Mr Sparrow-mate went on about funeral details, the time, the place, the number of people who should be invited back afterwards for a sandwich and a glass of wine at the cottage, it came back to me that after Hugo's disappearance there had been stories about Aggie and a handsome young actor whose name had been something like – yes, had positively been Peachey. At that time I had not been interested, later the name had been replaced by others, handsome young Peachey had shared the fate of many actors with little to recommend them except their looks and vanished from view, never to be heard of again. However had Aunt Aggie relit this old flame?

'So romantic,' rumbled Mr Sparrowmate.

'I beg your pardon?'

'I believe Mr Peachey had been – ah – seeking his fortune in the New World. On his return here he wrote to her, they met again, and within a month they were married. A wonderful character, Miss Elder or Mrs Peachey, wonderful. But in relation to the funeral arrangements, you need not concern yourself. Everything is in hand.'

As I drove down the A3 I reflected that the marriage explained Aunt Aggie's coyness. Peachey had presumably been out, perhaps been told to go out, when I came. If I had penetrated to the bathroom I should no doubt have found evidence of a masculine presence. Thinking about this, reflecting that this sunset marriage was perhaps an appropriate end to Aggie's tempestuous life, I hardly noticed that I was in a traffic jam until we stopped completely for several minutes, and then went on in hundred-yard spurts.

The result was that I arrived at the church after the service had begun, and found a place near the back where I sang a hymn unfamiliar to me, apparently called 'God be in my head'. The church was surprisingly crowded, and I looked round for people I knew, catching a glimpse of Justin at the front, and the back of a head that looked like Dodo's. The acoustics were as poor as in most churches, and my attention strayed. I looked at the sheet

235

given me when I came in, saw 'A Reading' by Leonard Peachey, and realised that the figure standing at a lectern thundering out Dylan Thomas's 'And death shall have no dominion' must be Aunt Aggie's husband. He had a red face, a mass of grey curly hair worn very long and an equally curly beard, wore a dark suit, white shirt and a big black stock at the neck. He declaimed the poem, and then one by Hugo called 'The Worm That Dieth Not', in a manner worthy of a Victorian parodist of Irving, even sketching a bow when he finished.

Afterwards, in the porch, I introduced myself and apologised for my lateness. Peachey clasped my hand in both of his, and said in a throbbing actor's voice how glad he was to meet me.

'My beloved Mary spoke of you so often and so warmly – I knew her first as Mary Storm and always thought of her by that name. And it is appropriate, for the stage was her reality, everyday life something to be endured, don't you agree?' I didn't express an opinion, but asked how they had met again. 'In the New World, where for my sins I spent most of my life in an attempt to conquer the Philistines, I followed Mary's triumphs, and wrote to her after the tragic blow that forced her to retire from the stage. We corresponded for years, and when I returned to the Old Country I naturally came down to see her. I came, saw – and was conquered. And then quite, quite tragically, she was taken from me, from us all. Of course you will join us at the cottage and raise a glass to Mary's memory.'

As I walked out of the churchyard a hand grasped my arm. It was Justin, a Justin who had expanded in every direction except height.

'How are you, brother mine? And how's the acting game?' He turned to his companion. 'Do you know, he's got a genius for landing himself in dead-end jobs that I have to drag him out of. But now he's an actor, what else is he fit for? Something in politics perhaps, they're all ham actors. Oh, this is Gloria Honey. Gloria, meet my brother Geoffrey. Her name's not really Honey, it's something Hungarian and unpronounceable, but Honey sounds better. She's a model.'

Gloria Honey was dressed from head to foot in black, with a thick black veil, through which she spoke in erratic, strongly accented English. 'You are really his brother? I do not know if he jokes.'

I said we were half-brothers, and Justin amplified it. 'Same father, different mothers. Father drove my mother potty, then put her away. But Geoffrey seems to have liked him. Here we are.'

He stopped beside a silver Rolls. I said I had my own car. 'Never mind that, I'll bring you back to collect it later. I want a word.' It was probably reluctance to have my old Ford compared to the Rolls that made me agree to get in. 'Come in front with me. Gloria, in the back for you.' Gloria passed me with a whiff of scent, settled in the back. Justin put the car into drive. 'Haven't seen you for years. I was in the States when the old b died, don't know I'd have gone to the funeral anyway, but I liked Aggie. Gloria tagged along because we're off for a weekend in Brighton. What about the acting game, it's a dead end, isn't it?'

I said it suited me, and asked what he was doing. He took a card from his pocket, gave it me. I read 'Justin Elder, Chairman and Managing Director', and beneath 'Euro-Belgian Credit Bank' with two addresses, one in Brussels, the other in Mayfair. 'If you ever think of moving into the good life out of Poverty Lane give me a ring. Don't say you've no head for finance, doesn't matter, might even be a good thing.' When he laughed his cheeks shook slightly, he had the beginning of jowls. 'I need somebody I can trust, and they don't grow on trees. Here we are.' There was a line of cars outside Aggie's cottage, but only one Rolls among them.

'I am disappoint in the death service,' Gloria said to me as we walked up the path. 'It has no drama, nobody weep. Only the husband, I think he is very good, show the emotion. But Justin he does not care, and you, you don't show the emotion.' She threw back her veil, revealing a small pretty face, great dark eyes. I thought for a moment of Melissa. I said it was not English to show emotion.

The parlour where Aggie had given me tea and crumpets retained her memorabilia on the walls but had otherwise been cleared of furniture, including the armchairs in which we had sat. Forty people were crammed into the little room, black-coated waiters fought a way through the crowd with bottles of champagne and bits of things to eat. Peachey was doing the thing in style.

'A word in your ear, Mr Elder.' The face was rubicund, smiling, the voice unmistakable. Mr Sparrowmate and I pushed a way through to a window embrasure. 'Since you were under the natural, though mistaken impression that you were the next of kin, I thought you might like to know the exact position. Mrs Peachey wasn't a good life, could have popped off at any time.' His mouth quivered, apparently with amusement, at the thought. 'She had made a will which, apart from a few odds and ends, left everything to you.'

'I don't suppose there was much to leave.'

'On the contrary.' Another quiver. 'During her years as a successful actress she had bought a number of small properties in London's East End. She took professional advice, but she was not without her own shrewdness, not by any means.' Now he permitted himself a positive chuckle. 'A few years back three of these properties were bought by a developer for what I would call a tidy sum, and the others have of course greatly appreciated in value. She was not a rich woman but quite comfortable, thank you, quite comfortable.'

'Are you going to tell me I've inherited?'

'I fear not.' He tried in vain to compose his features into solemnity. Somebody jogged his arm, and champagne splashed my suit. 'Dear me, what a pity. When she made this late romantic marriage I asked her – as, you will understand, was my professional duty – whether she wished to change her will, and she did so.' Mr Sparrowmate, an expert in creating suspense, paused. 'She left everything to her beloved husband, Leonard Peachey.' A pause. 'With the provision that her nephew Geoffrey Wild Elder should have any keepsakes or mementoes that he wished, and also the remainder of her papers, since some of them contain material relating to the past which he may find of interest. I am not sure that I am quoting verbatim, but that's the gist of it. I shall of course be writing to you, but I thought you might wish to know the position as soon as possible.'

'Yes. Thank you.'

There was an eager look on Mr Sparrowmate's face. 'I hope you are not too greatly disappointed.'

I told him I had expected nothing and so was not disappointed, and that was true.

When he had left me, I wondered what keepsake or memento I should like to have as a reminder of Aunt Aggie. A couple of her old theatre programmes? But I had little interest in Mary Storm the actress, and a lot of my own old programmes were stuffed into a cupboard at the flat. And why should she think I might be interested in her papers when the academic trufflehound Duffy had been through them? Looking round the little room, full of people unknown to me yapping at each other, I thought how little we care about people after they have gone. I said I had been fond of Aggie, and probably most of those in the room would say the same, but now that she had been put into the ground would any image of her remain in our minds, would any of our lives be changed in the smallest degree? Except for Peachey, I thought maliciously, Peachey's life had certainly been changed, and no doubt for the better.

I accepted another glass of champagne, and was halfway through it when I heard my name. The speaker was Dodo, but a Dodo so altered in appearance that for a moment I did not recognise him. The skin was drawn tightly across his face as if tucks had been taken into it at either side, his old ruddiness had been changed to a couple of faint red patches against a parchment surface, even his ears seemed to have shrunk. And his voice had the dullness I had remarked on the telephone, as if it were transmitted through a layer of material. He said I was looking well. I checked myself from reciprocating, and instead asked after Bella.

'She's talking to some old biddy who says she was Aggie's best friend here.' The language was that of the old Dodo, and it was painful to hear the vigorous words coming out in that dull voice. 'No need to ask about me, I've been ill. Better now though, or so the quacks say. Trouble with my gut, they've taken out yards of it.' I asked if he felt up to talking. 'Don't have much option, do I?

You said you've got a right to know things, perhaps you have. But not here.'

I said I was ready to go. We pushed our way towards the door, and Dodo waved to Bella, who joined us and gave me a smacking kiss on the cheek. At the door Justin and Gloria were saying goodbye to Peachey. Justin clasped a hand to his head.

'I said I'd take you back to your car. And of course I will.'

I said I was getting a lift from the Everards, and introduced them. 'You were an old friend of my father. I've heard your name,' Justin said. He looked surprised, wary, for once unsure of himself.

'Goodbye.' Gloria raised her veil and kissed me. 'I think there should have been singing. It should have been sad, happy and sad. But I have liked to meet you.'

'Come on.' Justin took her arm, said to me, 'I'll be in touch.'

'Splendid fellow, beautiful girl.' One or two curls had fallen over Peachey's forehead. He swept them back. 'Very good of you to come,' he said to Dodo and Bella, obviously with no idea who they were. Then he grasped my hand again in both his own. 'What can I say, Geoffrey? I shared her life for three wonderful months, but you were part of it from the beginning, her favourite nephew.'

'Her only nephew.'

'But always her favourite. I know, she told me. If there is anything you want, anything at all, it's yours.' His hand swept widely. I said I would be content with the family photograph, and a couple of framed theatre programmes. 'They are yours. I shall tell our good friend Mr Sparrowmate. And she mentioned papers, I shall see that everything is sent to you. Bless you.'

A few minutes later we were in a quiet café, Bella was pouring tea and saying it was lovely to see me again. She seemed almost unchanged, a little heavier, a little older, but recognisably the Bella who had worn the butcher's apron and stacked up guests' plates with food. Dodo shook his head when we asked if he would like a tea-cake, sipped his tea, and said if there were things I wanted to know, this was the time to say what they were. I told him about my visit to Newcastle, what Mrs Rackley had told me, and my conclusion that my father had an illegiti-mate son. When I had finished he shook his head.

'It doesn't sound like him.'

Bella was more emphatic. 'I don't believe a word of it. This Mrs Rackley was making it up.'

'I don't think so.' I said to him, 'You were at school with Father, weren't you? And you knew the family? Aggie told me their father believed in beating the devil out of children, and that if one of them was late home they missed tea or dinner. And she said Father was marvellous, looked after his brother and sister, took the blame for things they did. Is that right?'

'All true,' he said in that dead voice. 'Not that I saw much of them at home. It wasn't a house you'd want to go to, can't have been a comfortable place to grow up in.'

'So you knew him at school? And Cornelius too?' He nodded. 'What were they like?'

'Harry was what he grew up into, a good responsible boy.'

'And Cornelius?'

'Always in trouble, doing silly things. Harry must have been pleased when he went off to wherever it was. By that time I'd spent a few years in Canada doing this and that, then decided I'd had enough of it. Hard place to earn a living, Canada was then.'

'You never tried anywhere else?'

'No, one of our great colonies was enough for me. Wasn't easy back here either. I learned about antique furniture when I was trying to make a living as porter in a London auctioneer's.'

I asked Bella if she had known my father then. 'Lordy, no.' She wiped butter off her lip. 'I was brought up in Birmingham, my dad was a dustman, garbage collector as they say now. I did odd jobs, this and that, joined the ATS in the war, met Cy when it was over, he'd started up on his own and was just getting going. Never looked back, have we?' She put her plump hand over his thin one.

I went back to Dodo. 'You said what happened didn't sound like Father, and I think that too. There must be another explana-tion.' He said nothing. 'When did you get in touch with him again?'

'After I'd married Bella. That was in nineteen twenty-one. Then we met again when he was up in Yorkshire, came into my shop by chance.'

'And those names, Florence, Morgan, they don't mean anything to you?'

'No, except – I wouldn't take my oath on this, mind – but the Elders had servants. I don't mean lots of them, they didn't last long, old Silas would find fault with something or other and get rid of them. It's in my mind that one might have been called Florence.'

I told them Father had mentioned the name. 'I've been on the track of Morgan, but he's dead, walked out of a window drugged or drunk at a party. But someone rang me this morning.' I mentioned the woman on the telephone, my visit from the police, and their identification of the bones as Hugo's. Dodo sat staring at his teacup or at the tablecloth. Bella looked uncertainly from him to me, said nothing. Then Dodo spoke, the words more shocking because they were uttered in that monotone.

'What good do you think you're doing, why can't you let it go? Leave it alone for God's sake, whatever happened is over and done with.'

'It's not over and done with. The police think Father killed Hugo.'

He looked at me, eyes large in the parchment face. 'And if they do, what does it matter? It can't hurt him now.'

I said, only too conscious of sounding sanctimonious, that I had to find out the truth, and didn't believe Father was guilty of murder even though he might have had an illegitimate son. At that Dodo stood, rocking the cups and plates. Bella stood too, took his arm, but he shook her off. He said to me, quietly but emphatically, 'You're a damned young fool, Geoffrey Elder.' Then Bella, her voice shrill, cried, 'Why do you worry him like this, you must see he's not well.'

We said nothing more as we walked out to the café's car park. I got into my old Ford, they into a BMW. We both drove away.

At eight o'clock precisely the telephone rang, and the voice I had heard in the morning said, 'Okay, he'll see you, but you got to talk to me first. You know Villiers Street by Charing Cross Station? There's a pub called the Griffin, meet me tomorrow night there, seven thirty, saloon bar. I'll take you to him.' I asked again why the unnamed he couldn't come himself, but the telephone had been put down.

(iv) An Actor Involved with Reality

The next day it rained. I stayed in all day, brooding on what I might learn that evening, and wondering whether Aunt Aggie's papers might in fact contain something of interest. I rang Sparrowmate, who seemed surprised by my interest, but said Mr Peachey would have no objection to my collecting the papers if I wished. I found myself reluctant to face Peachey again, and asked him to post them. The day passed slowly. I contemplated calling Leila at her office, but decided against it. In the afternoon Justin rang. He said it had been good to see me, speaking with a note of warm sincerity I have learned to distrust from hearing it so often in the voices of producers and directors, the most unreliable people in the world. I asked after Gloria, and he said she was all you'd expect.

'We didn't have time to talk yesterday, but I'd like you to know I was serious about wanting you to join me. Let's not talk about money, but I can safely say you'd be making more than double whatever it is now. I need a right-hand man, someone I can trust, and there aren't many of them. I never put you wrong, did I? And I'm not putting you wrong now. If you row in with me I tell you, you won't regret it. All right, I can hear the silence saying no, but think about it. Another thing.'

'Yes?'

'That chap you were with, the one who looks like a mummy, Everard. Known him long?'

'Most of my life.'

'Is that right? I've heard things about him, that's all. Very sharp operator, friend of mine bought what was said to be some Louis Quinze furniture from him, paid an arm and a leg for it, had to sue when it turned out to be reproduction. Everard gave him a guarantee it was genuine, but my friend's house was burgled and a lot of stuff stolen, guarantee included. Funny coincidence.' I agreed it was funny, and he laughed. 'You're loyal, Geoff, it's a great quality. Give me a ring if and when.'

I don't know what sort of woman I had expected to meet in the pub, but not the obvious tart who came up to me in the saloon bar. She had hair that looked like brass, eyes loaded with make-up, a mini-skirt that ended halfway up her thighs, black stockings. Her age might have been anything between twenty-five and forty. She said, 'I'm Phyl. Mine's a large Scotch and water.' I got it for her, a glass of wine for myself. Her voice was hard and metallic as it had been on the telephone.

'Now then, you want to know what it's all about, right?'

'And how you got hold of whatever papers you're going to show me.'

She made an impatient gesture. 'Questions like that you'll have to ask Dermot. That's my feller.' I recalled Dermot as a name mentioned in the Dog and Compasses. 'You think I don't have a feller? I do, and you'll have to ask him stuff like that. What I'm telling you is there's a story here and it affects the family, yours I mean. We're selling it somewhere, and it can be to you.'

'I told you I'm not in the market. Anyway, I've got no money.'

'We're not unreasonable, payment could be on the instalment plan.' Her laugh was as harsh as her voice. 'Look, you want to know what it's all about.'

'You said that before.'

'Okay. I'll show you what Morgan knew.' She opened a large gaudy handbag, and took some papers from it. 'No point in snatching, they're xeroxed.'

'This is what Morgan was trying to sell to a publisher?'

244

'I don't know what he was selling. Morgan was a creep, only half there.'

One sheet was a copy of a birth certificate issued in Newcastle, saying that Edward Morgan Bentall had been born on the eighteenth of May, 1904, the son of Stephen James Bentall and Florence Williams. The father's occupation was given as cabinet maker, and his address as 9 Chapel Street, Newcastle. The other sheet was an affidavit given by Morgan before a solicitor, dated April 1936:

This statement is an account by me, Edward Morgan Elder, of the circumstances relating to my birth, as I have recently discovered them.

I was brought up in Newcastle by Mr and Mrs Rackley, and understood them to be my parents. I called them father and mother, and they never told me anything else, though I sometimes heard them discussing somebody they called Mr A. He paid them money, and they talked about what they would do when the payments stopped. I was only a child at the time, but understood them to be worried because Mr Rackley had business problems. Once or twice a gentleman came to visit, and talked to me, asking how I got on at school and what I wanted to do when I left. I now know him to have been Mr Harold Elder.

I discovered that Mr and Mrs Rackley were not my parents when I found a birth certificate in a drawer saying my name was Bentall. This was a shock to me, and I decided to leave home and look for a job. I also found in the drawer two snapshots, one with a note on the back saying 'S. J. Bentall', and the other saying 'Morgan's mother, Florence'. I took these with me, feeling they were my rightful property. Afterwards I did not use the name of Rackley, but called myself either Morgan Bentall or Edward Morgan.

Several years later I was working as a clerk at Stockport with the firm of Mortimer and Tatchell, and became friendly with a secretarial assistant named Ellen Price. I was using the name of Edward Morgan then, but one day I told her my name was not Morgan but Bentall, and showed her the snapshots. She recognised Florence Williams as a girl she had known at school, and told me that Florence had gone into service with a family named Elder. Florence said to her that she had become pregnant and was going to be married, although she did not name the father, saying this was a secret. Very soon afterwards Ellen Price left the neighbourhood, and did not see Florence again. Some time after this I saw a photograph of Mr Harold Elder in a newspaper, and at once recognised him as the 'Mr A' who had visited the Rackleys when I was a child.

I have suffered various misfortunes in my life, and have not been able to make a full investigation of all the circumstances of my parentage. There is no record at Somerset House of marriage between anybody named Elder and Florence Williams. So far as Stephen James Bentall is concerned, he was serving a prison sentence for robbery with violence from 1902 to 1905, so that he cannot have been my father. In 1910 his wife was convicted as an abortionist, and also went to prison.

It is my claim, based on the above circumstances, that I am the son of Mr Harold Elder, and I desire that fact to be openly and fully acknowledged. I have written to him on several occasions, but have received no satisfactory response. I therefore have no recourse but to make the matter public.

Edward Morgan Elder

I gave the papers back to her and said, 'Well?'

'Interested?'

'Not particularly. I know most of this already. I've seen Mrs Rackley, and she told me about Morgan. He doesn't mention here that when he left their home he stole their savings. Or that he's been in prison himself. And Mrs Rackley showed me a photograph of the person she called Mr A.'

'It was your father?'

'Yes. But that doesn't prove Morgan was his son. Even if he was, Morgan's dead and so is my father. If your friend Dermot thinks I'm going to pay for information like this, he's not the clever fellow you take him for, and you should find another boy friend.'

If you load your face with enough make-up it can serve as a disguise. I had no idea what she was thinking when she spoke. 'I said this was what Morgan knew, I didn't say it was all there was, it's only a beginning.' She snapped her bag shut. 'Dermot told me not to make any threats.'

'Very good of him. I said before, I'm not in the buying market.'

'You talk to him, he'll tell you the rest of it.' She stared at me, then took my arm. I got a whiff of scent, and felt her hard body.

As she marched me out of the pub, up Villiers Street, and into the tangle of small streets on the other side of the Strand, I caught a whiff of something else, a whiff of danger. Bad writing this perhaps, the scent's whiff being literal and that of danger metaphorical, but I leave it because there is also something tangible about danger's whiff. Something more than mere feeling is involved in one's awareness of it, a physical reaction which results in a sharpening of the senses. Hearing is more acute, touch enhanced so that rough cloth has the harshness of wire, heat and cold assault the body. After we had crossed the Strand and moved into the side streets Phyl released my arm, so that nothing stopped me from turning and leaving her. Yet in fact this was impossible, even though I dreaded what I might learn from Dermot. I was drawn by the attraction of the rabbit to the snake, or if that is too self-denigratory, by the fascination and fear of the unknown.

I asked if she knew exactly what had happened to Morgan, and she said he'd been high as a kite at a party, and fallen from a window.

'Sharkey seemed to think something different.'

'You know Sharkey?' She stopped. A nearby street light turned her face mauve. 'You never told me. Did you tell him you were meeting me?'

'Of course not. I saw him a few days ago. He thought Morgan had been thrown out of that window, not fallen. Would that have been to get hold of the papers you showed me? Or to get rid of him?'

She didn't answer this. 'He's mad, that Sharkey. I used to go with him. I'm a South Londoner, where we're going's my business address. You knew I was a business girl?'

247

'I guessed.'

'You *guessed*.' She laughed. 'But Sharkey never treated me right, used to beat me up. I wouldnta minded if I'd done something, but it was for nothing. Dermot's different.'

'I'm glad to hear it.'

We had begun walking again, and now were in a street so narrow it was almost an alley. She stopped by a Chinese restaurant with a placard in the window saying, 'Canton cooking. Takeaway,' and put a key in the green door next to it.

A room on the first floor was done out in pink. There were frilled pink curtains, a matching frilled dressing table, a heavy pile off-pink carpet, wicker chairs with pink covers, a large double bed with a pink satin quilt. A ceiling mirror reflected the bed. A man sat in one of the wicker chairs with a glass in his hand and a bottle of bourbon on a glass-topped table in front of him. He was in his twenties, dark, curly-haired, with an easy smile. He got up, came across the room, shook hands.

'Dermot O'Rourke. Good of you to come, Mr Elder. Phyl, you can find something to do while we're having our chat, can't you?'

'I can sit in the bleeding kitchen, if that's what you mean, but I don't know why I should.'

'No more do I, darling, we'll leave it to Mr Elder. Though I have to tell you that if she sits in the kitchen she can still hear every word.' I said she could stay in the bedroom, and she sat on the bed. As Dermot poured bourbon for us both, and freshened his own glass, I recognised him as a stage Irishman. I mean by this not only that he was the kind of Irishman often played on the stage, glib, good-looking and unreliable, but also that he was the sort who seems to be playing a national rôle for all and more than it is worth. And within a couple of minutes of talking to him I realised also that he was a crook.

I don't have a wide knowledge of criminals, but there is a particular kind of deceiving and self-deceiving conman familiar to me both from journalism and show business, where the type exists in large numbers. They may be trying to sell you a story (when I was on the *Record* a man produced a lot of superficially

248

convincing evidence that he had been a go-between carrying messages from Churchill to Hitler about a peace settlement, not after but before the fall of France in 1940), or a metaphorical gold brick, like a man who tried to dispose of the rights to several million acres in Arizona to an actor much more successful than me, producing in support a mass of documents in Spanish alleged to go back to the seventeenth century. Neither of these conmen had much chance of success, even though they had prepared their materials carefully, but I'm not sure that success was their prime object. Of course they wanted money, but along with that they were trying to sell themselves, their personalities. I recognised Dermot O'Rourke as one of the same breed as he told me his story about Morgan and Basher Bentall and Hugo, his manner confiding, easy, yet to me quite evidently deceitful.

While he talked I remembered I had heard the name O'Rourke mentioned long ago by the farmer in Seasalter, as a friend of Basher Bentall, and that Sharkey had cursed the name of Dermot. Put the two together – but Dermot was talking now about his father Rory. I paid attention, but was aware also of Phyllis at the dressing table, and something, an awkwardness perhaps in the way a pink-nailed hand was raised to pat hair into place, made me realise that Phyl was not a woman but a man.

His father, Dermot O'Rourke said, had spent much time in Australia in the years before World War I. (He paused, waiting apparently for a comment I didn't make.) He had been a salesman, at first for electrical equipment, then a space salesman for a newspaper group. When the war came he joined up, came to Europe, and afterwards got a job as space salesman for a London paper, and settled down. I interrupted, asked if Dermot was his son.

'Sure I am, not the first but the last fruit of his loins. He was a lovely feller, my da, a real Irish Aussie Englishman, had two wives and five children, neglected 'em all and we loved him for it. And a bit of a poet too in his spare time, which is how he met your friend the great poet Hugo Headley. And gave him some valuable information in the course of one of those drinking sessions the old man favoured. It was after one of them that he

passed away a few years back, the way he'd have wished to go.'
Again he seemed to invite a comment, but what did he expect
me to say? And why did he seem pleased that I failed to respond,
why did he give me one of his charming, untrustworthy smiles?
'Don't let me be making my da out a villain, he was honest as a
summer day, if he had a fault it was he never kept an eye on the
main chance. Not like his son, you'll be saying, and you'd be
right. And right too in saying I'm talking all round the houses
and not getting to the point, which I will here and now.
    'I told you me da's part in the Great War, fighting for the
Empire like a good Imperial Irishman. It was in the trenches, he
told me, he met Basher Bentall, and some time then or later the
Basher told him a tale he'd had from his mother about a
gentleman and his wife coming to stay with her, along with a
baby they wanted to put out for adoption. Now that was
Morgan, and you've read what he had to say, which was nothing
that interested anybody much but himself, though being
Morgan and just a little bit less than half-witted, he thought
different. But what Basher's mother did, Morgan never knew
that. I'll be bold enough to say you don't know it either.' He
cocked an inquisitive eyebrow. 'Basher's old mum told him how
this lady and gent lodging with her had a great row over the baby.
Seems she'd changed her mind about the adoption, wanted to
keep the baby. They had a fight, and that was the end of her. She
was kaput, finito, a dead duck. He killed her. Didn't mean to, I
dare say, but that's a kind of thing it's hard to prove. So you can
see the gent was in a spot, shadow of the gallows looming you
might say. But luckily for him Ma Bentall was a woman of
resource. She had a back garden and she had a spade, maybe two
spades, and there either the gent or Ma Bentall or more likely
both of them dug a hole, and put the lady in it. Mrs B didn't know
the name of either husband or wife, man or woman I should say,
and naturally the gent preferred to remain anonymous. But
that's what happened, take it from me.'
    My voice sounded strange in my ears as I said he had no proof
of anything he was saying, and that Mrs Bentall had been jailed
as an abortionist.
    'So she was. But as to proof, I'll tell you something, the street

where she lived in Newcastle, Chapel Street, that's not so much changed. Oh, the little houses have got baths and that, or some of them have, but it's still the sort of street you wouldn't want to live in, me neither, and as for Phyl she'd hate it, being a girl with ambition, isn't that right, darling?'

Phyl, whom I now thought of as Phil, shifted on the bed and said lovingly, 'You bastard.'

'But you were asking about proof. That strip of backyard they called a garden is still there. It could be dug up, and I guess you wouldn't have to dig very deep. Are you a betting man, Mr Elder? Would you like to bet it doesn't contain the bones of poor little Florence? And the gent who brought Florence and her baby to Ma Bentall and then planted the babe on the Rackleys, you know who that was, don't you? None other than your revered father, Mr Harold Elder.'

This last passage was said with a jocosity I have indicated, but along with it a contemptuous note that rippled with vicious feeling. And beside the jocosity, the contempt, and the tacit announcement of his own cleverness asserted by occasional glances at Phil or Phyl on the bed there was still something more, a wariness that contained a hint of uncertainty, as if he was playing a high trump but did not know whether or not I held the ace in my hand.

'Now we come to your friend Hugo, if I may call him that. I never met the gent, he was before my time, but from what I've heard he was a clever man, could put two and two together and when they made four he smelt money. You could say the whole fandango was like a jigsaw puzzle. Morgan held one of the pieces, Basher Bentall had some others, and Hugo found out some more from the lady who brought Morgan up, but it was my da who had what you might call the key piece, and in his good Irish innocence passed it on to Hugo. And then – bingo.' He snapped his fingers. I said I didn't know what he meant. 'Why did nobody miss Florence, that's what I mean.'

I became impatient. The pink room, the figure lolling on the bed, the smell of sex or drugs or both, disquieted and mildly disgusted me. I said I couldn't imagine why he had told me all this, or what he thought he could threaten me with. As I spoke I became angrier, and said he could peddle his story where he liked, nobody would be interested.

He held up a hand. 'Hold on now, hold on, no need for hard words. You wouldn't like it, would you, if it was said in print that your daddy had the best of reasons for wishing Mr Headley in a watery grave. I have one or two connections with the filth in a business kind of way, and they'd be interested in what I could tell them. I'm guessing you sure as hell wouldn't like that and there's no need for it. I'm suggesting to you we shouldn't use hard words about blackmail or threats about what might appear in the papers, but sit down like two reasonable men and talk about what you might call a small monthly retainer, something you wouldn't miss, something like what Basher Bentall had every month, regular as clockwork till he got greedy—'

I'm not sure at what moment I was aware of a sound down below, at first no more than a background of gentle thudding, that suddenly changed into a crash, followed by shouts, shouts that brought O'Rourke off his chair, and made Phyl sit bolt upright on the bed and scream to him, 'Get in the kitchen.' Then the door opened and shaven-headed Sharkey seemed to occupy the whole space of the door frame, his eyes red-rimmed and mad. Behind him was the man who had told me to get out of the pub. A revolver looked like a toy in one of Sharkey's great hands.

O'Rourke backed towards the kitchen door. 'Now, Billy,' he said, 'let's talk, Billy.'

'You killed Morgy,' Sharkey cried in his odd treble. 'You helped him out the window, then you steal my cunt.' He raised the revolver and shot O'Rourke between the eyes. Phyl screamed and screamed. Sharkey dropped the revolver, caught hold of her round the neck. His back was towards me and I jumped on to him, trying to pull him off. I heard a movement behind me, then felt as if I had hit my head against a wall or a cupboard.

I woke up in hospital.

252

(v) The Last Word in the Story

Accounts of time spent in hospital, or the ones I have read in books, are all similar and almost all boring. Everybody surrounding the patient is immensely cheerful, doctors and nurses smile, one is no longer a person but a thing, to be lifted out of bed and trundled along to the X-ray room, then back again, a thing pushed and pulled and prodded, fed through tubes, discussed as a non-person with the tolerance the hale, hearty and knowledgeable can afford to feel for the thing in the bed who is manifestly none of these things. I can't skip hospital altogether, however, because it was there I read the last word in the story, a word with the unmistakable stamp of truth.

Let me get the facts of what happened in the pink frilled bedroom out of the way first. O'Rourke was dead, Sharkey in prison charged with his murder. He and his sidekick had made so much noise bashing down the door that the police were there very quickly, in time to save Philip Wootton, the transvestite cause of their dissension, from anything worse than a bruised neck. Sharkey's sidekick Randy Richards was also in prison, charged with causing grievous bodily harm. I had been the object of this g.b.h., which consisted of hitting me on the head with a cosh when I jumped on Sharkey's back, and kicking and beating me about the kidneys as I lay on the ground. In consequence I pissed blood painfully for some time, and one of my kidneys suffered permanent damage, though the other functions well enough.

I thought about that bedroom scene a lot during my days in hospital. To be involved with actual violence is particularly strange for an actor who must inevitably be concerned with it in the course of some parts he plays, and my glimpse of the actuality showed something much drabber, quicker, more humdrum than it seems in police dramas. In my case it was all over in a minute or two. At one moment O'Rourke had been talking to me in his stage Irish way, and then, bang, he was dead. I had had no time to be frightened, or to be aware of reality. If I had been given a minute or so for reflection, I doubt if I should have jumped on Sharkey's back. As I played the scene over and over I was fascinated by the unreality, untidiness, absurdity of it. How ridiculous to be hit on the head and kicked while trying to protect a transvestite from being throttled by his ponce. I must have been out of my mind. Does participation in the real involve being out of one's mind?

There were visitors, Leila first among them, bringing flowers and fruit, rightly praising the doctors and nurses, and never once saying she had told me something not very nice would happen if I pursued my obsession with my father. Her presence was motherly, loverly, soothing as syrup. For a day or two I was disinclined to talk, and during the whole of one evening she held my hand without speaking. When I was a little better she said, 'Everything's under control, nothing to worry about, I'm back.'

'What about Ratty?'

'That was a mistake. She takes cocaine, she and her friends, they call it nose powder. Then they have parties, and things get quite out of control. I don't like things out of control, do you? Of course I think everybody should be free to do what they want, but they shouldn't want to do wrong things. Not if they're intelligent, and Ratty is. I agree with her ideas, you see, but I don't like it when she acts on them.'

'I could listen to you for ever.'

'You're making fun of me, but it's true. I mean, students should be able to do what they like, but that still means they have to work. We're free not to get married, but we have to behave as if we were.'

Other visitors came, some of them surprising. The Canon arrived one day, together with Olivia. He brought chocolates, and a book about the spread of Flower Power in the Far East, and told me he had been invited to give a series of talks in California about Weflap. Olivia looked at me with her habitual air of disapproval. 'You've got your own room.' I told her I subscribed to a private health scheme. 'The story I read in one paper said you were trying to protect a male prostitute, is that true?' I said it was, but he was in drag. 'I should have thought you could find better ways to spend your time. But Leila had left you.'

I could not bring myself to the effort of explanation, and said only, 'She's back now.'

Olivia said so she understood. I closed my eyes. The Canon said they mustn't tire me, and urged me to read the Flower Power book. I gave it to one of the nurses.

Other visitors: showbiz people who had seen the newspaper stories under headlines like 'Actor Attacked in Soho Killing', most of them as inaccurate as the heading that called Seven Dials Soho. Some of them inevitably implied what Olivia suspected, that I was in the pink bedroom for sexual purposes. Leila had never mentioned such a possibility, and I admired more than ever her monumental tranquillity.

Other visitors: the police. First of all a sergeant from Tottenham Court Road, who asked exactly what had happened, and seemed to think the whole thing was run-of-the-mill. Then, a couple of days later, my friends Herr Professor the Chief Inspector and his Sergeant. Herr Professor didn't waste time. He said he'd been told I was well enough to answer questions, and stepped in with both feet. Why had I been in the apartment, along with a known male prostitute? The Sergeant intervened to say, with barely concealed amusement, that they felt sure it hadn't been for pleasure. The Professor waved him down.

'No need for that. Mr Everard told us you were making a sort of private investigation, hoping to find out something more about your father's connection with Headley's death, right? I told you before I like to put my cards on the table, and I'll do it now. Our interest in O'Rourke's death is because of your connection with it, and some notes found in his apartment. O'Rourke is the name he was born with all right, though he used half-a-dozen others, and he had a string of convictions long as your arm for extortion, blackmail, false pretences, living off immoral earnings. We'd like to know what he was trying on you, some sort of blackmail? If so, what was the threat?'

'He said he would be able to expose my father as Headley's murderer, and the story would appear in the press.'

'What sort of proofs did he offer?'

I had no intention of telling them about Florence and the body possibly buried in the Chapel Street garden, and said O'Rourke had been shot before he could offer any proofs, though he'd told me that his father had known something vitally important, and had met Headley. I said also that he had asked for a monthly retainer, like that paid to a man named Bentall.

'Who got it from your father?'

'He didn't say that.'

'All right. I hope you're being straight with me, Mr Elder, as I am with you.' He said to the Sergeant, 'Tell him what we found in O'Rourke's rooms.'

The Sergeant went into his machine-on-automatic-pilot act. 'Papers belonging to Edward Morgan, claiming to be the son of Harold Elder.'

I interrupted to say I'd seen them, and asked if they had any further information about Morgan's death. It was the Sergeant who responded.

'Fell out of window at drugs party or may have been pushed by O'Rourke. Also in O'Rourke's possession list of names, Justin Elder, Geoffrey Elder, Cyrus Everard, Agatha Elder, question marks against all. Name of Florence Williams with "Friends?" put against it. Catalogue from Seven Seas Shipping Line plus note in O'Rourke's hand saying "Used to be Five Continents Line".' He moved into ordinary speech. 'Change from Five Continents to Seven Seas made in 1920. Any of that mean anything to you?' I shook my head. He resumed. 'Little map or chart, showing arrows leading to name of Headley. Arrows have got names attached to them, O'Rourke, Bentall, Morgan with Rackley in brackets. Under that, note saying "Headley in touch with all, found out the whole thing, Elder killed him."'

The automatic pilot cut out. The Chief Inspector cocked an eyebrow, the Professor interrogating a pupil. I said it didn't make much sense to me, although O'Rourke had told me different people knew parts of the story, and that Headley knew the whole of it after meeting O'Rourke's father. I pointed out, however, that the map or chart in itself proved nothing at all. The Professor nodded approvingly.

'Precisely. And unfortunately we can't talk to O'Rourke. What we do have, though, is his positive statement that Headley found out what he calls "the whole thing", and your father killed him. And it seems a fair presumption that those question marks put against the names of three family members and your father's close friend meant he was proposing to put the black on them all.'

I shook my head in irritation. 'He was stupid, if he thought that. I've got no money to spare, my aunt wasn't rich, Justin hated my father and would have been delighted to see his sins find him out, and I'd guess Everard would have reported any blackmail attempt to the police straight away. You may be right, he was certainly hoping to blackmail me, but if that was his idea he was stupid.'

A wintry professional smile. 'What should we do if the crooks were as clever as you and me? I've had years of knowing the way a man like O'Rourke thinks, and I'd lay odds I'm right. As long as *you're* not keeping some cards under the table.' I shook my head. 'All right then, I came to give you a bit of reassurance too. When we met last I told you I was going to find out all the facts about Headley, but O'Rourke's death changes things. There's no factual proof as you say, the file stays open, but that note O'Rourke made for his own information, not trying to kid anybody, saying your father killed Headley, is a clincher for me. It may be there's more to be found out, but we do have other things on our plates more urgent than a thirty-year-old murder. There's less doubt than ever in my mind that your father killed Headley, but until something turns up to prove or disprove it, we shall let the case lie.'

He nodded. The Sergeant said, 'And stay clear of those boys that look like girls.' Then they went, and I returned to brooding on the scene in the bedroom. Their visit brought it all back again, the fear on O'Rourke's face, his surprised look as a hole appeared in his forehead, his body slowly falling back against the kitchen door, the mad look in Sharkey's pale red-rimmed eyes, what seemed my slow-motion jump on to his back, the blow at the back of my head. And then in imagination I created things I could not have seen, the penis-shaped cosh as it landed on my skull, cords standing out on Phyl's neck, the eyes starting out and a dribble of saliva coming from the mouth so that the lipstick ran, the well-polished brown boots that kicked me relentlessly, sweat on Sharkey's face as he squeezed . . .

When Leila came that evening I told her of the Chief Inspector's visit, and his phrase about letting the case lie. I've said already that she had been a marvel of tact, but this was too much for her. 'You'll give it up now, won't you?' I said I supposed so. 'I mean, it's caused you nothing but worry and pain, and what have you learned?'

'One or two things. Those notes to Hugo mentioning M, which Duffy thought stood for Melissa, obviously referred to Morgan. Hugo had found out about Morgan, I discovered that in Newcastle.'

'I don't see it matters much.' I said it did to me. 'But you will give it up? I don't think I can go on if you don't.'

I said I'd give it up, and almost immediately began to feel much better, not only physically but emotionally. This was followed by a relapse. I was tormented by a feeling that I was betraying my father's trust, and in confused waking dreams he reproached me for failure to understand him. My temperature went up, I became delirious. I shall tell you the reason why I did it, he said, and then his features melted into Sharkey's, the two blending into a graven-faced sweating lipsticked visage that said something incomprehensible, so that I woke up screaming (if I was asleep, for I had the sensation of wakefulness), and had to be sedated.

Three days later I was recovering, although still suffering nightmares from which I woke to find the sheets drenched with sweat. I was unable to read for long, and fell into brief unsatisfactory daytime dozes. It was then that Leila brought me the bundle of papers sent by Mr Sparrowmate, in the hope that they would engage my interest. She was right. They acted like one of the tonics that doctors never nowadays prescribe for their patients. My inability to take interest in what I read vanished, my temperature dropped to normal. I set about sorting the papers and letters into groups, wondering as I did so at the variety and vividness of Aunt Aggie's life, and comparing it with the placid dullness of my own. Seeing somebody shot and being hit on the head might be called exciting, but it did not seem so at the time. Perhaps exciting things are always those that happen to other people.

Most of the papers were concerned with Aggie's career as an actress. There were dozens of letters from fans praising her performances, asking for photographs, saying they would like to meet her. A small group in a separate envelope came from people well-known in the years between the wars, including politicians and names I vaguely recognised as social lions and lionesses of the past. There was a clutch of letters that testified to the number of Aggie's love affairs, although of course everything relating to Hugo had been taken by biographer Duffy. And there were the letters from the Cissy she had mentioned as her only close friend in Plashet, and the only one tolerated by her father Silas.

There were twenty letters from Cissy, some undated, and it took me a little while to sort them into their probable sequence. They were written in a breathlessly enthusiastic style, and were mostly about the boredom of life in Plashet and Cissy's desire to join her friend in London. The ones that concern this narrative were a group that, along with accounts of dances, concerts and musical evenings, dealt with visits to the Elder home. I had assumed that the family lived above the shop, revealing my own ignorance of the position occupied in Edwardian days by a prosperous tradesman who was a pillar of local society. The family home was called The Hollies, and was evidently a good substantial house. The letters made it plain that Cissy's chief interest at the time was boys, and also that she was attracted by my father, whom she called Handsome Harry. She had names for them all. Silas was the King, his wife the Lady, Cornelius Cheerful Corny. Here are the extracts that concerned me.

5 January 1904

. . . went to The Hollies for supper, all *very* gloomy, something funny in the air. Not *all* gloomy actually, the King as usual, pulled my hair, said I was growing up, did I ever think

259

about boys? Do I *ever*, I'm nineteen, what does he imagine? But he was jolly for the King, especially when we had a sing-song. You should have heard him singing 'Father, dear father, come home with me now', and then 'England's Heart'. But the others! Lady was just very quiet, took me aside and said if I was writing send love to you – which I do, and *wish* I was there to see the lights of London – don't dare to mention you when the King's there. Thought Lady was rather miz – missing you perhaps, ha ha – and as I've said already, the others! Handsome H, well you know he's my ideal Strong Silent Man, but last night he nearly snapped my head off when I said I might go to stay with you in London and asked if he might come down. Told me not to be a silly little girl, his home and mine were here. Little girl – me! Even Cheerful C was grumpy, hardly said a word to me all night . . .

22 January

. . . met Handsome Harry in the street and he was *very nice*, said he was sorry about being snappy last time I was at the Hollies, had things on his mind. Told him I *quite under-stood*, I often had things on my mind too, and was very upset about Kaffirs being badly treated by Boers which there's a lot about in the papers, but he said he didn't mean anything like that, it was personal, and he hoped he might be offered a job in London, wouldn't it be heavenly darling A if he came down to live with you, and I was there too! I think perhaps I love him, he's so romantic, but he is *very* serious and you know me darling, I'm a flibbergibber (can't spell it, you know what I mean.) But does that matter??? . . .

February 1904

. . . you remember Jennie Green, tall thin girl with a funny nose? She's working at Tibbetts the dress shop now, I was in there, you've no idea of the prices but I suppose in London it's worse, and what do you think? She says Florence, your Florence, the one at The Hollies, is in the family way . . .

3 March 1904

. . . went round to the H, stayed to supper, almost invited

myself, don't think I was wanted, all gloomy again, can't bear it, I like people to *look* cheerful even if they aren't. The King especially had his lower lip going in and out in that way it does when he's cross, as if he's going to have a fit. I said I could see he was upset about something, and he caught hold of me and squeezed me so tight I almost cried out. 'Not with you,' he said, 'not with you.' Had a good look at Florence, seemed to me she was thicker round the waist but really couldn't tell, should have thought the King would have given her marching orders if it was true. Do you hear from H or C, have they said anything about it? . . .

12 March

. . . It's true!! And there's been the most awful schemossle (spelling?) at the Hollies, all shouting and screaming, and H and C are going to leave, H *will* be going to London and Cheerful C off to the Colonies. Perhaps you've heard?? How I know this is I went to a dance last night and a boy who's a friend of Cheerful C, Peter Pilley, you might remember him, head shaped like a cottage loaf but quite nice, though *of course* nothing like Handsome H, he told me. Cheerful C had told *him*, though a secret. Florence is still there at work!! And Peter says her father Joseph, strong union man, says whoever it is must marry her. So Peter says. Isn't it dramatic, *have* you heard about it? Can't wait to know who's the father . . .

18 March

. . . Very beastly of you to say you don't *really* know anything, what does that mean? I know you're still in trouble with the King because of running off, but either you know or you don't, and if you do I think it's mean not to say. And then to go on about petty provincial scandalmongering that doesn't interest you, my word it's funny how soon London changes people and makes them so stuck up, you *used* to be interested and I *used* to be your best friend, but I'm going to find out anyway and I'll tell you when I do, and I bet you *will* be interested . . .

22 April

... No reply to my last, haven't heard now for over a month, suppose you're cross with your Cissy or too busy with London Life, never mind, *I'm* still writing to *you*. I told you I'd find out about Florence and I have. Us provincials, when we want to find out something we *do*. Florence has left, they've got another maid now named Edie, face like the back of a bus. And it *is* true H and C are both going, H has a job in London, C off to Australia. I went round to tea yesterday, only Lady there, she told me about them, said it was time they branched out and made their way in the world, but then she cried and said all her children would have gone. I asked her what the King felt, and she said he was angry, thought it was the duty of the boys to go into the business when he retired. I thought she looked ill, the Lady. She said she never hears from you, and if I wrote send love, and she hoped one day the King would forgive you for running off as you had ...

... But now the news that will shock you as it did me, I still haven't got over it. You know my family still go in for evenings of poetry readings, Father says it's a fine old custom, a pity it's dying out, I think it's mostly because he fancies himself as a reciter. We had one on Thursday and invited your family, but only the King and HH came. The King read something by Alfred Austin, but HH wouldn't read, you know he's shy in some ways. I noticed he and the King were avoiding each other, and when we had the interval for high tea (made sure I sat next to him) I asked why, and he said the King didn't want him and CC to leave home. Then I cornered him afterwards in the conservatory, and said straight out, was it really about Florence? He asked why I thought that, and I said everyone was talking, and a lot of them were saying the King might be the father. Which is true, and people are saying too he's sent Florence off somewhere to have the baby. So then he looked at me directly in the way he does (makes me melt inside), and said that wasn't true. Then he said after he went to London he'd never come back to Plashet again. 'So you may as well know the truth. When it is born I shall be the father of that child.' I don't know what I answered, stammered something about keeping his secret and he didn't answer, just made a kind of little bow and left me ...

Aggie must have answered that letter with some more scathing remarks about scandalmongering, because there was only one more, in which Cissy said she'd not told anybody, she wasn't a gossip, and she'd done nothing to deserve the horrid things Aggie had said, and wouldn't write again.

For me those letters were the end of the story. I had begun my research (if I can dignify it by that name), on the surface because of indignation at the idea that Father had had an affair with Melissa, but really moved by a desire to know him, and to atone for my failure to return his unexpressed love for me. And what had I found out? The words he had spoken long ago to a silly curious girl in an Edwardian conservatory seemed to set the seal on the portrait of him. He had fathered an illegitimate child, possibly killed the mother, suffered blackmail by more than one person who knew of this, killed the most importunate blackmailer, Hugo Headley. Perhaps he had also been responsible for the death of Basher Bentall. I was not certain of this, and some details of Hugo's death remained obscure to me, but I no longer wished to know them. I was surprised to find that love for my father was unaffected by learning that he had become a murderer, but with that knowledge the quest was over.

Postscript by Julian Symons:

Reflections of an Armchair Detective

There were times when Sherlock Holmes played the armchair detective, solving a crime by a fresh interpretation of the given facts without leaving his rooms in Baker Street. In this he emulated Poe's Dupin, who solved the mystery of Marie Roget through deductions made from newspaper accounts of her death. Something similar seemed to me possible after I had finished reading Geoffrey Elder's story from which, as I said at the beginning, I have removed some personal reflections, but nothing related to his investigation of Hugo Headley's disappearance. His discoveries can lead to a very different conclusion from the one he reached. I wish he were in my study now, so that we could talk about it.

I should say something first of all about the other people in the story. Geoffrey's account was written, it should be remembered, in the Sixties. He died in 1979, and several of the people mentioned in the manuscript had predeceased him. In 1970 he attended the funeral of Dodo Everard, whose death's-head appearance as described in the manuscript had been caused by bowel cancer. Bella survived her husband only by a couple of years. Neil Paton died on the golf course in the early Seventies, suffering a heart attack after doing a hole in one. There is no mention in Geoffrey's papers that he ever saw Melissa again, but she survives and indeed flourishes, having extended her dog-breeding activities from St Bernards to Labradors and wolfhounds. She has appeared on TV in a series of programmes called 'Training Large Dogs'. Stout, firm-jawed, essentially doggy in appearance, she no longer shows any resemblance to the girl at Clempstone.

Norma kept up a correspondence with Geoffrey and came to his memorial service, which I also attended. We talked a little, and she told me that Hal had both loved and admired his son, though he had found it difficult to say so. At the time this meant little to me, for Geoffrey had hardly mentioned his father, and I had not then looked at his manuscript. After reading it I wrote to her, and learned that she had left her sister and opened an art gallery at Castle Cary in Somerset, where she sold Victorian watercolours and small landscapes. She had got rid of all the Prattertons which, she told me, were Hal's taste rather than her own.

At the memorial service I also met Justin, who surprised me by saying Geoffrey had always spoken of me as one of his closest friends. Again, as with Norma, I knew nothing of Justin, and was amused by the accuracy with which Geoffrey described him when I read the memoir, although his view was more generous than mine would have been. I should have put Justin down as a red-faced overweight rich businessman. However, he was very friendly, and before driving away in perhaps the same Rolls in which he attended Aunt Aggie's funeral, said we must have lunch one day. He was as good as his word, taking me a week later to the Savoy Grill.

There, attacking his steak as if it were a business enemy, he told me about his mother being put in a loony bin by the old b. He turned to Geoffrey while savouring the Mouton Cadet, and telling me how good it was.

'I was fond of him, y'know, though I'm not sure he ever believed it. Blood thicker than water, that kind of thing. He was a fool to himself, you know that? I wanted to take him in the organisation, he'd have had a wonderful life, travelled round the world, had a decent place in London and an apartment in Brussels, but what did he do? Stayed in his poky little Pimlico dump with that great slug of a Leila. Ever go there?' He snorted when I said it was a nice comfortably run-down flat, and perhaps Geoffrey had preferred that kind of place and that kind of life. 'Like saying you'd prefer a slum to Park Lane, I don't understand things like that. He had some queer ideas, Geoff, fixated about his father. Our father, I should say, though I never had any cause to say thank you to the old b. I've told you what he did to my mother.'

'But Geoffrey liked him?'

'Not sure that's the word. Geoff, you know, he wanted to love somebody, and his bitch of a mother wasn't a candidate, so he

265

tried to love his dad. Ever meet his mother, Deirdre? You didn't miss much, though she was a wonderful looker. Couldn't keep off men, they were like dope to her. She's dead now, ran out of stallions and died of a broken heart. And his dad was a cold fish. A cold fish disguised as a stuffed shirt. Am I shocking you?' His laugh showed some splendid bridgework.

What was the reason for this excellent lunch? A writer of crime stories assumes there must be reasons for such hospitality to a stranger, just as he believes every problem must have a rational answer. Sure enough, a reason emerged with the brandy, when Justin asked casually whether Geoffrey had ever told me he was writing something about Hugo Headley's disappearance. As I've said, I had done no more than glance at the manuscript, and replied only that Geoffrey had once said something about making an amateur detective's investigation.

'You don't know what he found out, if anything? He never mentioned writing something about it to you? Thought he might have done, as you're a specialist in that sort of stuff.' Justin's description of my writing was the reverse of persuasive, and I said I knew nothing about it. He went on rather brusquely, 'Geoff told me he'd written a lot of stuff, and might show it to you in case you could make something out of it. Publish it, I suppose he meant. I wouldn't like that.'

I told him Geoffrey had left me a manuscript, but I hadn't looked at it. I don't think he believed me.

'There might be things in it that reflected on the family. I didn't like the old b, or most of the others, but I've got a reputation. I'm looking for a K in the next Honours List, or maybe the one after, and I've heard tales about the old b and Headley I wouldn't want to see in print.'

I refrained from laughter, and told him I would get in touch with him in what seemed then the unlikely event that I wanted to put any of Geoffrey's story in print. I looked at the Honours List for the next two, three, four years, but Justin never got his K, or so far as I know any other acknowledgement of what would I suppose have been called service to British business, or something of the kind. I never heard from him again. He died in 1985, and received an obituary in *The Times* which said he was the image of a self-made man, and was thought by some to exemplify what Mr Heath meant when he spoke of the unacceptable face of capitalism.

And now, with the fates of the characters disposed of, I am firmly settled in my armchair, trying to decide what happened to Hugo Headley.

First of all I set myself to discover the meaning of that little drawing O'Rourke had made, in which he said Headley had known the whole story, and been killed for trying to use his knowledge. What had Headley learned from the others? And why was the whole apparently so much more than the sum of its parts?

Morgan had known, or believed, that he was Harold Elder's son. He knew nothing more, and only somebody as stupid as Morgan would have thought the knowledge of any value.

Bentall had learned from his mother the story of Florence's murder and burial. Equipped with this knowledge he was able to blackmail somebody into paying him a small monthly income, and there was a strong presumption that the somebody was Harold Elder. But when Bentall met O'Rourke senior he found out something more, something that as he told Bellinger meant he was coming into a fortune. What was it?

O'Rourke senior had this information, which he gave to Hugo and later to Bentall. Why had it not meant a fortune for him too? Perhaps because he was an honest man who passed on the information without realising its importance, but it was possible also that what he knew was only meaningful in combination with what Hugo, and later Bentall, had already learned. Bentall had told the farmer that the fortune he was coming into had nothing to do with his small monthly income. This must mean, then, that there were *two* subjects for blackmail, not one. And it was this second subject, the one being asked for the 'fortune', who had paid a visit to Bentall's caravan, bringing a bottle of Château Fantin-Latour, and disposed of the threat. Hugo clearly knew the same secret. Was O'Rourke junior right in his statement: 'Elder killed him'?

Having got so far with conjecture I cast back to Cissy's letters, and the identity of the man who made Florence pregnant.

Geoffrey had accepted what his father said to Cissy as unquestionably true, but that was by no means certain. Aggie had stressed to her nephew that Harold was held responsible for the behaviour of his brother and sister, and readily accepted such responsibility. It was obvious from her letters that Cissy would not have rested until she had been given a name for the prospective father. Realising this, and knowing that he was leaving the district for London and had, as he said, no intention of coming back, it was quite in character that Harold would have acknowledged prospective paternity, whoever the father might have been. Since it was almost certainly somebody at The Hollies, the possibilities were Silas, Harold and Cornelius. Silas, in spite of his semi-amorous approaches to Cissy, was ruled out by the fact that Mrs Bentall had told her son Florence's husband was young. Could it have been Cornelius?

Once thought of, he was obviously the most likely candidate. What was it Aggie had said? Corny did silly things, Harry was the dutiful one, accepted responsibility, took the blame. And then Florence had said she was going to be married, yet had agreed to have her baby given to foster parents, and in fact hadn't got married. If Harold was the father this seemed to make no sense, but if it was Cornelius, then Silas might well have opposed his son's marriage in England. To Silas the whole thing would have been a disgrace, something to be hushed up. Florence's father, Cissy had been told, would insist on marriage. Very well, then the couple could get married in Australia, but without the baby, which would be a millstone dragging them down in a strange country. Silas would probably have added the inducement of a cash settlement if they did as they were told. So they agreed, but at the last moment Florence refused to leave the baby, and Cornelius killed her. Then, panic-stricken, he told Harold, who took the child away for adoption, and paid for its board and lodging, probably out of his own pocket, perhaps with money provided by Silas. Cornelius, meanwhile, went to a new life in Australia unhampered by either wife or child.

This would provide a new answer to the phrase: 'Elder killed her.'

So far went what seemed a plausible theory about what

happened at Newcastle long ago, a theory that turned Harold from villain into something more like a saint. Yet if the theory was correct it would still not provide an adequate basis for Bentall's glee at having discovered something that would make his fortune. Nor did it explain the sense Geoffrey had when talking to O'Rourke junior that another card was hidden up his sleeve. I returned to the idea that there were two subjects for blackmail. Harold was one, vulnerable because he was thought to have fathered a bastard, and could not deny it without opening a can of worms that could lead to the discovery of Florence's body and an investigation of the facts relating to her death. Who was the other? It could only be Cornelius, a Cornelius not killed in a train accident as Geoffrey had been told, but alive and in England. What Hugo had discovered, and O'Rourke junior worked out for himself, must have been Cornelius's identity. Where was he, what had happened to him? There could be no doubt of the answer: in England he called himself Cyrus Everard.

It will be seen that like many armchair theorists I reasoned from effect to cause, and having reached a conclusion looked for discrepancies to support it. Not facts, for there could be no evidential proof: but the theory was supported by many discrepancies in Geoffrey's narrative. An outstanding one was Aggie's statement that Harold had always been a loner, had no friends at school, and certainly none who came to The Hollies. Yet Dodo, talking to Geoffrey after Aggie's funeral, had said he visited the house although it wasn't one you'd want to go to, an uncomfortable place to grow up in. That he had known Harold when they were young, and been friendly with him, was made clear by the nonsense song they sang together at Clempstone, and the closeness of the relationship emphasised by their singing of 'Friend of Mine'. A clincher to this was provided by the local education authority, to whom I wrote. The school at Plashet had long since been turned into a comprehensive, but a local archivist had produced a privately printed account of the school's history, and had retained the register of pupils. It contained the names of Harold and Cornelius Elder, but not of Cyrus Everard.

A check on Aggie's statement that Cornelius had died in an Australian train crash while still in his twenties proved more difficult. Armchair detection, or laziness, precluded a visit to the Newspaper Library at Colindale to check on Australian papers, but in response to a letter the Australian High Commission in London said they could find only one bad train accident in the relevant period, and the name of Cornelius Elder was not among the dead and injured. So Aggie had deliberately misled her nephew, and had also tried to warn him off his quest. How much more had she known? Obviously she was aware that Dodo was Cornelius, but I doubted if she knew or wanted to know what had happened to Florence. If she knew, she stayed silent. Blood in the Elder family was much thicker than water.

There was one more obvious discrepancy. Cornelius Elder had gone to Australia but Cyrus Everard had, he said, spent the years after he left England in Canada. Asked by Geoffrey if he had been a great traveller he said he hadn't, the wide open spaces of Canada had been enough for him. Yet years before, at Clempstone, he had incautiously talked about an experience in Melbourne. He had stopped abruptly, Geoffrey thought out of embarrassment, but in fact no doubt because he was revealing something that contradicted the story of the past he had invented.

Then there was the catalogue from the shipping line in the possession of Dermot O'Rourke, a man obviously much less stupid than Geoffrey had thought him. I wrote to them and again struck lucky, in that they were able to check the passenger list of the SS *Ottoman Prince*, which sailed from Newcastle to Sydney in May 1904. My luck didn't extend much further, however. A husband and wife had booked passages in a name that, from the manifest, might have been Elder, but could also have been Arden, Eiden or Andrew. And had they both sailed? On that the manifest was mute.

So what did happen to Hugo Headley? In my armchair reconstruction it ran like this. Cornelius had presumably not made a great success of life in Australia, and in any case had thought it safe to return to England after the war. As Cyrus Everard (initials unchanged) he had established himself as a dealer, and made contact again with his brother and sister. The past must have seemed over and done with, even though Harold or his brother was paying a little hush money to Bentall because of what had happened in Newcastle. It was revealed only through Hugo's pertinacity when, as Dermot O'Rourke put it, he smelt money. He put together the whole story, in part from Mrs Rackley, in part from Bentall, the vital element from Rory O'Rourke, who may have known Cornelius slightly or well, but in any case recognised him as Cyrus Everard when they met by chance again in England. Probably O'Rourke senior was as honest as his crooked son said, but in any case the knowledge was of no value unless you could fit in the other pieces of the puzzle. Hugo had done just that and to him, desperate for money and totally unscrupulous, it must have seemed a godsend. He wrote to Harold, telling him he knew Morgan was Harold's son, and when he was threatened with legal action played his trump card by saying he knew Cy Everard was Cornelius Elder, and mentioning also what he had learned from Bentall about Florence's death. There is a marked difference in tone, surprisingly unnoticed by Geoffrey, between Harold's first two letters to Hugo and the third, in which he backs down and in effect says he is ready to pay blackmail if Hugo leaves the country. It would seem certain, from the pretext of the cottage sale, that Harold was prepared to pay off Hugo. Then he got in touch with his brother, and Cornelius came down to Clempstone.

But Cornelius was a different character from his brother, reckless, and as Justin suggested not particularly scrupulous in his business dealings. If Harold was prepared to pay off a blackmailer, Cornelius was not. The most likely reconstruction of what happened on the night of the party is that after Harold found Deirdre in the gardener's shed he was too stunned to take any further part in the negotiations, and that Cornelius then suggested to Hugo that they settle the final details at his cottage. When they got there he attacked Hugo and stunned or killed him, removed his clothes, and drove him to the site at Lightchurch which he had visited with Harold, using his own converted Daimler. On returning he put Hugo's clothes into the back of his Austin 7, and drove it up to Parker's Point.

271

It is possible, but very unlikely, that Harold helped to dispose of the body. His shocked reaction on the following morning, when he learned that Hugo's car had been found at Parker's Point, is almost proof of his innocence. But he must have realised at once, or almost at once, what had happened, yet he said nothing. Blood was thicker than water, but the burden of guilt stayed with him. Hence his various remarks to Geoffrey about acquiescing in things one knew to be wrong.

And Bentall's death? He was already receiving his monthly stipend, and died because he too met up with his old Army friend O'Rourke, learned that Everard was Elder, became greedy and approached Dodo direct. Dodo paid him a visit, bringing down a bottle of wine perhaps to celebrate their agreement. The wine may have been doped, or he may have hit Bentall over the head as he did Hugo. He was a very successful murderer, disposing of the body ingeniously in one case, and in the other leaving murder unsuspected.

Is that what happened? It is the only solution that covers all the facts, as other armchair detectives have said about similar deductions. But it is not finally provable, and I am content to set down the story, leaving you to find another answer if you can. The chief interest for me has been less the puzzle than Geoffrey's quest: a quest dominated by the search for his father and the image of that crucial coupling witnessed by him, but also an attempt on his part to recreate differently the for ever unrealisable past.